DATE DUE

Dec30'85			
Mar2290			
Jul 1290			

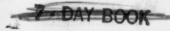

THE MURDERS
OF
RICHARD III

Also by Elizabeth Peters

THE MURDERS
OF
RICHARD III

Elizabeth Peters

DODD, MEAD & COMPANY · NEW YORK

ISBN: 0–396–06936–3
Library of Congress Catalog Card Number: 73–21160
Printed in the United States of America
by The Haddon Craftsmen, Inc., Scranton, Penna.

To Marge

A dear friend and a fellow-traveller along
the thorny by-ways of Ricardian research

THE MURDERS
OF
RICHARD III

1

THE portrait was that of a man. Recent cleaning had brought out the richness of the colors: a background of smoldering scarlet, the crimson of rubies in the jeweled collar and hat brooch, the gold threads in the undertunic displayed by open collar and slashed sleeves. Yet the over-all impression was sober to the point of grimness. Shoulder-length brown hair framed the man's spare face. It was not the face of a young man, although the subject had been barely thirty years of age when it was painted. Lines bracketed the tight-set mouth and made deep vertical indentations between the narrowed eyes, which were focused, not on the beholder, but on some inner vision. Whatever his thoughts, they had not been pleasant ones.

The portrait had an odd effect on some people. Thomas Carter was one of them. He had seen it innumerable times; indeed, he could summon up those features in memory more clearly than he could those of his own father, who was enjoying an acrimonious eighth decade in Peoria, Illinois. Thomas could not explain the near-hypnotic spell cast by the painted features, but he sincerely hoped they were having the same effect on his companion. He had private reasons for wanting Jacqueline Kirby to develop an interest in Richard III, quondam king of England, who had met a messy death on the field of battle almost five hundred years earlier.

Thomas had not changed a great deal since the day he and Jacqueline had first met, at the eastern university where Jacqueline was employed at one of the libraries. He had acquired a few more silver threads, but they blended with his fair hair. His baggy blue sweater tactfully concealed a slight tendency toward embonpoint. Thomas was a fair golfer and a good tennis player; but he was also an amateur chef, and this latter hobby left its marks on his figure. The blue sweater and the shabby tweeds were British made, but Thomas was not, although he was presently lecturing at one of England's oldest universities.

His prolonged bachelordom had given rise to predictable rumors. Thomas knew of the rumors and did not resent them; indeed,he encouraged them by his abnormal reticence about his personal affairs. Although he would have denied the charge indignantly, he was a rather old-fashioned man who believed that gentlemen do not boast of their conquests. He also found his reputation a useful tactical weapon. It reassured the ladies and put them off guard.

Neither this device nor any other had aided Thomas's campaign with Jacqueline. He had begun his pursuit the first day he saw her enscounced behind the desk in the library, glowering impartially on all comers from behind her heavy glasses. Thomas noted the emerald-green eyes behind the glasses, and the rich coppery bronze of the hair pinned back in a severe knot. He even judged, with fair accuracy, the figure under the tailored wool suit. The job offer from England ended the campaign before it had fairly begun. However, he and Jacqueline had become friends, and Thomas appreciated Jacqueline's quick unorthodox mind and weird sense of humor as much as he did her other attributes. When Jacqueline wrote him that she was spending part of the summer in England, he had replied enthusiastically, offering his services as guide to the glories of London. He had not, at that time, had ulterior motives. The motives had arisen in the interim, and had directed them to the place where they presently stood. The National Portrait Gallery, though one of London's accepted tourist "sights," was not high on Jacqueline's list of things to see. Thomas glanced at her uneasily. If she resented his arbitrary choice she would say so, in no mellow tones.

Jacqueline was regarding the portrait with a fixed stare. Her horn-rimmed glasses rode high on her nose, but she had left the rest of her tailored working costume at home. She wore a short, clinging dress of her favorite green; the short sleeves and plunging neckline displayed an admirable tan. Tendrils of bronze hair curled over her ears and temples. Without turning her head, she spoke. The voice could not by any stretch of the imagination be called mellow.

"The Tower of London," she said. "Westminster Abbey. Buckingham Palace. I'm just a little country girl who has never been abroad. What am I doing here? I want to see the Changing of the Guard. I want to have tea, a real English tea, in a real London tea shop. I want—"

"You just had lunch," Thomas said indignantly. "At Simpson's on the Strand. You had an enormous lunch. Don't you gain weight?"

Instead of replying, Jacqueline let her eyes drift sideways. They focused on Thomas's midriff. Reflexively

Thomas sucked in his breath, and Jacqueline went on with her mournful monologue.

"I don't even mind looking at portraits. Elizabeth the First, Charles the Second . . . I adore Charles the Second. He was a very sexy man. I could contemplate Keats and Byron and Shelley without resentment. And what do I get? A bad portrait—if it is a portrait, and not a seventeenth-century painter's imaginative guess—of a famous villain. Old Crouchback himself."

"Old Crouchback!" Thomas was indignant. "Look at him. See anything wrong with his back?"

Jacqueline studied the portrait again and Thomas let out a little sigh of relief as the glasses began to slip slowly down her narrow, high-bridged nose. The glasses were a barometer of Jacqueline's moods. When she was interested in, or worried about something, she forgot to push them back into place. In moments of extreme emotion they perched precariously on the tip of her nose.

"No," Jacqueline said finally.

"There is a slight hint of deformity in the set of the shoulders; one looks higher than the other. But that could be due to bad painting. He certainly was not a hunchback. He's even good-looking, in a gloomy sort of way. It is a contemporary portrait, of course?"

Thomas glanced at her suspiciously. She continued to contemplate the portrait of Richard III with candid interest, but Thomas was not deceived. Art history was one of Jacqueline's specialties.

"No. It's been dated to about 1580. Like most of the other portraits of Richard, it was probably copied from a lost original. The only one that might be a contemporary portrait is in the Royal Collection. When it was X-rayed recently, the experts found that parts of it had been painted over. Originally the right shoulder was lower, even with the left, and the eyes were not so narrow and slitlike."

Jacqueline's eyebrows lifted. She would never admit it, but Thomas knew that he had caught her interest.

"Retouched, to suggest the hunchbacked, squinting villain? That does suggest that the original was a contemporary portrait, too flattering to suit Richard's enemies. Let's see; if I remember my history lessons, Richard's successor was Henry the Seventh, the first of the Tudor kings and the last heir of the house of Lancaster. Richard was the house of York. Henry got the crown by killing Richard at the Battle of Bosworth—"

"Henry Tudor never killed anyone in a fair fight," Thomas said contemptuously. "At Bosworth he was running for the rear when Richard was cut down by a dozen men. It was Richard's good name Henry tried to destroy. Henry had no real claim to the throne and no popular support. He'd have lost the Battle of Bosworth if his widowed mother hadn't been smart enough to marry one of the most powerful nobles in the kingdom. Lord Stanley and his brother marched to Bosworth field as Richard's vassals and then treacherously attacked him. The only way Henry could justify his seizure of the throne was to show Richard as a usurper and a tyrant. Otherwise Henry was the usurper, and a rebel against the rightful king. Henry began the Tudor legend about wicked King Richard. He literally rewrote history. He—"

"He wasn't sexy," said Jacqueline regretfully. She had moved on; Thomas joined her in front of the portrait of Henry VII. "Grasping hands, and a mouth like a steel trap.

And a shifty, suspicious expression." She turned to the neighboring portrait. "Who's the simpering doll-faced blond lady?"

"Henry's queen, Elizabeth of York. His marriage with her united the houses of Lancaster and York, and ended the Wars of the Roses. She was Richard's niece, the daughter of his elder brother, Edward the Fourth. Whom you see before you, in this portrait. He was supposed to have been one of the handsomest kings England ever had—a big blond six-footer, with an eye for the ladies."

"He doesn't look very sexy," said Jacqueline, eyeing the flat, doughy features of Edward IV critically.

"Sexy, hell. If I had realized you suffered from historical necrophilia, I'd never have brought you here. Ready to leave?"

"Oh, no. You brought me here, and I'm not leaving till I've seen all my heroes. Keats, Shelley—and of course King Charles. Where is he? 'Here's a health unto his Majesty—' "

"I had forgotten your regrettable habit of bursting into song at odd moments. Jacqueline . . ."

It took Thomas over an hour to extract Jacqueline from the gallery. The portrait of Charles II had to be admired and the long line of his official mistresses subjected to a scathing commentary. Jacqueline said they were all too fat. When Thomas finally got her out the door, Trafalgar Square was raucous with late-afternoon traffic, and Jacqueline said she was faint from hunger.

"No wonder I love England," she remarked some time later, after devouring most of a plate of cream-filled buns. "People eat so often here. Morning tea, breakfast, elevenses, lunch, afternoon tea—"

"I don't think I can afford you," said Thomas.

"I know you can't." Jacqueline gave him a look that left him momentarily speechless. She pushed her glasses firmly back onto the bridge of her nose and regarded him severely. "All right, Thomas. I know you're up to something. First you invite me to a country weekend with a lot of people I've never met; then you deluge me with information about one of the most mixed-up periods in English history. There must be a connection, but I can't figure out what it is. Go on; I can see you're dying to lecture about something. I recognize your classroom scowl."

"I'm not going to lecture," Thomas said self-consciously. "How much do you know about—"

He stopped, staring at Jacqueline. She had slipped sideways in her chair. One arm dangled; the hand at its end was out of sight under the tea table, but it seemed to be making violent motions.

"For God's sake," Thomas snapped. "What are you looking for? If it's cigarettes, I'll buy you some. You'll never find anything in that purse. Or is it a briefcase? Anyhow, I thought you had kicked the habit."

Jacqueline resumed an upright position. In one hand she held a ball of white thread; in the other, a metal shuttle. Thomas watched, openmouthed, as she wound the thread around her fingers in a pattern that resembled a one-handed form of cat's cradle.

"I have kicked the habit nine times since you last saw me. I have taken up tatting in order to help me kick it once again. I tried knitting, but that didn't work; every time I reached in my purse I stabbed myself on a knitting needle."

"I suspect this isn't going to work either," said Thomas. "Forgive me for mentioning it, but your fingers are turning blue. I think the thread is too tight."

Jacqueline put the shuttle down and began unwinding the thread.

"Thomas, you are too easily distracted. If I should choose to chin myself on the chandelier, it should not interrupt your discourse. I am listening. How much do I know about what?"

With an effort Thomas wrenched his eyes away from the struggle between Jacqueline and her fancywork.

"It wouldn't surprise me if you did. Chin yourself, I mean . . . How much do you know about Richard the Third?"

For answer, Jacqueline arranged her features in a hideous scowl. Out of the corner of her mouth, in the accents of a movie gangster, she said,

" 'I am determined to prove a villain, And hate the idle pleasure of these days!' "

"Oh, forget about Shakespeare," Thomas said. "He based his *Richard the Third* on the Tudor historians, and they maligned Richard to please Henry the Seventh. Shakespeare's version is great theater, but it isn't history. Let's try another question. How much do you know about the Wars of the Roses?"

"I know a little bit, but not enough, about everything," said Jacqueline. "I'm a librarian, remember? Oh . . ."

The last word was a low moan. Tenderly she freed her swelling fingers from entwined thread, wadded the whole mass up, and thrust it back into her purse. The second failure had soured her temper. She went on disagreeably,

"I never did understand the Wars of the Roses. I don't think anybody understands the Wars of the Roses. I don't want to understand them . . . it . . . the Wars of the Roses. The houses of Lancaster and York—the red rose and the white—were fighting for the throne. That's what the Wars of the Roses were about. That's all I know and all I need to know."

"Okay, okay," Thomas said soothingly. "The last of the Lancastrian kings was Henry the Sixth—not to be confused with Henry the Seventh, the first of the Tudors. Henry the Sixth was a nice ineffectual old idiot—part saint, part mental defective. His successful Yorkist rival was Edward the Fourth, the big handsome blond, whose contemporaries considered him sexy, even if you don't. Edward got rid of Henry the Sixth, and Henry's son, and a few miscellaneous malcontents, and settled down to enjoy himself. His biggest mistake was to marry a widow lady, Elizabeth Woodville by name. Everyone was shocked at this marriage with a commoner; they resented Edward's failure to strengthen England with an alliance with a foreign princess. Elizabeth had a couple of sons by her first marriage and a crowd of brothers and sisters. They were a predatory crew, and Elizabeth helped them advance. The noblest families in England were forced to marry the queen's sisters; the marriage of her twenty-year-old brother with the Dowager Duchess of Norfolk, aged eighty, scandalized the country. Edward begat a clutch of children on his beautiful wife—two sons and a number of daughters. The eldest daughter was also named Elizabeth."

"These people all have the same names," Jacqueline grumbled. "Edward, Elizabeth, Henry. Can't you call them Ethelbert or Francisco or something?"

"I could," said Thomas coldly. "But those weren't their names. Stop griping and concentrate."

Jacqueline reached for a cucumber sandwich. They were having the genuine English tea she had demanded, in the lounge of one of London's dignified old hotels. The chink of silverware and the subdued rattle of china were no louder than the genteel murmuring voices of the other patrons.

"Edward the Fourth," Thomas went on. "The Yorkist king—Richard's brother. Got that? Okay. Edward died at the early age of forty, worn out by riotous living. He left two sons. The eldest, on his father's death, became Edward the Fifth . . ." He ignored Jacqueline's grimace and went on relentlessly. "Yes, another Edward. He was only a kid—twelve years old, too young to rule alone. A protectorate was necessary; and the obvious candidate for the role of Protector was the kid's only paternal uncle, Edward the Fourth's younger brother—a brilliant soldier, a first-rate administrator, devoted to his wife and little son, loyal, honest, popular—Richard, Duke of Gloucester."

"Three cheers and a roll of drums," said Jacqueline. "Gee whiz, Thomas, to think that all these years I've had the wrong idea about Richard the Third. He was a swell guy. I'm surprised they haven't canonized him. Beloved husband, fond father, admirable brother. . . . Loving uncle?"

"You have a tongue like a viper."

"Thanks. Look here, Thomas, what is the one thing people do know about Richard the Third—if they know anything? He was the wicked uncle par excellence. He murdered his nephews—the two little princes in the Tower—and usurped the throne that was rightfully theirs."

"He did not!" Thomas shouted.

Heads turned. A waiter dropped a fork.

Thomas subsided, flushing.

"Damn it, Jacqueline, that is the most fascinating, frustrating unsolved murder in history. There is no evidence. Do you know that? Absolutely no proof whatsoever that Richard had those kids killed. Only rumor and slander on one side—"

"And on the other?"

"Richard's character. The otherwise inexplicable behavior of other people who were involved. Simple common sense."

"I wouldn't say his character was exactly—"

"I mean his real character, not the one the Tudor historians invented. Everything that is known about Richard's actions supports the picture of a man of rare integrity, kindness, and courage. At the age of eighteen he commanded armies, and led them well. He administered the northern provinces for his brother the king, and won lasting loyalty for the house of York by his scrupulous fairness and concern for the rights of the ordinary citizen against rapacious nobles. He supported the arts. He was deeply religious. As for his personal life—oh, he sired a few bastards, everybody did in those days, but after he was married, to a girl he had known since they were children together, he remained faithful to her while she lived and mourned her sincerely when she died. The death of his little son threw him into a frenzy of grief. In a time of turncoating and treachery, he never once failed in his loyalty to his brother, Edward the Fourth. There was a third brother, the Duke of Clarence, who tried to push his own claim to the throne and even took up arms against Edward. Richard persuaded Clarence to come back into the fold, and when Edward finally got exasperated with Clarence's plotting and ordered his execution, Richard was the only one who spoke up for Clarence."

"That ain't the way I heard it," said Jacqueline, eating the last sandwich.

"No, you heard the Tudor legend—the myth of the monster. By the time Sir Thomas More wrote his biography of Richard, in the reign of Henry the Eighth, Richard was being accused of everything but barratry and arson. According to More, Richard murdered Henry the Sixth and Henry's son; his own wife; and his brother, the Duke of Clarence. He had his nephews smothered, usurped the throne, and decapitated a group of noblemen who objected to his activities.

"Modern historians admit that Richard was innocent of most of these charges. He did execute a few nobles, including some of the queen's Woodville relatives. He said they had plotted against his life, and there is no reason to doubt that they had. When Richard killed people he did it in broad daylight, with plenty of witnesses, and made no bones about it. But the little princes just . . . disappeared."

"Very interesting. But what does all this have to do with the mysterious house party? You've been very cryptic about it, and I don't see—"

"I'll get to that. Stop looking wistfully at the waiter; I'm not going to order any more food, you've had enough for two people already. Pay attention. I'm not just trying to improve your knowledge of English history; all this has bearing on a very contemporary problem.

"We return, then to the time right after Edward the Fourth died. Richard was in the north when it happened, at his favorite castle of Middleham. The new young king had his own household in Wales. At the news of his father's death he started for London, with his Woodville uncles—the queen had made sure her brothers had control of the heir to the throne—and an escort of two thousand men. Richard, on his way south for the funeral, had only six hundred. He obviously didn't anticipate trouble.

"But somewhere along the way, he got word that the Woodvilles were planning to seize power and cut him out of the job of Protector. They may have planned to kill him. They virtually had to; he had the popular support and the legal rights they lacked, and he was not the sort of man to turn the other cheek.

"Two men warned Richard of what was happening. One was Lord Hastings, his brother's old friend and drinking companion. The other was the Duke of Buckingham, of royal descent himself, who had been forced to marry one of the queen's upstart sisters.

"Richard moved like lightning. He caught up with the young king's entourage, arrested the boy's Woodville relatives, and escorted young Edward to London. The queen rushed into church sanctuary, taking the other children with her. Later she was persuaded to let the younger boy join his royal brother. The two kids were lodged in the royal apartments in the Tower, which was the conventional place for kings to reside in before their coronations. Up to this time, Richard's behavior had been perfectly reasonable and forthright."

"Richard the Forthright," murmured Jacqueline.

Thomas pretended he had not heard.

"Then, around the middle of June 1483, all hell broke loose. England was astounded to learn that Edward the Fourth had never been married to Elizabeth Woodville. He had entered into a precontract with another lady, and in those days a precontract was as binding as a marriage ceremony. That meant that all Edward the Fourth's children were bastards, and that young Edward the Fifth had no right to the throne.

"The Tudor historians claim Richard invented this story, but all the evidence indicates that it was true. The man who broke the news was no fly-by-night flunky of Richard's; he was one of the great prelates of England, the Bishop of Bath and Wells. The story was accepted by Parliament and embodied in a formal decree, *Titulus Regius*, that proclaimed Richard's right to the throne. Both his brothers were dead; Clarence's children were barred from the succession because their father had been executed as a traitor; and if Edward's children were illegitimate, the rightful heir was Richard himself."

"Oh, that's all right, then," said Jacqueline. "If the boys were bastards, Richard had every right to smother them."

"Damn it, he didn't smother them!" Thomas felt his face reddening. He got control of himself with an effort. "The boys were seen, playing in the Tower, in the summer of 1483. Except for a few doubtful references in the official royal account books, that is the last anyone ever heard of them.

"In 1485, two years later, Henry Tudor landed in England. Thanks to the treachery of the Stanleys, Richard was killed at Bosworth and Henry became King Henry the Seventh.

"Now what would you have done if you had been Henry? Here you are, occupying a shaky throne in a country seething with potential rebellion. Your claim to the throne comes via your mother, who is descended from an illegitimate child of a king's younger son. There are a dozen people still alive who have stronger claims than that. The man you succeeded is dead, but he is by no means forgotten, especially in the north of England. You propose to strengthen your claim by marrying young Elizabeth, Richard's niece, but a lot of people think she is illegitimate; and if she is not, then her brothers, if they are still alive, are the real heirs to the throne. There have been rumors that the boys were killed, but nobody knows for sure what happened to them.

"If you had been Henry, surely one of your first moves would have been to find out the truth about the princes. The Tower of London is in your hands. You would look for those pathetic little bodies, and question the attendants who were on duty when they were killed. The Tower is a huge fortress, full of people—servants and warders and scrubwomen and cooks and officials. There are dozens of people still alive who must know what happened. You can't eliminate two state prisoners without someone noticing that they have vanished between sunset and sunrise.

"Henry did nothing of the sort. I don't think he could —because the boys were still alive when Henry entered London in 1485. But they wouldn't stay alive, not for long."

Jacqueline nibbled a piece of bread and butter.

"Someone confessed to the murder, didn't he?" she asked tentatively.

"Yes—a man named Sir James Tyrrell. *Twenty years later*, after the supposed murderer had been arrested on another charge. The confession was never published. It was not made public until after Tyrell's execution on another charge. The version given in Sir Thomas More's biography of Richard bristles with contradictions, misstatements, and downright lies. It is such a palpable tissue of—"

He broke off, eyeing Jacqueline with a sudden wild

surmise. She stared owlishly back at him over the rims of her glasses; and Thomas, who seldom did so, swore imaginatively.

"You know all this! You, who claim to have read every detective story ever printed . . . Of course you know it. You've read *The Daughter of Time.*"

"Sure."

"Then why didn't you say so?"

"I lo-o-ove to hear you talk," said Jacqueline silkily.

"There are times when I could kill you."

"I read all Josephine Tey's mysteries," Jacqueline said. *"The Daughter of Time* is absolutely brilliant. But it's a novel, not a work of serious history. It is far from unbiased."

"What else have you read?" Thomas asked with resignation.

Jacqueline reached for the last bun.

"Once a librarian, always a librarian," she said, nibbling. "When I read historical fiction I always check to see what's real and what's made up. Tey got her material from one of Richard's apologists, and she is just as biased as the Tudor historians, only on the other side—Saint Richard the Third, full of love and peace and flowers. I read some historical novels about Richard," she added, finishing the bun with a snap of her white teeth. "Most of them portrayed him as a sensitive martyr, wringing his slender hands and sobbing. I doubt that he cried much."

"You are really—"

"So now we come to the house party," said Jacqueline. She eyed the crumbs on the empty plate regretfully, and went on, "I assume the party has to do with your hero. What is it, a meeting of some organization? There is a group that is concerned with Richard's rehabilitation.

They call themselves Richardians, and are not to be confused with the followers of the economist, David Ricardo. They put *In Memoriam* notices in the *Times* on the anniversary of the Battle of Bosworth."

Jacqueline's tone gave this otherwise innocuous statement implications that made Thomas's eyes narrow with exasperation. His sense of humor triumphed, however, and he smiled sheepishly.

"There are several groups interested in Richard the Third. I suspect ours is the freakiest of them all."

"That's nice."

"You needn't be sarcastic."

"I'm not being sarcastic. There is no happier outlet for our inherent aggressive instincts than the belligerent support of an unorthodox cause. I myself," said Jacqueline proudly, "am a member of the friends of Jerome." She watched Thomas sort through his capacious memory for potential historic Jeromes, and added, "Jerome is a place, not a person. It's an absolutely marvelous ghost town in Arizona. It sits on top of an abandoned mine, and if we don't get busy, it is going to slide right down the hill into—"

"That's even crazier than our organization."

"One attribute of eccentric groups is their lack of sympathy for other eccentrics. Tell me about Richard's friends."

"Don't call us that. It's one of the names of the older organization from which we reneged when they denied Sir Richard's illegitimacy."

Jacqueline had again produced her tatting. She studied it fixedly for several seconds before she looked at Thomas.

"Just say that again, Thomas. Slowly."

"Our founder and president is Sir Richard Weldon,"

Thomas explained. "He claims to be descended from one of Richard the Third's illegitimate children. The Richard the Third Society wouldn't accept his claim, in spite of well-documented—"

"Thomas!"

"Well, it could be true. Richard had several bastards; everybody did in those days."

"That resolves all my doubts. You tempt me, Thomas," Jacqueline said pensively. "I'd like to meet Sir Richard . . . Weldon. That isn't the department store?"

"Stores, not store. They're all over England. But you'll like Sir Richard," Thomas added with seeming irrelevance. "He's a nice guy, even if he does have an *idée fixe*. The house party is to be at his home in Yorkshire. It is a special meeting of the executive board of the society. Usually we forgather on the anniversary of Richard's birthday—October second."

"He was a Libra," said Jacqueline, interested. "That's a point for your side. Libras are well-balanced individuals, not liable to bursts of passion or ungoverned rage. They are sensitive to beauty, fond of justice—"

"Now stop that!"

Jacqueline grinned. Then she sobered and shook her head.

"Thomas, I'd adore coming to the meeting, but I don't think I can manage it. I had planned to go home early next week."

"Why must you? College doesn't open till the middle of September. You're not worried about the offspring, are you? Surely they're old enough to manage for another fortnight."

"Oh, they'd be delighted to have me stay away permanently. They have my car, my TV set, my refrigerator, and my bank account—such as it is—at their mercy. They are probably having nightly orgies."

"They can't be doing anything too bad. . . ."

"Oh, yes, they can. However," Jacqueline said, brightening, "they manage to keep me unwitting. So far they seem to have buried the bodies and settled out of court."

"You're a damned unnatural mum. I don't know how they put up with you. Jacqueline, you've got to come. I'm counting on you."

"It's not polite to visit people without an invitation. I was brought up to be a lady."

"I've already told Sir Richard you're coming. He's delighted."

"Oh, you have, have you?"

"Don't be so hostile. You haven't asked me why the meeting is extraordinary."

"Why," said Jacqueline in the same steely voice, "is the meeting extraordinary?"

"We've found the letter. The one from Elizabeth of York, Richard's niece."

The bald statement had the desired effect. Jacqueline's hard stare softened.

"You're kidding."

"No."

"The letter in which the girl says she's in love with her uncle and wants to marry him? That she wishes the queen would hurry up and die? That Richard is her—"

" 'Only joy and maker in this world,' " said Thomas, thoroughly pleased with himself. "That's the letter."

"The girl was at court," Jacqueline said thoughtfully. "Her mother let her and the other princesses leave sanctuary after Richard was crowned. He agreed to provide for them, and not to force them into unsuitable marriages.

But the letter is apocryphal, Thomas. I remember; it was quoted by one of Richard's earliest defenders, back in the seventeenth century—"

"Buck."

"Yes, Buck. He said he had seen the original, in Elizabeth's own handwriting. But then it disappeared. Most authorities doubt it ever existed. Because, if it did—"

"Uh-huh," said Thomas. "If it exists, it absolves Richard of one of the Tudor slanders—that he tried to force his unwilling niece into an incestuous marriage in order to improve his claim to the throne."

"Yes, I remember. I was particularly struck by one part of that story—the Christmas party at court, where Queen Anne and young Elizabeth appeared in identical dresses."

"Everyone at court was struck by it. The gesture was in singularly bad taste. The queen was dying of tuberculosis; she must have looked like a haggard ghost next to a handsome, healthy young girl. Richard was accused of thinking that one up, of course."

"A man would never think of a thing like that. It's a woman's trick. Not the queen's; she wouldn't give another woman a gown like hers, especially if the other woman was younger and prettier. I thought, when I read about it, that Elizabeth must have planned the trick herself—had the dress copied."

"Excellent," Thomas said approvingly. "I hadn't thought of that, but it bears out my own theory. There certainly was a rumor going around that Richard planned to marry the girl. When Richard heard it, he denied the story, publicly and emphatically. It would have been an extremely stupid move from his point of view. The girl was illegitimate, a commoner, his own niece, one of the hated Woodvilles. He had everything to lose and nothing to gain by such a marriage.

"No, I'm sure young Elizabeth started the rumor herself. Wishful thinking. Richard was only about ten years older than she was, and the queen was dying. . . ."

Jacqueline shook her head violently. "No, Thomas, it's too much. Granted that the girl was ambitious—granted that she was in love with her uncle. Even so . . ."

Thomas finished the sentence. ". . . it is inconceivable that she should want to marry the murderer of her brothers. I couldn't agree more. It's hard enough to explain how the queen mother could have entrusted her daughters to Richard's protection after he had ruthlessly slaughtered her sons. She accepted a pension from him, even wrote to her son by her first marriage, who had fled abroad, urging him to return because Richard would treat him well."

Jacqueline was still shaking her head. "Maybe the two Elizabeths didn't know the boys were dead. The date, Thomas. What was the date of the letter?"

"That won't wash. The letter was probably written in January or February of 1485—a year and a half after the boys were supposed to have been killed. All England prayed for saintly Henry Tudor to come over and rescue them from the monster. You can't have it both ways. Either the truth was known—and in that case the boys' family couldn't help knowing it—or the boys were still alive and the accusations were malicious lies spread by Henry's agents. Agitprop is not a modern invention, you know."

"Hmm." Jacqueline acknowledged his logic by abandoning the argument. "The letter would support your second alternative. It isn't absolute proof, but. . . . Good heavens, Thomas, it's an important document! And your little society is sitting on it like a broody hen. Who found it? Where was it found? Has the provenance been checked? Have any reputable authorities seen it?"

"An authority is about to see it."

He had rarely seen Jacqueline taken aback. Now she gaped at him, unable to believe her ears.

"Me? Is that how you got me invited? Thomas, I'm not—"

"You took a course in authenticating manuscripts, didn't you?"

"Oh, for God's sake—just the usual survey sort of thing. I'm no—"

"And you studied handwriting analysis, didn't you?"

"I can read your fortune in the Tarot, too, if you like. That has nothing to do with—"

"Could you spot an out-and-out fake?"

Jacqueline studied him thoughtfully. Her indignation faded as she realized his concern was genuine.

"A crude one—of course. Errors in vocabulary, spelling, and the like. . . . So could you. For anything more complex I'd need a laboratory. They can test the paper, the ink. . . . And I'm no expert on fifteenth-century orthography. What's wrong, Thomas? Do you think one of your fellow enthusiasts forged this letter?"

"I don't know! I'm sure the letter did exist. Buck couldn't have invented it out of whole cloth. But it's too damned fortuitous to have it turn up now, after all these years. The scholarly world and the press think we're a bunch of crackpots now. If we make a big public spectacle of this—as we are planning to do—and then some goateed expert strolls in and says, 'You've been had, ladies and gents; this is Woolworth's best stationery. . . .' You can see how idiotic we would look. And . . . maybe you won't understand this. But we honestly are concerned with a little matter of justice, even if it's five hundred years late. A fiasco like this . . ."

". . . could hurt Richard's cause," said Jacqueline, as he hesitated. She spoke tentatively, as if the words were too bizarre to be uttered; but as she studied the flushed face of the man across the table, her own face changed. "My God. You really feel . . ."

"I guess it sounds silly," Thomas said, with no sign of anger. "I can't explain it. In part, it's the fun of an unsolved puzzle; in part, the famous Anglo-Saxon weakness for the underdog. But it's more than that. Do you remember what they wrote about Richard in the official records of the city of York, after they heard the news of Bosworth? 'King Richard, late mercifully reigning upon us, was . . . piteously slain and murdered, to the great heaviness of this City.' The men of Yorkshire knew him well; he had lived among them for many years. It took guts to write that epitaph with Henry Tudor on the throne and Richard's cause buried in a felon's grave at Leicester. . . . If there is such a thing as charisma, maybe some people have an extra-large dose. Enough to carry through five hundred years."

Jacqueline's eyebrows went up. "That's a scary idea, Thomas. I refuse to pursue it. . . . Okay. If you feel that strongly, I'm your woman. In a limited sense," she added. "What is going on this weekend? Do you reenact the Battle of Bosworth, or what?"

"It's like a regular professional meeting," Thomas explained. He didn't thank her; they knew each other too well for that. "We start on Friday with a dinner at Dick's place; after dinner we'll hear papers, have discussions, the way they do at the scholarly society meetings. More lectures, etcetera, on Saturday. Saturday night we're having our big banquet and ball. The Sunday afternoon meeting is when Dick is producing the letter. God, they've invited the BBC, and I understand half the papers in England are sending reporters. Not because the find is important, you understand; they just want to see a bunch of nuts making a spectacle of themselves."

"It sounds rather dull."

"Well . . ."

"Ah! Come clean, Thomas. You *are* going to reenact the Battle of Bosworth. Only this time Richard wins?"

"That's an idea," said Thomas interestedly. "History as it should have been. I'll have to propose that some time."

"Thomas."

Thomas came as near to squirming as a dignified adult male can come. "We—er—dress up," he said reluctantly. "In costume of the period."

"Indeed."

"You don't have to, it's optional. And then we—well, we take parts. Various historical characters."

He looked at Jacqueline and saw with regret, but without surprise, that her green eyes were sparkling. Her mouth was fixed in a line of exaggerated composure.

"Really, Thomas? What fun! And who are you, darling?"

"Clarence."

"Richard's brother, the Duke of Clarence? The one who was drowned . . ."

"Yes, that one. Really, Jacqueline, for a woman of your age and supposed refinement, you have the most raucous laugh."

"I'm sorry." Jacqueline wiped tears of mirth from her

eyes. "I had a sudden mental picture of you, head down in—"

"That story about the butt of malmsey is ridiculous! Can you imagine anyone drowning an enemy in a barrel of wine? It would ruin the wine, for one thing." Thomas grinned unwillingly. "Sorry to disappoint you, but I'm not going to dive into a barrel with my feet kicking in the air just to entertain you."

He was to remember this statement later as a particularly dazzling example of "famous last words."

✤ 2 ✤

THOMAS had tomato on his tie.

"I'm getting tomato on my tie," he said.

"Lean forward and drip on the floor," Jacqueline advised.

She was also eating an egg-tomato-and-cucumber sandwich. Thomas was irked to see that there wasn't a spot on her snowy-white pants suit.

He followed her advice and her example. At least there was no one to see the ridiculous picture he made. They were sitting side by side in the front row of seats on the top of the double-decker bus. There were only two other passengers on this level; both were local people, far at the back, and superbly disinterested in the foreigners up front. An occasional bird or squirrel in the leafy branches that brushed past the windows might be observing his graceless posture, but they were probably equally disinterested.

Thomas dabbed at the spot on his maroon tie. It bothered him more than it ought to have done, and this fact made him wonder, in his introspective fashion, whether he was as indifferent to worldly concerns as a scholar ought to be. He had been only mildly vexed when Jacqueline insisted on traveling into Yorkshire by local bus; he was undisturbed at the idea of disembarking from one of the lumbering green monsters, along with a crowd of yokels, at the gates of his titled host's country residence. At least his conscious mind was undisturbed. Then why, he asked himself, had he been relieved when Sir Richard suggested that they disembark in the next village but one, where they would be met by Sir Richard's chauffeur? Why did he hope the bus would be early and Jenkins would be late with the car? He had encountered Jenkins before, and the thought of the supercilious chauffeur watching him descend from this plebeian form of transport induced a definite qualm. Jenkins, who doubled as Sir Richard's valet, would certainly notice the spot on his tie.

Jacqueline, who had been staring at the panorama of English countryside unrolling before them at a genteel speed of ten miles an hour, delved into her purse and eventually produced a small tube.

"Spot remover," she said, proffering the tube without looking at Thomas.

"I don't see why we couldn't have a decent lunch instead of munching sandwiches on top of a bus," he grumbled.

"We'd have missed the bus," Jacqueline said patiently. "And there isn't another one till tomorrow."

"Ridiculous idea, anyhow." The spot remover worked beautifully. Thomas went on, in a more affable tone, "We have had to transfer three times already."

"You've lived in England for years. Have you ever taken local buses before?"

Memory gripped Thomas, so unexpectedly and so strongly that he felt an actual physical pain.

"Thirty-five years ago," he said. "Before the war. I was sixteen. It was my first trip abroad."

Jacqueline was silent, which was just as well; Thomas would not have heard her. What was the name of that girl? He had written to her for almost a year. . . . He had forgotten her name, but he could see her as vividly as if he had parted from her, in the bluebell-carpeted woods, only yesterday. Hair like pale-yellow silk and eyes as blue as the flowers . . .

With a nostalgic sigh he turned to Jacqueline.

"You're a witch. Are those rumors about your purse true?"

"What rumors?"

"The students claim it's magic. That you can produce anything you want out of it."

"Such nonsense."

"You mean you always carry spot remover?"

"When I'm wearing a white suit and taking buses to visit a noble peer of the realm I do. Be sensible, Thomas."

II

In the year 1466 Sir John Crosby, alderman of London, built a town house in the city district called Bishopsgate. The Great Hall of this handsome residence still survives in a new location on the Embankment. Since Richard III, for whom Jacqueline was developing a distinctly ambivalent attitude, had once rented Sir John's house, Jacqueline had been taken to Chelsea to see Crosby Hall. Ricardians liked to visit the place and gaze sentimentally at the walls that had once enclosed their hero. They are perhaps among the few who appreciate the irony of the Hall's present location. The adjacent building was the home of the saint and martyr and questionable historian, Sir

Thomas More, whose biography of Richard infuriates that king's modern admirers.

The Yorkshire copy of Crosby Hall looked just as out of place as its London original. It was an exact replica, but instead of building a house to go with it, Herman Weldon, the father of the present owner, had attached the Hall onto an existing country residence. This mansion, Georgian in date, seemed to turn its back on the addition. The mellow red brick did not clash with the pale stone of the Hall; it ignored it.

Jacqueline didn't comment directly on the unfortunate juxtaposition. She merely remarked that bastardized combinations of architectural styles sometimes succeeded, but only, in her opinion, when they grew naturally through the centuries. Thomas said nothing. He agreed with the aesthetic judgment, but the romantic appeal of a fifteenth-century Hall superseded taste; he would have liked it if it had been built onto a high-rise apartment building.

He could tell by Jacqueline's face that the architectural monstrosity had confirmed her prejudice against its owner. He had given her a brief biography of their host. Sir Richard had inherited his title, his house, and his Ricardian enthusiasm from his father, who had been a highly successful merchant. It was inevitable that the merchant's son should be named Richard, but far less likely that old Crouchback's namesake should have reacted so positively to his father's obsession. Instead of rejecting it, as a healthily antagonistic offspring is supposed to do, the boy had embraced it with even greater fervor. The Weldon fortune having survived war, post war inflation, and death duties, Sir Richard was a member of that increasingly rare breed, a gentleman of wealth. He lived with, for, and among his collection of Ricardiana.

Jacqueline and Thomas were received at the door by a member of that equally rare breed, a genuine butler. As he took their suitcases, a door at the far end of the hall opened, and from the shadow of the arch the original of the portrait at the National Gallery came walking out of time to greet them.

Weldon wore his brown hair at shoulder length. His head was covered with a black velvet hat pinned with a jeweled brooch—copied from the portrait, as was his long fur-trimmed gown. The pleated garment was belted in at the waist. The neck was open, showing the high-necked undertunic, or paltock.

Thomas heard Jacqueline's breath catch at the first sight of this fantastic figure; as it moved out into the light he heard another sound, which was one of courteously suppressed amusement. He smiled to himself. Whatever Jacqueline's prejudices, they would soon be dispelled. No one could dislike a man as cheerful and gentle as Richard Weldon.

The resemblance to Richard of Gloucester was cultivated and not really very close. Weldon's short, slight figure suited the image, but his snub-nosed face had no resemblance to Gloucester's somber countenance. It was pathetic to watch Weldon struggle with his facial muscles; he tried to keep his face as sober as that of its painted prototype, but his features were not designed for melancholy.

He was beaming as he marched forward, both hands extended. After greeting Jacqueline warmly, he turned to Thomas.

"Brother!" he exclaimed, and flung both arms around Thomas. "Noble Clarence! God wit ye well!"

"Now, now," said Thomas, disentangling himself from yards of loose velvet sleeve. "Hadn't we better stick to our own names? It's confusing enough as it is."

"Oh, dear," said Weldon, looking chagrined. "Of course you're right. Do come into the drawing room and meet the others."

The drawing room was a lovely Georgian chamber, but its fine lines and discreet ornament were obscured by an outré collection of bric-a-brack and furniture, an overflow from the famous Weldon collection of Ricardiana. A mammoth carved chest, black with age, loomed threateningly over a little ormolu table. An ivory sofa was disfigured by a plush cushion with the legend "Souvenir of Middleham Castle." Clearly Weldon could not bear to throw anything away if it had the slightest connection with Richard of Gloucester.

All the people present were wearing medieval costume. Some were sweating inelegantly under the muffling folds of velvet and the heavy fur trim. The feminine garb of the period, romantic and graceful as it was, only suited the slim. The woman who strode forward to meet them, with the air of one who knows her rights of precedence, was far too massive for the dress. The full skirts were supposed to be belted in just under the breasts, but in this case it was hard to tell where that area was located. Her massive bosom went out and out and further out; from its extremity the crimson cloth of gold billowed instead of falling in graceful folds. The neckline and skirt of the dress were trimmed with bands of ermine. Against the white fur the woman's neck was scarlet, streaked with runnels of perspiration. She had a visible moustache, and her iron-gray hair was almost concealed under a velvet-banded hennin—the tall pointed hat popular with assorted fairy princesses. From its peak a long gauzy veil stood straight out every time the wearer moved. It was an impractical appendage, as the tears and snags in the fragile fabric indicated.

"Mrs. Ponsonby-Jones," said Weldon in a subdued voice. "My late cousin's wife."

"And your queen," said Mrs. Ponsonby-Jones, in a voice that made her gauze veil flutter. She gave Weldon a coy glance and a dig with her elbow. "Richard's wife, Queen Anne. Good day, Thomas—dear brother Clarence, I should say, though you were not very kind to poor little Anne, were you? You must get into costume at once, we are having such a jolly time pretending." Thomas, who had been opening and closing his mouth, had no chance to reply. Mrs. Ponsonby-Jones turned her attention to Jacqueline, not liking what she saw and making no effort to conceal it. "Hem. Yes, as Richard's hostess, let me welcome you, Miss—er—hem. Of course you will want to join our little game of make-believe. I fear that all the major parts are taken; but you will no doubt enjoy portraying one of the ladies of the court, or perchance a serving wench. I am sure I can find some costume for you in the old-clothes basket, Miss—er—Mrs—hem."

"How nice of you, Mrs. Ponsonby-Jones," said Jacqueline. She turned to the other older woman in the group, and Richard Weldon said quickly,

"Lady Isobel Crawford."

The only word for Lady Isobel was "skinny." "Thin" would have been an understatement. She was barely five feet tall, and thirty years earlier she might have been a petite, dainty little woman. Her robe was a copy of one worn by Edward IV's queen, Elizabeth Woodville, in a National Gallery portrait. The truncated hennin of gold brocade matched the metallic sheen of her bleached hair and was adorned with a butterfly veil, supported by three fine wires that gave it its shape. Her gown of black velvet was trimmed at cuffs and neckline with matching gold brocade. The neckline was cut low, showing an embroidered undertunic and a pair of bony shoulders. Chains and pendants jangled when she moved.

"How do you do, Dr. Kirby," said Lady Isobel. She went on, with an amused glance at Mrs. Ponsonby-Jones, "I fear our little charades must strike you as foolish. I assure you, they are not—to those of us who share a touch of the divine spark of creativity. . . ."

Modestly she examined her fingernails, and Weldon said,

"I'm sure you have read Lady Isobel's novels, Dr. Kirby. Her book about Richard is particularly admired."

The Gallant Young King," said Jacqueline. "Oh, yes. I read it."

"How sweet," murmured Lady Isobel. She examined Jacqueline. Suddenly she gave a little squeal and clapped her hands. "Oh, my dear, you must participate. You've no idea of the mystical insight of identification—the understanding one derives of the person one is representing— the passions, the suffering, the—I've always thought . . . the aura, in short. One feels it—here." She clasped her hands over her flat bosom, and smiled at Jacqueline. "Unfortunately, all the major parts do seem to be taken. I would offer you my own part of Elizabeth Woodville, but I'm afraid you would simply pop out of my costume!"

"So sweet of you," said Jacqueline enthusiastically. "But I couldn't take such an important part—a visitor like myself. Oh!" It was a diabolical imitation of Lady Isobel's squeal. Jacqueline clapped her hands girlishly. "I know! I shall be Richard's mistress. That is, if Sir Richard doesn't mind?"

She beamed at Sir Richard, who was looking a little bewildered.

"Not at all," he said heartily. "Jolly good."

"Mistress!" Lady Ponsonby-Jones exclaimed. "Richard, I really do not think it is suitable—"

"Get on with the introductions, Dick," said Thomas.

Weldon presented the third woman in the party. She was young and slim. Her pale-pink robes were trimmed with brown fur and belted high under shapely breasts; the lifted skirt showed an embroidered underskirt of deeper rose. Brown curls escaped from under her tall cap with its dependent veil. Her features would have been unusually pretty if they had not been marred by a sulky pout and by the latest in mod makeup. To Thomas's conservative eyes her face looked like a mask; but the over-all effect was not unpleasing.

Certainly Weldon did not find it so. His eyes shone with fond affection as he made the introductions.

"Here is our young Elizabeth of York. Her real name is Elizabeth Ponsonby-Jones, so that's one less for you to remember, Jacqueline. I may call you that, I hope? We are all friends here."

"Well, don't call me Elizabeth," drawled the girl. "Liz or Bessy or Hey-you, but not Elizabeth. I'm an unwilling sacrifice on the altar of family feeling. I think I ought to be Diccon's mistress instead of ghastly Elizabeth of York. She's the sickest character of the lot."

"You are Elizabeth of York?" Jacqueline asked. "The writer of the famous letter?"

Liz laughed. "Yes, that's me. I'm Dickon's niece and I'm supposed to show a hopeless incestuous passion for him."

She leered at Sir Richard, who smiled fondly.

Mrs. Ponsonby-Jones moved in. She was so much larger than Sir Richard that she seemed about to engulf him like a giant amoeba, and the look she gave her daughter held no maternal warmth.

"Don't be offensive, Elizabeth. You are distracting your cousin Richard from his duties as host."

"Elizabeth distracts all of us." A man sauntered toward them. "My name's Kent, Dr. Kirby. I'm glad you could join us. As the only heretic in this group, I welcome support. Hello, Thomas."

Kent's short, stocky body appeared almost cylindrical in his long black-and gold-robe. He wore his gray hair clipped short. All his hirsute efforts had been concentrated on his moustache, which curled out and up like the horns of a buffalo. The sleeves of his robe were slit to the shoulders, and the heavy hanging folds were fur-trimmed, as was the hem of the garment. On Kent's head was perched an absurd tall hat with a rounded top and a yellow padded edge.

"Major General Sir Archibald Kent?" Jacqueline asked, shaking hands.

"Thomas has briefed you?"

"He had no need to do so. Even in the wilds of America the newspapers follow your career with interest. Don't you find Ricardian research a little dull after your—er—activities in the Middle East?"

"Not at all." Kent displayed long, yellowing teeth in a wolfish smile. "The Arabs and Israelis are easy to deal with compared with my colleagues."

"Why do you regard yourself as a heretic?" Jacqueline asked. "I thought membership in this society was contingent upon belief in Richard's innocence."

"You make us sound rather like a peculiar religious sect," Weldon said with a smile.

Kent gave a brusque, barking laugh. "That's what we are, Dick. You see, Doctor, the others admire Richard because they believe he was innocent of the vital crime —the murder of his nephews. I admire him because I think he was guilty. They want to make him a medieval liberal left-winger; I see him as a practical politician and a damn good soldier. It was sound policy in those days to rid yourself of disinherited princes; they were a focus for rebellion."

"Fascinating," said Jacqueline.

"Disgusting," said Mrs. Ponsonby-Jones.

"He doesn't mean it," said Lady Isobel, with a high-pitched giggle. "He loves to tease us."

Jacqueline hadn't taken her eyes from Kent. "What part are you playing?" she asked.

"Buckingham." Kent barked again. "Very appropriate, eh? I insisted on the role. The duke is one of the strong suspects for the murder, you know. His behavior was damn peculiar; first his solid support of Richard against the Woodvilles—he was one of the first to urge that Richard take the crown. Then suddenly he is leading a rebellion against his former ally."

"It was peculiar behavior."

"Not at all," Kent said promptly. "Buckingham wanted to be the power behind the throne. Richard wouldn't stand for it. So Buckingham decided to play Kingmaker with Henry Tudor, who might prove more malleable. Perhaps he planned to claim the throne himself, after he had made use of the Tudor. Perfectly sensible plan."

"It makes more sense than you do," Thomas said, scowling. "Ignore him, Jacqueline; he'll argue on either side of a question just for the fun of it. No more debate, colleagues, until the formalities are over."

There were only three others to be introduced. Donald Ellis, a chubby man with eyes of luminous innocence, wore gorgeous purple velvet and a crown. A pastor of the Church of England, he had chosen to portray the lusty, virile Edward IV. Thomas's eyes, meeting Jacqueline's, saw the amusement in them and knew she had not missed the implications. The roles played by these people had meaning on a number of levels.

John Rawdon looked alarmingly like Abraham Lincoln, even to the wart on his cheek. He was a Harley Street specialist who was prominently featured in the newspapers because of his advocacy of natural foods. His reputation as an internist made it difficult for his exasperated colleagues in the medical profession to denigrate his recent enthusiasm. Certainly the doctor was a living testimonial to his eating habits; his tall, thin body moved with the vigor of a young man's, and his coarse black hair had not a touch of gray. His head was uncovered; the chaperon, a cap with a formal version of the medieval hood, was flung back over his shoulder and attached to his belt by a long liripipe. His velvet skirts did not suit his vigorous stride; he kept kicking them out of the way as he walked. He represented the last Lancastrian King. Saintly, feeble Henry VI.

Then the last member of the group rose from behind the grand piano, which had hitherto concealed all but his head and shoulders.

Alone of the men, Philip Rohan had chosen to wear the short tunic. And short meant very short. It was belted in at the waist like the long robe, but its skirts were only six inches long. The rest of Rohan was covered by tights as revealing as those of a dancer. Thomas couldn't even suspect him of padding the tights. The ripple of muscle fore and aft indicated that the shape was all Rohan. And Jacqueline was taking it in with fascinated interest.

Finally her eyes moved up from the pale-gray tights to the green-and-silver tunic, with its padded sleeves and fur-trimmed neck. Rohan's chest was broad enough without the extra width of the sleeves; he looked almost wasp-waisted. The chaperon, which he wore on his head, was very becoming. The fall of cloth along one side of the face softened features that were too hard for conventional handsomeness, but which had a rakish appeal. He too wore his hair long. It was fair, so pale a gold that it looked like silver, and as fine as a girl's. But there was nothing girlish about the rest of him.

"Well, well," he said softly, surveying Jacqueline as candidly as she had observed him. "What a pleasant surprise. I expected any expert Thomas collected would be hawk-nosed and hideous."

"You are an actor, of course," said Jacqueline.

"How did you know?" The deep, controlled voice quivered with amusement. "I am also Hastings, Richard's best friend, whom he beheaded one morning between elevenses and lunch."

"After he had treacherously plotted against Richard," squeaked Lady Isobel indignantly.

"And conspired with the Woodvilles," added Weldon. "It is difficult to explain Hastings' change of loyalty. No doubt he was seduced by—"

"You sound like one of your own articles," Liz interrupted. "Do be quiet, darling Uncle Dickon, and let Jacqueline have some tea."

"She'd much rather have a drink," said Philip. "Wouldn't you, darling?"

"No," said Jacqueline. With Philip's assistance she removed her jacket, displaying a sleeveless green jersey top. Looking cool and relaxed, she settled on one of the sofas and smiled at Weldon. "Tea would be splendid."

For a time no one spoke. The silence was unusual and, to Thomas, slightly disturbing. It was as if they were all wary in the presence of a stranger—afraid of giving something away.

"Why all the cops and robbers about our arrival, Dick?" he asked, to break the silence.

"I meant to ask if you had had any difficulty," Weldon said.

"Difficulty? Why should we?"

"The wolves are gathering," said Mrs. Ponsonby-Jones melodramatically. "We are virtually besieged, Thomas."

"I did notice the village was unusually crowded. You mean those people are—"

"Newspaper persons," said Lady Isobel, as one might say "burglars." "Frightful people! One of them actually tried to creep into the house."

"But you're going to admit the press on Sunday," Thomas objected. "What's all the fuss about?"

It was Kent who answered, with his barking laugh.

"They want to catch us—what's your popular phrase?—with our pants down. Attired in ludicrous costumes, playing childish games—drunken and lecherous, hopefully. Fleet Street is quiet this week; no crises, only the same boring old wars."

"The silly season," Jacqueline said. "You must admit

you make good copy. Many of you are famous in your own fields."

"And some of us simply adore being good copy," said Liz. Her eyes moved from Lady Isobel, who pretended not to notice, to Philip, who laughed aloud.

"I've no objection to being photographed," he said, striking a pose.

"Well, the rest of us do object," said Mrs. Ponsonby-Jones vigorously. "I cannot imagine why people are so ill-bred!"

"Piltdown man," said Jacqueline unexpectedly. They all stared at her; most of them looked blank, but a few got the point. The vicar chuckled, and Philip's mouth widened in a cynical smile.

"The disclosure of the Piltdown hoax made headlines," Jacqueline went on. "People love to see the experts deflated. You have publicized your find extensively. If, after the publicity, it should turn out to be another hoax . . ."

"Impossible," cried Lady Isobel.

"I only wish we could be certain."

It was the rector who spoke. Ruffled white hair framed his rosy face like a halo, but the cherubic features were worried.

"But you were the one who found the letter," Weldon said.

"I did not find it," said Mr. Ellis irritably. Thomas sensed that he had tried to make this point before, without convincing his fanatical audience of its importance. "It was sent to me anonymously, and if that is not significant. . . ." He glanced at Jacqueline, who was watching him steadily, and smiled. "Yes. Mrs. Kirby sees my point, if the rest of you do not. Now, Mrs. Kirby, I have stated the fact somewhat baldly. The letter enclosed with the manuscript gives adequate reasons for the sender's wishing to remain unknown at present. It also provides a plausible history for the manuscript, which was last seen by Buck, in the seventeenth century. We are not so naive as we appear; all of us are familiar with manuscripts and letters of this period, and there are no egregious errors in this letter which would suggest forgery. All the same . . ."

"Yes," Jacqueline said. "All the same . . . Frankly, Mr. Ellis, I wouldn't touch it with a ten-foot pole. What prompted you to go ahead with this unnecessary publicity?"

"I deplore it!" Ellis looked like a vexed baby. "I have always argued against that aspect. After I had shown Sir Richard the letter, we agreed that the executive committee should examine it. Sir Richard very kindly suggested a weekend here, so that we could discuss the problem at leisure. I don't understand quite how these arrangements evolved. . . ."

"All sorts of strange things evolve when this committee meets," said Kent sarcastically. "However, Ellis, you are too timid. What do we risk? There can be no question of legal fraud, since our anonymous donor has not asked for money; he is willing to wait until the manuscript has been officially authenticated before he is paid, and even then he throws himself on our generosity. How can we object to that?"

` "But the embarrassment . . ."

"Bah," said Kent. He was the only man Thomas had ever met who actually said "bah," and he said it with emphasis. "There will be controversy in any case. Have you ever known two experts who can agree on a technical point? Every important scientific or cultural discovery has been greeted with mingled cheers and hisses. The Piltdown skull was accepted by experts for years; the authentic cave paintings of Altamira were considered fakes by most of the historians of the day. If our letter is a forgery, it's a damned good one. Some experts will accept it and some will reject it, and the same thing will happen if it is genuine. I'm not keen on the publicity either, but it can't do any harm—unless we manage to make asses of ourselves in some other way."

Silence followed this pronouncement, which was, Thomas had to admit, a perfectly reasonable summary of the situation. Kent was no fool, for all his outspoken belligerence and his deplorable tendency to punch reporters in the nose.

Jacqueline looked at Weldon.

"Why not call in an expert?" she asked.

"But we have." Weldon smiled engagingly at her.

"Have we, though?" Lady Isobel giggled maliciously. "As an *expert*, Mrs. Kirby, you surely are familiar with Sir Richard's reputation. He is one of the foremost authorities in the world on fifteenth-century manuscripts."

"Yes, I surely must be familiar with that, mustn't I," said Jacqueline. She glanced at Thomas in a way that boded no good.

"Well," said that gentleman hastily, "I think I'll just run upstairs and change. All that bus travel—"

"I'm being a bad host again," Weldon said sadly. "Dr. Kirby, you must be tired too. I'll ring . . ."

Before he could do so, the door opened.

"They have arrived, Sir Richard," said the butler.

"They?" Thomas repeated. "Who is missing?"

"Why, Thomas," said Liz, in an affected drawl. "Don't

tell me you haven't noticed that my fiancé is not here? Frank is so conspicuous."

"Frank is a nice young fellow," Thomas said. "I like him. It's just that the rest of us are rather obtrusive."

Liz smiled mockingly. Mildly embarrassed, Thomas went on, "Who else is coming?"

"A most distinguished guest," said Mrs. Ponsonby-Jones. "The new president of the American branch of our society is flying over in order to be present at this great moment. His name is O'Hagan."

"Frank is the only one of us coming by automobile," Weldon explained. "That is why I asked him to meet Mr. O'Hagan at Heathrow. O'Hagan has never been out of the States before, and I gather from his letters that he is somewhat apprehensive about traveling alone. This is a difficult place to find. . . ."

Two men appeared in the doorway. After his *faux pas* Thomas made a point of greeting Frank Acton with particular warmth.

All the same, he had to admit that Frank did not stand out in a crowd. He was of medium height and build, with one of those pleasantly nondescript faces that blur in one's memory. His dark hair was long but neatly barbered and his clothes were conservative. Thomas remembered that the young man was a budding solicitor, a very lowly member of the firm that handled Sir Richard's affairs. It was through this connection that he had met Liz. Thomas had wondered, when their engagement was announced, what the girl saw in him.

The American Ricardian was a tall, stooped man of about Thomas's age. His square-jawed, hawk-nosed face might have been attractive if it had not been set in an expression of timid terror. Projecting front teeth increased his resemblance to a nervous rabbit, and a bushy white moustache vibrated like whiskers when he was agitated. There was no doubt as to his identity; fastened to his left lapel with a large safety pin was a name tag. Thomas had an insane vision of the American society affixing the label as they pushed their president onto his plane like a bundle. Or had O'Hagan labeled himself? It was an equally insane idea. Weldon had said the American sounded apprehensive. That was an understatement. What was wrong with the man? Maybe he couldn't talk.

He could. The voice was a high-pitched whine and the moustache vibrated like a hummingbird's wings.

"Frightful, frightful," he exclaimed. "Those people at the gate—like a howling mob, ladies and gentlemen! I felt quite hunted, I assure you!"

"Not very bright of you, Frank, old boy," Philip said. "You ought to have driven in the stable gate instead of coming to the front of the grounds."

"No one bothered to warn me." Frank's voice was low and well modulated, with impeccable vowels, but he sounded irritated. He glanced betrayingly at Liz, who raised a languid hand in greeting, before he went on. "I hadn't realized you were turning this meeting into a circus. It's been a rotten day. I had difficulty finding Mr. O'Hagan; he wasn't where he was supposed to be—"

"It is such a confusing place," said Mr. O'Hagan pathetically. "All those *large* buildings—and people running around, bumping into you and pushing you—"

"The worst is over, Mr. O'Hagan," Weldon said soothingly. "You are perfectly safe with us. Do you . . . do you feel up to meeting the others?"

Mr. O'Hagan was able to nerve himself to the ordeal, but the introductions were marred by Liz's tendency to giggle. As soon as they were completed, Thomas excused himself. Jacqueline followed suit, and a neat parlormaid showed them to their rooms.

They needed a guide. Weldon House was like a maze. The copy of Crosby Hall was not the only accretion; wings and annexes proliferated. As they paced along behind the maid, Thomas heard Jacqueline mutter something about rabbits. He didn't know whether she was referring to the warren of corridors and rooms, or to Mr. O'Hagan, and he didn't inquire. He was not looking forward to his next conversation with Jacqueline.

Their rooms were adjoining. Thomas wondered whether this was accidental or not. The maid was certainly well trained. She didn't even blink when Jacqueline reached out a long arm and dragged Thomas into her room.

"I've got to unpack," he said, retreating.

"I expect you have been unpacked. I see I have. Doesn't the maid unpack for guests at these high-class affairs?"

"They do here, at any rate, and I hate it," said Thomas, still backing toward the door. "I always feel as if I have holes in my underwear even when I know I don't. Maybe I can get there before—"

"Close the door," said Jacqueline ominously.

There was no use putting it off. Thomas obeyed. When he had done so, Jacqueline dropped into a chair and beamed at him.

"Thomas, you are the love of my life. How can I ever thank you for bringing me here?"

"You aren't mad? I didn't warn you about Sir Richard—"

"Being an expert on the fifteenth century? Oh, that's all right. His appraisal is meaningless anyhow. He wants to believe in the letter. That's fatal to objectivity."

Masochistically Thomas continued, "And those frightful old women! I'm sorry you had to put up with their insults. Of course both of them are after poor Dick, and they regard every other woman as a rival. He's years younger than either of them, but he is quite a matrimonial catch."

"He's a catch, all right. He's sweet. Oh, Thomas, I am enjoying this! Let me see if I've got everybody straight in my mind. Sir Richard is Richard the Third, of course; no one else could possibly play Richard. And that enormous Ponsonby-Jones women copped the role of Richard's queen—pale, frail consumptive Queen Anne. How did she get away with that?"

"The Ponsonby-Joneses are Sir Richard's only relatives. They are distant relatives, but he feels responsible for them. He's particularly fond of young Elizabeth Ponsonby-Jones."

"Who is Elizabeth of York," Jacqueline resumed her summary, "Richard's niece, and later the queen of Henry the Seventh. The nice little rector is Edward the Fourth, Richard's brother—does he see himself in his secret day-dreams as a lusty lecher? Dr. Rawdon is poor, weak Henry the Sixth, which is equally inappropriate—he's so healthy-looking, it hurts to look at him. General Kent isn't suited to the role of Buckingham, either; Buckingham must have been a vacillating character; he changed his mind so often. Kent is certainly not indecisive. Lady Isobel—oh, Lord, Thomas, have you read any of her ghastly books?— is Edward the Fourth's queen, Elizabeth Woodville. She probably would have preferred to be Richard's queen, but she wouldn't object to playing Elizabeth Woodville, the fabulous beauty with the silver-gilt hair who seduced a king into marriage. Philip Rohan as Lord Hastings—yes, but he could play any part. He's a gifted actor. He has a beautiful voice."

"It wasn't his voice you were admiring," said Thomas.

"Now, Thomas. Whom have I forgotten?"

"Well, you know I'm playing Clarence, the brother of Richard and Edward. You've forgotten Frank, Liz's fiance. Everybody forgets the poor guy."

"I know one reason why I forgot him; I don't know what part he's playing. Did you tell me?"

"I guess not. He's Edward of Lancaster, the son of Henry the Sixth. He was the first husband of Anne, whom Richard later married. Edward was killed in battle, but the Tudor historians accused Richard of murdering him."

"I know that. Okay, I guess I've got them sorted out. Thomas, do you realize what this is? It's an English house party, darling, straight out of all those British detective stories I revel in. These people are classic characters. They couldn't be better if you had invented them. The doctor, the vicar, the village squire; the catty middle-aged hags and the sulky, beautiful young heroine, and the two juveniles—homely and nice, handsome and rakish. There is one missing. But I suppose it would be too much—"

The door burst open.

"Ah," said a voice. "You must be thinking of me—the missing character! The offensive, precocious small boy!"

The final adjective could only have referred to the apparition's relative age. His cheeks were still soft and downy, his voice high tenor. Otherwise he was more than large; he was elephantine. His puffy pink face was perfectly spherical. His features were regular and well shaped, but they were drowned in fat. His costume was unfortunate. The tights, stretched to bursting point, enclosed legs like Karnakian pillars, and his tunic was dragged up in front by a pot belly that would have disgraced a middle-aged beer drinker. The front of this garment was streaked with food and drink stains.

"Offensive is right," said Thomas distastefully. "Jacqueline, this is Percival Ponsonby-Jones, the son and heir of the lady you met downstairs. I needn't introduce you to him; he knows who you are. He knows everything. How long have you been eavesdropping, Percy?"

"Long enough to hear my mother referred to as a middle-aged hag." Percy came into the room and dropped heavily onto the bed. From a pouch at his belt he took a handful of cookies and began to eat them, scattering crumbs deliberately.

"Hag was an ill-chosen word," admitted Jacqueline. "It suggests someone who is haggard and undernourished. . . . What part are you taking in this charade, child? The court jester? Or perhaps Clarence's son, the one who was mentally retarded?"

Thomas blinked. Jacqueline was not usually so brutal. The attack disconcerted the boy. He hesitated, trying to decide which insult to answer first.

"I'm Edward the Fifth," he said. "The one who was murdered by Henry Tudor."

"Not smothered in the Tower by Richard?" Jacqueline asked.

Percy finished the cookies and extracted an apple from the same place.

"Everyone knows Richard didn't kill the princes," he said scornfully. "That's a Tudor slander. I expect you don't know who the Tudors were."

"But I thought the bones of the boys had been found in the Tower," said Jacqueline gently.

Percy expanded. Thomas felt a faint twinge of pity for

the boy; he ought to have been warned by Jacqueline's earlier comments, but he was too young and too conceited to know better.

"The bones were found in 1674, when some workmen were demolishing a staircase outside the White Tower. It wasn't till 1933 that the bones were examined by a doctor and a dentist. *They* said the skeletons were of two children, aged about ten and twelve.

"Now . . ." Percy took another bite of apple and continued in a muffled voice, "you wouldn't know this, of course, but the very precision of the ages given is suspect. In order to blame Richard for the crime, you have to prove that the boys were exactly ten, and between twelve and thirteen, when they died, and you can't prove that because it's impossible to determine the ages of bones of young people that accurately. You can't even tell whether they were boys or girls before puberty. The description of where the bones were found doesn't agree with Sir Thomas More's story, either, but I won't go into that, because it's too complicated for you to understand."

He smirked at Jacqueline and took another huge bite.

"More says they were buried 'at the stair foot, meetly deep in the ground under a great heap of stones,' " Jacqueline murmured. "The accounts of the seventeenth-century workmen who found the bones imply that they were under the foundations of the stairs. Not only would that have been a much more laborious operation than the one More describes, but it doesn't agree with his statement that the bones were later removed and reburied elsewhere by a certain priest. There is also the evidence of one anthropologist consulted by Kendall, who believed that the older child could not have been more than nine years of age. In the absence of a dating process, which cannot at present be used effectively on human bone, we do not know how long the remains were in the Tower. They could have been buried at any time after 1100 A.D. I must admit I share your doubt as to the identification of these skeletal remains with the two princes."

Percy's mouth hung open, giving the viewers an unattractive vista of masticated apple.

"Think you're clever, don't you," he said feebly.

"I don't think, I know," said Jacqueline. She added parenthetically to Thomas, "There is no point in being subtle with him, Thomas. Now, Percy, go away. Don't ever come in here again without knocking and waiting for permission. If you do, I will belt you one—as we crude Americans are wont to say."

"You wouldn't dare. . . ." Percy stood up.

"But you can't be sure. Taking chances lends variety and interest to life."

Percy began to look trapped. "I'll tell them you've got Thomas in here. I saw you drag him in. My mother would like to hear *that.*"

Jacqueline laughed.

"What a little horror you are," Thomas said. "If young Edward was anything like you, it's no wonder he was smothered."

"You're wasting words," Jacqueline said. "Never tell them more than once. Never bluff. Act."

She rose and advanced purposefully on Percy, who proved her point by retreating, at full speed, and without further comment. In the doorway he collided with Sir Richard, who was passing along the corridor.

"So there you are," Weldon said. "Your mother is looking for you, Percy. Run along now."

Percy left, with an eloquent look at Jacqueline, and Weldon shook his head.

"I do hope he hasn't been bothering you. He's a rather difficult child. Extremely intelligent; but it's not easy for his mother, lacking a man's authority. . . ."

He looked wistfully at Jacqueline, who smiled brightly.

"Don't apologize, Sir Richard. I enjoyed my chat with Percy very much."

II

At the hour appointed, Thomas made his way back to the drawing room. He was wearing slacks and a sport shirt; Weldon had decreed that the evening meeting and meal were to be informal. Thomas was relieved that he did not have to wear his medieval robes. It was an unseasonably warm evening, and he was shy of displaying himself before Jacqueline's ironical eyes.

He found the drawing room deserted except for Wilkes the butler, who was sourly studying the drinks tray. Thomas rather liked Wilkes; he was as well trained and as formal as Jenkins, but his manner was not so supercilious as that of the tall chauffeur. A stout, balding little man, he looked up as Thomas came in.

"Am I the first one down?" Thomas asked, accepting a whiskey and soda. He didn't really like whiskey and soda, but it seemed the proper thing to have.

"They have retired to the library," Wilkes said. "I proposed to Sir Richard that I should follow with the tray, but he assured me they would return immediately."

Thomas understood the butler's air of pique. Soothingly he said, "I'll go after them. Maybe I can casually mention the passage of time."

Wilkes's melancholy expression did not change. Thomas had to agree that his errand was probably vain. When Sir Richard got into the library it was hard to get him out, especially when he had a new audience.

The door of the room stood open; from the corridor Thomas could hear Weldon's voice rising and falling in gentle, uninterrupted cadence. He paused in the doorway for a moment, enjoying the chance of watching the others before they realized they were being observed.

Most of them had abandoned medieval garb, but Percy still wore his messy costume. Either he didn't know how terrible he looked, or he didn't care. Philip, leaning gracefully against the carved stone mantel, was also in costume. Unconsciously Thomas pulled in his stomach.

He was next struck by the unnatural alliance between Mrs. Ponsonby-Jones and Lady Isobel, who were seated side by side. They looked comical together, the ample girth of the one emphasizing the scrawniness of the other. They were united by a common emotion; two pairs of narrowed eyes stared intently at the enemy. Jacqueline was wearing her favorite green, a misty shade that set off her tanned arms and shoulders. It clung to her tall body, and the ladies weren't the only ones who were staring.

Weldon had taken Jacqueline's arm in order to lead her around. He was still talking.

There was plenty for him to talk about. High-ceilinged, with French doors opening onto the terrace, the room contained two tiers of bookshelves with an open gallery running around three sides and stairs leading up to it. Another flight of narrow circular steps went up from the gallery. It opened, as Thomas knew, into the private sitting room of Sir Richard's suite, so that the scholarly gentleman could reach his beloved books without a long walk through the house.

A big library table and an equally mammoth desk were dwarfed by the dimensions of the room. Fat leather chairs and sofas were scattered about. Thick wall-to-wall carpeting muffled voices and footsteps. Glass cases, spaced at intervals, contained some of the rarer items of Weldon's collection, and there were other exhibits on the wall over the fireplace—an impressive array of medieval weapons. Prominent among these was an enormous two-handed sword. It was this object Weldon was discussing as Thomas entered.

"I am convinced it was Richard's. It comes from Leicester, near Bosworth, and the tradition—"

Kent interrupted with a snort.

"Nonsense. The weapon is certainly sixteenth century. You may be the handwriting expert, but I'm the authority on armament, and I assure you—"

Weldon turned. He looked almost grim enough for Richard III.

"I beg your pardon. The historical tradition—"

Kent gave another volcanic snort and Frank said tactfully,

"I can't understand how any soldier could wield a weapon so heavy. How long is it precisely, sir?"

Instead of answering, Weldon climbed nimbly onto a chair and lifted the sword down. Jacqueline stepped back as the mammoth blade left its support, but Weldon handled it easily.

"It only weighs fourteen pounds and a bit," he said.

"Overall length, eighty-nine inches," Kent added. "The blade is well over six feet."

The startling dimensions of the sword became clearer when Weldon held it upright. He was several inches under six feet; the hilt topped his head by a foot and a half.

"You are thinking in terms of modern dueling," Kent said to Frank. "That didn't begin until the seventeenth century. In Richard's time the idea was to whack your enemy as hard and as often as you could. The sword was used for cutting, not thrusting."

He demonstrated, taking the weapon from Weldon. The blade cut the air with a deadly and surprising precision; even Thomas, in the distant doorway, stepped back a pace.

"There's a knack to it," Kent warned, as the others crowded forward, wanting to try their hands. "Don't swing it as I did, you'll lop an ear off someone."

Frank was the first to try; he was properly cautious, remarking on the poor balance of the weapon. Lady Isobel made a show of trying in vain to lift the weight. Jacqueline gave her a thoughtful look and hoisted the sword without difficulty, remarking, "My purse weighs more than that." But when Percy swaggered forward and reached for the sword, Thomas decided it was time to intervene.

"Hey," he said. "You're all supposed to be back in the drawing room. Wilkes is sulking . . ."

It was too late.

"Dinner is served," said Wilkes, and gave Thomas a reproachful look.

III

They were dining early so that the business meeting could start at a reasonable hour. It was still light outside; from his seat Thomas could see out across the wide lawns toward the maze and the rose garden. The softening light made the fabulous turf look like smooth green velvet. It was a lovely view, a scene out of the England of glamorized history and legend.

Then two figures appeared, one human, the other four-legged. A watchman, with a large mastiff on a leash.

It was ridiculous, Thomas thought sourly. All this fuss and furor over a few reporters. You'd think the place were under siege by howling Lancastrians waving pikes and thirsting for Weldon's head.

Thomas was sulking, although he would not have chosen that word. Rohan and Kent, the most aggressive males in the group, had grabbed the chairs next to Jacqueline. Weldon had disposed of the two older women with the skill a hunted man develops. Mrs. Ponsonby-Jones sat triumphantly at the foot of the table as hostess, but Lady Isobel had won the seat at her host's right. Thomas was stuck between Mrs. Ponsonby-Jones and Liz, and was getting no attention from either. Liz was preempted by Frank, on her other side, and Mrs. Ponsonby-Jones was preoccupied with her son. Percy was directly across from Thomas, and the latter watched Percy eat with fascinated disgust. Eat was hardly the word; the wretched boy swallowed food like a python, and his besotted mother kept urging him to eat more. Thomas averted his eyes and let fragments of conversation drift through his ears into his brain. The discussion, as might have been expected, was predominantly Ricardian.

". . . Richard blamed the Woodvilles for Clarence's death. They had a pressing motive for wanting him out of the way if, as seems probable, he knew about the precontract."

". . . try to eat another teeny bit of beef, darling. A

growing boy must keep up his strength."

". . . wore German armor. It was the best available."

". . . might have won if Northumberland had not remained aloof from the battle. Richard ought to have known he was treacherous . . ."

"Why? He had loaded the rascal with favors."

The rector's voice rose over those of the other speakers. He and the American visitor were refighting the Battle of Bosworth, and Thomas smiled to himself as he saw others turn toward the debaters. He was reminded of Southern friends talking about a more recent war. "If Stonewall Jackson hadn't been killed . . . If England had come in on our side . . ." The lost causes, the romantic failures . . . the flight to Varennes, the Forty-Five, Bonnie Dundee and the Lost Dauphin. "If only . . ." Futile speculations, impractical and thoroughly irresistible.

The American answered.

"Richard's popularity in the North threatened Northumberland's position in that region. If Henry Tudor won, Northumberland could expect to be supreme—"

"He didn't have to risk supporting the wrong side," Kent interrupted. "All he had to do was sit tight and refuse to move. Shrewd—very shrewd."

"Despicable, you mean," squeaked Lady Isobel.

"Ah, the gentle illogic of women," Kent said, with a vicious smile. "I regret Richard's betrayal as much as you, dear lady, but I must admit he did not act with his usual good sense. If he had anticipated the treachery of the Stanleys—"

A chorus of voices drowned him out.

"Yes, the Stanleys were the decisive factor."

". . . incredibly naive of Richard. Stanley was the husband of Henry Tudor's mother."

"What do you mean, naive? Richard had Stanley's own son as hostage . . ."

"Stanley knew Richard wouldn't kill the boy. He was too damned soft-headed."

"Too sensitive and kind! No, poor dear Richard's greatest error was in attacking Henry Tudor personally. He ought to have remained safely in the rear!"

"Balderdash. That was a brilliant move, and it came damned close to winning the day. Richard was a bonny fighter and Henry was a coward. Five more minutes and Richard would have smashed the rascal's skull—"

"Five minutes? Two minutes! Richard struck down the biggest brutes in Henry's bodyguard. . . ."

Thomas was shaken by a vertiginous shock of confusion. Had it happened five hundred years ago, or only yesterday? Turning, he met the eyes of the girl beside him and saw his own incredulity mirrored in her face.

"We're all mad," she muttered.

"It's a harmless madness," Thomas answered slowly. "And you at least seem impervious. . . ."

Liz shook her head. Her fine brown hair shifted silkily.

"I'm as bad as they are. 'King Richard, alone, was killed fighting manfully in the thickest press of his enemies. . . .' It was his enemies who said that about him; even though they hated him and murdered him, they couldn't deny him that tribute. And I . . ." She laughed softly, but there was a note in her voice Thomas didn't like. "I've got a schoolgirl crush on him. I'm too sophisticated to fall for the pop musicians and the nude centerfold types. I dream about a man who's been dead and rotten for five hundred years."

"Liz . . ."

The girl shook her head again. The cloud cleared from

her face, which regained its habitual expression of sulky boredom.

"Thomas, you are too much," she said lightly. "One can't resist teasing you, you're so trusting."

Without giving Thomas time to reply, she raised her voice in a shout.

"Mother! Isn't it time for the ladies to retire? We'll never start the meeting at this rate."

Mrs. Ponsonby-Jones glared. She was not quick at repartee. It was Weldon who replied amiably,

"What conventional circles you move in, Liz. I thought your generation lingered over the port along with the men."

"Port is not what we linger over," said Liz. "You're close, though."

"None of us is going to linger tonight," Weldon said, as Philip laughed and Mrs. Ponsonby-Jones pondered Liz's comment. "We'll have coffee later, at the meeting, if that is agreeable. In the Great Hall at eight, then. Frank, you're giving the first paper."

"Right, sir. I'd better go up and get my notes together."

Weldon gave the younger man a friendly pat on the back.

"Not nervous, are you?"

"Oh, no, sir."

"Nothing to be nervous about. We're all friends."

Frank glanced from Philip's wide white grin to Kent's anticipatory smile. His affable face took on a look of deep gloom.

IV

The reverberations of a gong summoned the members to the meeting. Thomas had been refreshing his memory with Kendall's *Richard III;* when he reached the Hall, most of the others were already present. He stopped in the entrance to enjoy a moment of sentimentality; the reconstruction of Richard's former home delighted him. Jacqueline, also late, came up behind him, and Thomas moved aside so she could see.

It was a vast room, its floor of unpolished Purbeck marble stretching away like a skating rink. The fireplace was a simple rounded arch of carved stone, without mantel or hood. At the far end a minstrel's gallery, balustraded in dark oak, was reached by a winding stair. Windows filled the upper half of the Hall; each light rose to a pointed arch framed in stone trefoils. Panes of stained glass replaced some of the diamond-shaped panes, and Weldon had made sure Richard's coat of arms was included along with those of other characters in the Ricardian drama. The lower half of the walls was covered with priceless old tapestries from Weldon's collection.

The real glory of the room was its ceiling. Sculptured, painted beams intersected in complex patterns, with bosses and hanging ornaments at the points of intersection. Enough of the natural wood had been left to provide a mellow brown background for the designs in crimson and green and shining gold. Thomas had never asked, but he felt quite sure that the gilt was genuine gold leaf.

On the dais at the far end Weldon had placed a table, as long as a fallen oak, surrounded by chairs that were copies of fifteenth-century furniture, with high, carved backs and seats of crimson velvet. Weldon was already seated at the head of the table. His mammoth chair dwarfed his slight body, and Thomas's mouth pursed in a silent whistle as he observed the chair. It was new since his last visit, and from the crown on the back to the shape of the arms it rather suggested a throne.

Perhaps it was the throne that had cast a hush over the assembled group. The silence continued as Thomas escorted Jacqueline down the length of the room. He felt like the victim of some formal ceremony, marriage or investiture or coronation, and he wondered if the floor was as slippery as it looked. Jacqueline paced solemnly at his side, looking neither to right nor to left. Thomas knew she was enjoying herself immensely.

Liz winked at him as he took his seat. Philip was sitting next to the girl; he nudged her and said something in a whisper, so close to her ear that his breath stirred the curls on her cheek. Liz giggled. Her mother glared.

Frank was the only one who had not arrived. Thomas wondered if the boy really was nervous. Surely a lawyer ought not suffer from stage fright. It was a hard audience for a novice to face, though. Frank was new to Ricardian controversy, having joined the society after he became engaged to Liz. Now he had to perform before a group of critical experts, and in the presence of his fiancé's equally critical family—including the wealthy, expert head of that family.

Thomas glanced at the program. Weldon didn't do things by halves; the document was printed on expensive paper and bound in calf. Frank's was the first paper of the evening, and Thomas sighed inwardly as he read the title.

"Who Murdered the Princes?"

That was the trouble with amateur societies, they kept rehashing the same old material. The "murder" of the princes had been written about so often; there was nothing to be said that hadn't been said a thousand times. But it fretted Ricardians like a bad tooth. They couldn't leave it alone. And some of the poor innocents couldn't tell the difference between logic and wishful thinking, between the relevant and the extraneous. They threw everything in together and served it up, assuming that the warmed-over mixture of fact and fancy would appeal to an audience.

However, Thomas had to admit that amateur historians were not the only ones who suffered from this particular weakness. The scholarly journals were full of trivia and faulty argument.

Absorbed in his own mildly pompous thoughts, he was unaware of the rising murmur of impatience until Philip called out,

"Sir Richard, what's happened to Frank? It's nearly half past eight."

"Probably he's hiding under the bed," said Percy, with a hoarse chuckle. He was eating jelly beans, or some form of confectionery that resembled them, brightly colored and very slippery. There was a constant rattle of fallen candies from his direction.

"Can he have fallen asleep?" Lady Isobel wondered. She looked groggy herself, and if there was the odor of jelly beans from Percy's direction, a scent of another kind wafted from Lady Isobel. Seeing her flushed face, Thomas felt sure she had taken a nip or two in the privacy of her room before coming to the meeting.

Jacqueline glanced at her watch.

"Is he often absentminded?"

"Quite the reverse; most methodical young fellow I know." Weldon looked worried. "It's foolish—a healthy specimen like that, nothing could have happened, but perhaps we had better . . ."

"Quite right," Kent said briskly. "Let's hunt him out. You ladies stay here, we'll soon find him."

Lady Isobel didn't look capable of movement, and Mrs. Ponsonby-Jones inclined her head in majestic acquiescence, but Jacqueline was already on her feet, and Liz followed suit. In a disorganized group they trailed one another up the stairs.

The most logical assumption was that Frank had fallen asleep. In fact, Thomas thought with a small shock, there was no other logical assumption. If an emergency had kept the young lawyer from the meeting, he would have sent a message.

Percy was the first to reach Frank's room, not because he was more nimble, but because the others tended to hang back. The fat boy flung the door open, and as Weldon came forward, he announced with the relish some people feel at proclaiming bad news, "He's not here. Unless he's under the bed."

He was not under the bed. Feeling like a fool, but driven by an inexplicable compulsion, Thomas looked.

For a few moments they stood staring at one another. Then Kent said brusquely, "Ridiculous. Organization, that's what we need. Ring for Wilkes, Dick. Perhaps one of the servants has seen the lad."

None of the servants had, not since the whole group had gone upstairs after dinner. This was not surprising, since the staff had been at its own dinner in the servants' hall; but the news cast a pall over the group. Percy's was the only cheerful face.

"All right," Kent said, after the butler had gone back to his duties. "Let's keep the servants out of this; it's bound to be a tempest in a teapot. I'm going out to inquire of the outdoor staff. Perhaps Frank went for a walk and dozed off. Dick, look in the library, lounge, drawing room. Philip . . ."

"We'll investigate the bedrooms," said Philip, taking Liz's hand.

"But what would he—" Liz stopped. The enameled facade of her face was beginning to crack.

"He might have fainted," Thomas said. "He looks healthy enough, but I suppose he might have a heart condition, or epilepsy, or something . . ."

"No," Liz said positively.

Weldon gave her an odd look and then said firmly, "We are becoming fantastical. I feel sure there is some unalarming explanation."

They separated. Kent, moving briskly, was soon out of sight. The doctor and the rector followed. Weldon gave the others a hesitant smile before heading for the stairs. O'Hagan trailed after him. Percy followed Philip and Liz along the corridor; he had, Thomas thought, a propensity for bedrooms. That left Thomas and Jacqueline, and when they were alone Thomas turned toward her.

"You've been very quiet. What are you thinking?"

Jacqueline didn't answer immediately. She reached into her bag and took out her glasses. The purse was a good deal larger than it looked, as was characteristic of Jacqueline's purses. Settling the glasses firmly on her nose, Jacqueline said,

"I think something is wrong. I've thought so ever since we arrived. If I were psychic, I'd roll my eyes and mumble about auras. Thomas, it is almost nine o'clock. Can you think of any reason why that young man should not be where he is supposed to be?"

"None that convinces me."

"Nor I. Let's go look for him."

"Where?"

"We'll check the Hall first; he may have appeared in the

meantime. If not—I suppose this place has a cellar?"

"It has a cellar the size of Mammoth Cave. Why do you suppose—"

"I don't suppose anything. But all the other parts of the house are being searched."

Frank had not gone to the Hall. The two older women were still alone there. Lady Isobel had fallen into a tipsy doze, her head at an uncomfortable angle and her mouth wide open. Mrs. Ponsonby-Jones was watching her with a malicious smile. She did not see the pair in the doorway, who beat a hasty retreat.

The cellars had, of course, been electrified. They were almost as large as Thomas claimed, stretching the full length and width of the house. Thomas saw Jacqueline shiver as they descended into clammy, dust-shrouded silence.

The house was well staffed, but not even Weldon's fortune could pay enough servants to keep the lower regions dust-free. There was a light coating on the floor, and almost at once they saw signs that someone had been there. There were no footprints, but rather a scuffed, faintly visible path.

"It needn't have been Frank," Jacqueline said, as Thomas squatted to peer at the marks. "The servants must come down here, at least to the wine cellar."

"There are no other marks," Thomas said. "If he was down here, he went this way."

It took some time to carry out the search. The lighting was poor and the switches were located in obscure corners. The scuffed trail branched off from time to time, toward storerooms and the furnace room. The heating plant was a vast monstrosity, antique but still capable of functioning. Weldon had enough food stored to withstand a siege. Thomas got lost twice.

"Yes, I've been here," he said irritably, as Jacqueline made a sarcastic comment. "Weldon showed us over the house the first time we came. But that was a couple of years ago, you can't expect me to . . . That must be the wine cellar, over there. It's about the only place we haven't looked."

"Then we'll look there."

"This is silly," Thomas grumbled, trailing Jacqueline. She had lifted her skirts, and her silver sandals twinkled in the dim light. "I'll bet they found him snoring in the garden."

Jacqueline opened the door of the wine cellar. She stood quite still; only her fingers moved, a bare fraction of an inch. The shadowy green skirts came whispering down to the floor.

Thomas ran forward.

Frank lay face down in the center of a gleaming dark puddle. Red stained the back of his white shirt and shone wetly in his hair. The only light was the feeble glow from the bulb outside the small room; monstrous shapes loomed in the shadows beyond the fallen body, and sparks of light winked like a thousand squinting eyes.

✤ 3 ✤

IT was several seconds before Thomas identified the shapes as barrels and realized that the light was reflected from the rows of bottles neatly racked along the back wall. There were winking sparks on the floor as well. Broken glass.

He groped for a light switch and found a hanging cord instead. He pulled it. The overhead light came on, giving the scene a distinctness that made it even more unbelievable.

Jacqueline lifted her skirts. Thomas held her back.

"Stay there," he said, relieved to find his voice even. "No point in ruining your dress."

"He's alive," Jacqueline said.

"Of course he is," Thomas said soothingly. "That's wine, not blood. Must have broken a bottle."

He picked a careful path through the shattered glass and spilled Burgundy, and ran his hand over Frank's hair. When he took it away, his fingers were red and sticky, but not with blood.

"Just a bump," he announced with relief.

Frank groaned and stirred. Thomas put his hand on the

young man's shoulder.

"Take it easy, Frank. You have quite a lump on the head. You must have fallen, knocking down a bottle as you collapsed."

Frank muttered something unintelligible.

"How did he get wine on the back of his shirt?" Jacqueline inquired softly.

Thomas looked at her in surprise. Then Frank rolled over and sat up. Jacqueline gasped, and Thomas saw his comfortable theory go glimmering away down a dark corridor of improbability.

There was only one way of accounting for the marks that disfigured the young man's face. He had been in a fight—and if Frank hadn't lost it, Thomas thought, he would hate to see the other guy. Dark bruises marked jaw, cheekbone, and temple. Cuts ran like jigsaw pieces over the whole of his face, and the crusted stains above his mouth were certainly not wine.

"Good Lord," Thomas said. "Jacqueline, go for help. We'll have to carry—"

"No, no, I'm all right," Frank said unconvincingly. "Oh, Lord—what happened?"

"We hoped you could tell us."

"I don't remember a thing after I followed that fellow in a trench coat down the stairs."

Thomas glanced at Jacqueline.

"Get him upstairs," she said. "This is not the time nor the place for a debate."

II

It was ten o'clock before the meeting finally began, and the topic of conversation was not the murder of the princes. Frank was present. After vigorous ablutions he had convinced them that the damage wasn't as bad as it looked, and Rawdon had confirmed the diagnosis. Most of the blood on Frank's face came from his nose. Sheepishly he had explained that he was very susceptible to nose-bleed. The cuts were mere scratches. The chief damage was to his self-esteem, and on this subject he discoursed with vigor and fluency.

"He must have hit me with a bottle," he finished bitterly. "I don't remember a thing—not even a fight—but I couldn't have dislodged one of those bottles accidentally. If I could only remember!"

"Temporary amnesia is not uncommon after a blow on the head," the doctor said reassuringly. "It will probably come back to you."

"What he does remember is bad enough," said Kent. "Some intruder made his way into the house. How?"

"It doesn't seem possible," Weldon said. "I've men patrolling the grounds. . . ."

"Nevertheless, someone did get in. Frank, you haven't given us a very good description. A trench coat and a wide-brimmed hat, you say?"

"I never saw his face," Frank said. "Just caught a glimpse of the fellow ducking under the stairs as I came down them. I was early—wanted to get my thoughts organized before the meeting began. I followed him—saw the door of the cellar wide open—and that's all I remember."

"Obviously one of those horrid reporters," said Lady Isobel, whose nap had revived her. She shuddered fastidiously. "Isn't that the costume they habitually wear?"

"You ought to know, dear," said Lady Ponsonby-Jones. "You claim the creatures are always pursuing you."

"We'd never be able to identify him," Kent said. "Not from that description."

Mrs. Ponsonby-Jones gave a little scream. They all jumped.

"Perhaps he is still here!" she cried. "Still in the house!"

"No, no," Weldon said. "That would be foolish of him, to remain after committing an assault."

"I'm not sure," Philip said thoughtfully. "He might assume we would reason along those lines and feel it safe to remain. We'd better all look under our beds tonight."

His handsome rakish face was sober, but he glanced at Mrs. Ponsonby-Jones, who cried out again.

"Richard, I'll not be able to sleep a wink!"

"I'll have the servants search the house," Weldon said reassuringly. "Just to be on the safe side."

He rang and gave orders to the butler. Percy followed Wilkes out.

"Philip might think it safe to stay," Liz said. "He's that sort of fool. But I'm sure most reporters have better sense."

Philip smiled at her, and the rector said,

"Quite right, quite right. After all, dear lady, these chaps are not criminals; you would be in no danger if you did find one under . . . that is . . ."

Liz burst out laughing.

"You certainly wouldn't need to worry, Mother."

Kent brought his fist down on the table with a crash.

"Of all the irresponsible fools I've ever seen, this lot is the worst. We're wasting valuable time. If this chap was a reporter, there's no harm done. I can deal with reporters." A reminiscent red gleam shone in his eyes. "But what if it wasn't a reporter?"

The others stared at him.

"I've heard a rumor," Kent went on. "They say that there is a stranger at the village inn. A stranger to them, but not to us. . . . Ladies and gentlemen, I suspect that the man is no other than—James Strangways!"

An unenlightened outsider would have thought Kent had told them there was a bomb in the room. Faces turned pale; eyes glazed; Lady Isobel sank back in her chair with a gasp, and Mrs. Ponsonby-Jones tried to faint.

Thomas glanced at Jacqueline. He suspected she recognized the name. She gave no indication of it. Clasping her hands in a gesture of exaggerated horror, she gave Sir Richard his cue.

"Good heavens! Sir Richard! Who is—James Strangways?"

Weldon's round face was grim.

"He is the worst enemy I have in the world."

Mrs. Ponsonby-Jones changed the scene from melodrama to farce.

"Your enemy? What about me? Don't you remember that dreadful insulting letter he wrote about my little article on Richard's religious beliefs?"

"Oh," said Jacqueline. "That Strangways."

Weldon nodded solemnly.

"Perhaps I should call him Richard's worst enemy. The man is a menace. One might call him a renegade, because he was once a strong supporter of Richard's."

"He wrote a biography of Edward the Fourth," Jacqueline said. "The authoritative biography."

"That is correct. In an appendix he asserted his belief in Richard's innocence of the murder in very strong terms."

There was no need for Weldon to explain which murder he meant; in Ricardian circles the young princes were the only victims worth mentioning.

"But that was ten years ago," Weldon went on, "when

Strangways was a rising young scholar at one of your American universities. Since then he has changed his attitude. Not only has he written derogatory articles about Richard, but he attacks pro-Ricardians on every possible occasion. Until recently he was a member of the American branch of the society, but our colleagues in the States finally had to expel him."

"For treason?" Jacqueline inquired seriously.

Sir Richard looked at her reproachfully.

"Indeed, Jacqueline—"

"Forgive me; I didn't mean to poke fun at the society."

"Of course not." Sir Richard smiled at her. "I suppose we do sound a bit foolish to outsiders; but Strangways is really a most unpleasant chap. We consider him our most pernicious opponent, for the man has prestige and a certain literary style—"

"A most disgusting, cynical style," Lady Isobel said. Her sallow cheeks were flushed. "It has no literary merit. Pure invective, that is all it is."

"Strangways was extremely rude about *The Gallant Young King*," the rector chirped sympathetically. "The review was rather widely read; it appeared in one of your local American newspapers."

"*The New York Times*," Thomas said, straight-faced. "It does have a moderate circulation."

Philip gave Thomas an appreciative look.

"Your little local papers," he said grinning. "Well, we know about Americans, don't we, Lady Isobel? No taste. Barbarians."

"I resent the implication," O'Hagan said suddenly. "You denigrate the valiant efforts of the American branch, under whose auspices I am proud to appear here."

He was an indignant rabbit. His face was flushed and his white moustache twitched vigorously. The group hastened to make apologies, which were interrupted by another bang on the table from Kent.

"Good Gad, are we going to sit here babbling all night? Dick, I move we adjourn normal business until tomorrow morning; we can have an extra session at ten A.M. to hear the papers that were to have been read tonight. At the moment—"

"This is not proper procedure," said the rector, looking shocked. "You must entertain a motion—"

"To hell with procedure," Frank said. "Sorry, Mr. Ellis, but I agree with the general, and so do all my scrapes and bruises. This affair may have more serious implications than you realize. If the intruder was not a newspaperman, he may have been after something more important than scandal."

Surprisingly, few of them had considered this possibility. Weldon was the exception.

"The letter is locked in my safe," he said. "No one but myself has the combination."

"Strangways may not know that," mumbled the doctor.

"But how do we know—"

"Just a minute," Thomas interrupted in exasperation. "We're beginning to babble again. First of all we ought to find out whether this business about Strangways is anything more than an idle rumor. One of us must go to the village in the morning and investigate. Is the stranger really Strangways? If so, can he provide an alibi for tonight?"

"I'm sure he'll be delighted to describe his movements to you," Liz said sarcastically.

"We needn't ask him. Discreet questioning of the personnel of the inn—"

"Good thinking," Kent said approvingly. "I'll go 'round in the morning."

"Not you," Weldon objected. "Every reporter in England knows your face."

"Humph," said Kent.

"I'll go," Thomas offered. "Jacqueline and I are of no interest to the press."

"Your faces may not be known," Philip said, with a cynical smile, "but do you know the face you hope not to see? Do any of us know the notorious Strangways by sight?"

A damp silence fell. Finally Jacqueline said mildly, "Would there perhaps be a photograph on the jacket of his book?"

Weldon went trotting out to get the book. When he returned, the others crowded around the head of the table and stared at the small photo on the inside back flap of the jacket.

"No good," Frank said. "Just a head and shoulders."

"I like his nose," Jacqueline said pensively. "Big and bold and Napoleonic. And a good square jaw."

"This is not a male beauty contest," Thomas said in exasperation. "The point is that the photo isn't much use as a means of identification. I'll bet it's ten years old. That square jaw you admire may be buried in double chins, and the hair—pardon me, Jacqueline, the thick black hair—may be gone altogether."

The door burst open. Percy appeared, coated with a blend of cobwebs and crumbs, and followed by the butler. Before Wilkes could speak, Percy announced shrilly, "No one. But we found a window open."

"That is correct, Sir Richard," said Wilkes, icily proper. He shot Percy a glance of burning hatred.

"Thank you, Wilkes."

The butler left. Percy dropped heavily into one of the chairs and his mother exclaimed, "Darling boy, you are absolutely filthy. You must pop straight into a hot tub."

"No," Percy said insolently. "I might miss something. What happened while I was gone?"

"Isn't he amusing?" asked Lady Ponsonby-Jones fondly. "To summarize, darling boy—"

"Do you mind summarizing on your own time?" Jacqueline inquired. "I'm rather tired, and Frank ought to be in bed. His injuries may be superficial, but he suffered quite a shock."

"Of course." Weldon got to his feet, running his hand distractedly through his mane of brown hair. "This has been a confusing evening. I'm sure you are all tired and distressed."

But they weren't, Thomas realized. They were having the time of their lives. Even Frank's abused face showed more anger and excitement than worry. As he had often done before with this group of engaging monomaniacs, he felt as if he were the only adult in charge of a nursery class. He looked at Jacqueline, and thought he saw a similar sentiment on her face. She had once mentioned that she didn't much care for children.

III

Thomas was up early next morning. Weldon had implied that it would be nice if they all made it to the meeting scheduled for ten o'clock. The society was touchy about its rituals. And after Frank's nonappearance and its melodramatic sequel, a missing member would arouse general hysteria. Before the meeting Thomas and Jacqueline had to undertake their espionage operation in the village, seeking the nefarious James Strangways.

On a sunny summer morning the breakfast room at Weldon House looked particularly charming. It suggested a photograph out of *Country Life*—a prewar *Country Life*, when such items as Georgian silver and Chippendale tables were commonplace. Silver chafing dishes sparkled along the mahogany sideboard, and Thomas's nostrils sorted out a variety of tempting odors. It was not power that corrupted, he thought—it was soft living. Any invading barbarian would succumb to this fare. Bacon—solid English bacon, like thick slabs of ham marbled with fat; scrambled eggs, boiled eggs, coddled eggs; oatmeal, and a variety of cold breakfast cereals—removed from their plebeian cardboard containers and elegantly encased in crystal; rows of toast in silver toast racks; cut-glass pots of jam; black cherries glowing like dark rubies in crystalline syrup; thick orange marmalade, solid with rind; amber honey from Weldon's own hives; hot biscuits, and . . . Thomas's eyes widened as he identified a platter of jelly doughnuts. He had mentioned his passion for jelly doughnuts the last time he stayed at Weldon House. Damn it, he thought affectionately, you couldn't help liking a man who remembered a trivial remark like that. He wondered if the tastes of the others had been catered to also, and decided in the affirmative as he saw the rector piling his plate with what appeared to be deviled kidneys. He waved his fork, adorned with kidney, at Thomas as the latter joined him at the sideboard.

"Good morrow, brother Clarence, good morrow! How is it with you?"

Thomas rolled an eye toward the table, where Jacqueline sat in more than oriental splendor. The sunlight streaming through the bay windows made her hair glow like fire; she was wearing white slacks and a silky garment printed in shades of green, peacock blue, and gold. She looked up from the austere cup of tea and piece of toast on which she was breakfasting, and winked. Reassured, Thomas turned back to the rector, who was, he recalled, his Ricardian brother, Edward IV.

"Hail, my liege," he said valiantly. "How is it with you?"

The doctor, who had just entered, clucked disapprovingly.

"No, no, Thomas; 'your Grace' would be more suitable." He put a heaping spoonful of a pale-gray substance on his plate and studied the rector's pile of kidneys disparagingly. "As for my fellow king here, he isn't going to be at all well if he eats that frightful mess. I shudder, friend Edward, to think of the lining of your stomach."

"Then don't think about it," said Mr. Ellis cheerfully. "Really, Rawdon—forgive me, King Henry—we ought to exchange roles. Not that I claim to be a saint, and there are those who believe poor mad Henry qualified for that position—"

"As a man of the cloth you are closer to the role of saint than I," Rawdon admitted. "Actually, I believe Henry was a mental case, not a saint, but that may be a professional prejudice."

"You may both be right," said Thomas, helping himself to bacon. "Henry was a gentle, kindly man who was also considerably confused. I suspect your diet would appeal to him at that, Rawdon. What is that stuff?"

The doctor's long face brightened.

"Barley cereal, honey, malt, and a few other of nature's

gifts to man. It's my own invention. Weldon is good enough to have it prepared for me when I come. Really, Thomas, you ought to try it. It would do wonders for your—"

"No, thanks," Thomas said. He didn't want to hear what organs the revolting mess would do wonders for, much less eat it.

The rector chuckled.

"It's better than malmsey wine—eh, brother Clarence?"

Thomas acknowledged the witticism with a sour smile. He was getting tired of references to the famous butt of malmsey.

He retreated to the table and sat down beside Jacqueline, who turned emerald-green eyes upon him.

"Hail, brother George. I may call you brother, I hope? As the mother of Richard's bastard children—"

"Cut it out," growled Thomas.

"Certainly not. I have decided to fling myself wholeheartedly into the spirit of the thing. Have I told you my name is Katherine? Nobody seems to know who Richard's mistresses were; I have formed a theory that one of them was Hasting's wife Katherine. That would explain why Richard was so hasty—" a flicker of long dark lashes emphasized the pun, and Thomas made a wordless grimace of disgust—"so hasty in executing Hastings. We know that Richard's illegitimate daughter was named Katherine; what would be more natural than for her to be named after her mother? Richard dedicated a chapel to Saint Katherine—"

She broke off as Kent came to join them. In the bright light of day the general's face looked like that of a well-preserved mummy, but his eyes were snapping with energy and appreciation as he surveyed Jacqueline's cool elegance. He put his plate down, and Jacqueline eyed it with consternation. Two white-eyed fish looked back at her.

"Very interesting idea," Kent said, beginning to debone the nasty-looking specimens. "Don't believe I have ever heard it before. Would you give us a lecture, Jacqueline?'

"I was just joking," Jacqueline said meekly. She seemed subdued by the fishy stare.

"Mustn't joke about serious matters." Kent chuckled. "Do you know, the more I think about it, the more it attracts me. Lady Hastings as Richard's mistress . . ."

"Now wait a minute," Thomas said. "That's a ridiculous idea. She was too old in the first place, and in the second place—"

Kent paid no attention. Turning to the rector, who had taken the chair beside him, he began to recapitulate Jacqueline's theory. Rawdon, eating with slow, well-chewed bites, also listened attentively. Jacqueline caught Thomas's eye and lifted her own eyes in pious resignation.

"Fascinating," the rector said. "Indeed, Jacqueline, you must write an article for our little journal. Or—no! May I call you Katherine?"

"Oh, do," said Jacqueline wildly. "Do."

"Where are the others?" inquired Thomas, in an attempt to change the subject before Jacqueline waxed violent and profane.

"Let me see." Ellis considered the question, as if it were an exercise in historical research, which it did rather resemble. "Our good host and his lady have come and gone, as has my own excellent spouse. Young Edward—

your son, my dear doctor—has also breakfasted, as has the other young Edward, my son and heir. I do not know about the others."

It took Thomas a few moments to sort out the aliases. "Sir Richard, the two older ladies, Frank, and Percy," he translated, for the benefit of Jacqueline, whose eyes were glazed. "I'll bet Percy was the first to come and the last to leave."

"No doubt." The idea seemed to distress the doctor. He put his fork down and considered his half-empty plate doubtfully. "The boy has an excellent appetite. . . ."

"The boy is a menace," Thomas said. "He won't live to grow up."

"Being overweight is unhealthy," the rector agreed innocently.

"I didn't mean that. I mean someone will kill him before he grows up. It might be me. Rawdon—what's the matter?"

The doctor was bent over his plate, his hands covering his mouth. Suddenly he leaped up, overturning his chair. Thomas caught a glimpse of his face as he bolted from the room. It was pale pea-green.

The remaining breakfasters stared at one another.

"Sick," said Kent succinctly. "No wonder, that ghastly mess he's been eating—"

"He eats it every morning," Thomas said. "I hope he isn't coming down with something—a virus—"

"I had better see if I can be of help," said the rector. He popped the last kidney into his mouth. Thomas couldn't blame him for the smug look on his round face.

The rector trotted out. Jacqueline was staring at the doctor's plate.

"I wonder . . ."

"No time to wonder," said Thomas briskly. "Come on, Jacqueline. If we're to be back by ten, we'd better get moving."

Jacqueline went upstairs to get her gloves—"I can't possibly go to the village without *gloves*, Thomas!" Thomas took the statement in the spirit in which it was offered. He knew what Jacqueline was going to get. The Purse, in one of its giant manifestations.

As she started up, the butler approached Thomas. He proffered a note on a silver salver.

"This was found in your room, sir, by the maid."

The envelope had Thomas's name on it in a hurried scrawl. Thomas opened it.

Jacqueline, on the landing, leaned over the banister. Her hair gleamed like an infernal aureole.

"What is it, Thomas?.'

Thomas read the note again. It didn't take long; the message was brief.

"Come down to the wine cellar after breakfast. I think I've found something. Frank. P.S. Don't tell anyone. This could be dangerous."

The word *anyone* was heavily underscored.

"Thomas, what does it say?"

Thomas looked up.

"Nothing much. I'll meet you here in five minutes."

The cellar lights were on. This might have alerted Thomas or reassured him, depending on his state of mind; but in fact he didn't even notice. He was sure Frank had nothing of importance to show him, but he wanted to check it out before he went haring off to the village on what was probably a wild-goose chase. He was also moved by a less noble motive. Jacqueline was lovely and charming and witty, but she was also irritating, with her amused contempt and her air of omniscience. If he could find out something she didn't know . . .

Absorbed by these ignoble but satisfying thoughts, Thomas was taken unawares by the blow that struck him down. He saw stars, but that was all he saw, except for the blackness that swallowed him as he felt himself falling.

He came to his sense after an indeterminate period of time, and it took more time, equally impossible to calculate, before he figured out where he was. His position seemed to be the product of delirium or delusion; it couldn't be real. The growing congestion in his aching head finally convinced him. He was standing on that very head—upside down, to put it plainly. His arms were tightly bound to his sides and his legs were tied together. A gag covered his mouth. He was blind. Literally blind; his eyes were uncovered and open, but he could see nothing. He could smell, however. The smell filled his nostrils and increased the nausea which his position and his injury had instigated. One other sense, normally unused except by the genuinely blind, came feebly to his assistance—the generalized sense of location centered in the nerve cells of his face. Thomas's brief state of consciousness was fading again, but he was a man of considerable intelligence; his reeling brain put the data together and came up with an incredible answer. The smell of stale wine, the sense of enclosure in something narrow and confining, the absurd, humiliating position. Thomas tried to swear, choked, and fainted again.

When he regained consciousness the second time he opened one eye to check the stimuli before deciding whether to retain his senses. The result was reassuring. He was prone and horizontal; his limbs ached, but they were free; light greeted his eyes, and there had been a fleeting suggestion of a face, haloed in flame and pale with what Thomas hoped was anguish on his behalf. He opened his mouth and croaked like a frog.

"What did you say?" The voice was Jacqueline's. It was cool and controlled and mildly querulous.

Hurt, Thomas opened both eyes and blinked them till they got used to the light. It seemed blinding after the darkness that had surrounded him earlier, but it was only the dim bulb in the ceiling of the wine cellar. He was lying flat on the dusty floor, and beside him, turned over on its side, was an empty barrel—a large barrel, fully five feet high when erect.

Someone put a glass to his dry lips. Thomas drank. The liquid tasted like vintage champagne to his dusty throat. He realized that it was champagne. Jacqueline had opened a bottle. Thomas swallowed, and repeated his question.

"I'm afraid so," Jacqueline said regretfully.

"I was in a barrel?"

"That's the third time you've asked that."

"I still can't believe it. I won't believe it. Oh, God—" Thomas sat up and glared wildly. "Who else saw me?"

"This is no time to be worrying about your male ego," Jacqueline said. She spread her knees and received Thomas's head neatly in her lap as he fell back. "Thomas, darling, you aren't hurt, you know. Only the classic bump on the head. But—you really did scare me for a minute!"

The wobble in her voice restored some of Thomas's battered vanity. Her lap felt comfortable—soft, cool, silky. He wriggled his head into an easier position and relaxed.

"It took you long enough," he said grumpily. "It's a wonder I didn't die of congestion of the brain or something."

"You were only in—in that thing for a couple of minutes."

"How do you know? It felt like days."

"I waited for ten minutes before I started to look for you. Considering the time it took to knock you out, truss you up, and—er—insert you . . ."

Jacqueline's voice was still unsteady, but Thomas suspected another emotion than concern. He squinted up at her, saw the corners of her mouth quiver, and suddenly smiled with the good humor that was one of his most endearing characteristics.

"I must have looked like an absolute fool," he said. "My feet sticking up out of that thing . . . I don't blame you for laughing."

"I'm not laughing," said Jacqueline.

Thomas sat up. He gathered Jacqueline into his arms and for a time they sat in silence while she made gulping noises into his shirt front. Finally she detached herself and sat up on her heels. Her face was smudged with dust and her eyes were still damp; two tendrils of hair had come loose and curled wickedly over her ears.

"No," she said, fending Thomas off as he reached for her again. "That's enough of that."

"Is that all I get for being knocked on the head and stuck into a barrel upside down?" Thomas inquired plaintively. "If I lost an arm and a leg, I suppose you might—"

"You're drunk," Jacqueline said coldly. "Thomas, be serious. I got something of a shock, that's why I acted so silly; but this is no joke. And I'm afraid your male ego is going to suffer, although I was the only one to see you *in situ*. We'll have to tell the others."

Jacqueline's therapy had been amazingly successful.

Except for a slight headache, Thomas felt fine. He reached for the champagne bottle, which was sitting on the floor beside him. After a long drink, he nodded.

"Yes, I see what you've got in mind. Oh, well. At least I won't have to hear Lady Isobel recite her poem about gallant King Richard."

IV

The emergency meeting was in full swing, and it was getting absolutely nowhere. Thomas's head was aching. He no longer felt like a kindly adult watching the antics of cute children; he felt like a lion tamer with a cageful of feline schizophrenics. People were pacing around the room shouting questions at each other. At the head of the table Weldon pounded his gavel. No one paid the slightest attention. The pounding only increased Thomas's headache.

As he had feared, the first reaction to the news of his misadventure had been hilarity. Outrage soon replaced the laughter, but this emotion was just as noisy and just as ineffectual. Frank was the most indignant; he kept insisting that he had not written the note that had lured Thomas to his doom. Thomas kept reassuring him, but Frank demanded paper and pencil and produced a specimen that was certainly quite unlike the handwriting Thomas remembered. He had to depend on his memory, for the note was no longer in his pocket.

Jacqueline was curled up in one of the big chairs. She was wearing her glasses. Her green eyes flickered as she glanced from one gesticulating speaker to the next.

Finally she rose. Conversation gradually died as she walked slowly to the head of the table. She smiled at Weldon, who stepped back and, with a wordless gesture, invited her to take his place. When she faced the group, the silence was almost complete.

"I'd like to say a few words," she began in a soft voice. "May I please have your attention? No comments, no questions—and no bloody interruptions!"

A mouse's squeak would have been distinctly audible.

"Very well," Jacqueline went on, glaring at them over her glasses. "I'll begin at the beginning. "Last night Frank was attacked by a figure that was in essence that of a masked man. Or perhaps I should say masked person. . . .

"In your Ricardian charades, Frank is taking the part of the Lancastrian Prince Edward, the son of Henry the Sixth. The Tudor propaganda accuses your hero, Richard, of being responsible for the death of this young prince. Edward was killed in battle, and the earliest commentators simply state that fact. Later historians imply that he was killed after he had surrendered, by the attendants of the victorious Edward the Fourth. One of the Tudor propagandists says Richard stabbed him as he knelt and begged for mercy.

"I apologize for repeating what you all know. I do so in order to set the record straight and clarify my thoughts as well as your own."

It was admirably done, Thomas thought. A professor of English history couldn't have sounded more pompous.

"The death of this prince," Jacqueline continued, "may be considered the first of Richard's murders, if one follows the Tudor line. Edward's injuries are not specified, but we might suppose that a man killed in battle would suffer wounds from sharp-bladed instruments such as swords and daggers, plus blows from maces, battle-axes, and the like. His body would have been bruised and cut."

She went on without waiting for a reaction. The reaction had begun; the sharper-witted listeners showed signs of horror and disbelief.

"The second of the murders of which Richard has been accused was that of Henry the Sixth, who was a prisoner in the Tower of London. The Tudors added this death to Richard's account, saying that he had personally stabbed the poor old man. I don't know whether anyone suggested that Henry was poisoned, but the body, when publicly displayed, as was the custom, showed no marks of violence, and poison was often suspected in cases of sudden death.

"This morning Dr. Rawdon, who represents Henry the Sixth, was taken ill after eating a dish specially prepared for him.

"Up to this point no one could have seen the connection between the seeming accidents. Thomas's adventure makes the connection explicit. The comedian among us is getting more direct. Thomas, who represents the Duke of Clarence, was knocked on the head and placed in a barrel of wine. Fortunately the barrel was empty, but the joker went to considerable lengths to make the position ignominious. Thomas was held erect—if I may use that word—by rope attached to his ankles and then looped around the top of the barrel.

"No reputable historian believes that Richard was really responsible for the death of his exasperating brother, but the Tudor legend blamed him nevertheless. Now," said Jacqueline, in the same mild, pleasant voice, "do you really want us to go to the village looking for imaginary villains, or shall we start collating our alibis?"

The amazed Ricardians stared dumbly, too thunderstruck to speak at first. Thomas leaned back in his chair and folded his hands across his stomach. By finding a common denominator, Jacqueline had reduced his ludicrous adventure to part of a puzzle. One does not mind being made a fool of quite so much if one has plenty of company.

"I cannot believe it," the rector said finally. His ruddy face had paled. "Dear lady, are you certain—"

"Let's not waste time denying the obvious," Kent interrupted. "The connection is there. But I question your conclusion, Jacqueline. Alibis?"

"It seems equally obvious to me," Jacqueline said. She looked so smug that Thomas wanted to throw something at her. "We cannot completely eliminate the possibility of an outsider. But in order to act, such a person would have to have access to the house as well as knowledge of the roles you are playing. The first is not impossible. Despite Sir Richard's precautions, this place is not really secure. It is not a medieval castle with a moat and a drawbridge, but an open, modern house surrounded by a wall that I can guarantee to climb in ten seconds flat. As for the special knowledge required, that, too, might have been accessible to an outsider. The servants could have been bribed; none of them would feel they were betraying a trust by divulging such trivial information. Some of you may have talked to your friends. However—"

"But you've just contradicted your own suggestion," Frank said, frowning. "You've proved that an outsider could have the necessary opportunity. As for the motive —obviously someone wants to make us look foolish. None of us would do such a thing."

The rector made noises of enthusiastic agreement. Mrs. Ponsonby-Jones, whose slow-moving brain had finally grasped the situation, nodded her massive head. The others were silent; and gradually all eyes focused on a single object.

Percy giggled.

"I wish I had thought of it. I'd love to have seen Thomas in the butt of malmsey."

"Now, young man," Sir Richard began angrily.

He was interrupted by Mrs. Ponsonby-Jones, whose wits moved more rapidly in the face of a threat to her son and heir. With a piercing cry of indignation she gathered Percy to the maternal bosom.

"How dare you accuse Percy? Why, the poor boy hasn't the strength, even if he were capable of imagining such nasty things."

Thomas had to admit that the woman had a point. Most of Percy was fat, and he doubted that the boy had the muscle to overpower and move a grown man. Otherwise Percy was a perfect candidate. Childish, precocious, malicious . . . Malice. As he considered the word, Thomas understood why Jacqueline looked so grave.

A squeaky cough from the end of the table drew everyone's attention. The American visitor cleared his throat.

"Must be an outsider," he said, breathing agitatedly. "And I know who. Strangways! The man is capable of anything. Must be here. Look for him!"

"Do you know him, Mr. O'Hagan?" Jacqueline asked.

"Good gracious, no." The suggestion seemed to infuriate O'Hagan. His moustache quivered. "Would I associate with such a scoundrel? Know of him, though. Capable of anything."

"You said that before," Philip remarked. "I've another idea. Some particularly enterprising newsman could have engineered these tricks. It would make a marvelous article—the mad Ricardians carrying their roles to insane extremes. If the chap carried a camera and took pictures of the victims . . ."

A low groan of horror issued from Thomas's unguarded lips. Frank didn't actually groan, but he looked as if he wanted to.

"My God, I'll have to emigrate," he muttered.

"Me, too," Thomas said. "If my students ever saw a photo—"

"Nonsense," Jacqueline exploded. "What's wrong with all of you? Theoretically an outsider might have played these tricks, but he'd have to have had the luck of the Irish and the cloak of invisibility to play them without being caught. If this is not an inside job, I'll—"

Liz said something under her breath. She seemed more shocked than any of the others; under the mask of makeup her face was pale.

"What?" Jacqueline asked.

"I think everyone is mad," Liz muttered. "I'm tempted to pack up the whole business and clear out of here."

"There's no need for you to worry, darling," Philip said. He was no longer smiling, and his handsome face looked hard and dangerous. "Elizabeth of York survived Richard for a good many years. I'm the one who ought to pack it up. Hastings was Richard's next victim—if our comedian continues to follow the Tudor chronology."

"Think about that for a while." Jacqueline dropped the words like stones into the stricken silence. "Come on, Thomas, let's go to the village. If we can eliminate the possibility of an outsider, maybe your friends will face the facts."

She walked out of the room.

Thomas had to run to catch up with her. They were

outside the house, walking along the terrace, before Jacqueline was calm enough to speak rationally.

"It's not the logic of the situation," she muttered. "It's the atmosphere. Can't they see it? The malice, the nasty sense of humor—it's a domestic crime, that's what it is. People don't play vicious practical jokes on total strangers. And if they aren't practical jokes . . ."

Thomas took her arm as they descended the shallow steps that led from the terrace into the rose garden.

"That's precisely why they won't face the facts. The facts aren't very pleasant. Stop seething, love, and smell a rose. It's too nice a day to stay mad."

"I'll bet it will rain before night," Jacqueline said.

But the beauty of the morning would have moved a stone; her face cleared as she took a deep breath. She stopped on the path and cupped a full-blown rose gently in her hand. It had a heart of pure pink that shaded off into ice-white petals.

"I've never cared much for roses," Thomas said placidly.

"What are your favorite flowers?"

"What red-blooded American male will admit to having a favorite flower? I don't think much about 'em. Deadly nightshade? It reminds me of you."

He put his arm around her, and Jacqueline burst out laughing.

"Thank you, Thomas, I'm touched. Was I too awful just now?"

"No, they had it coming." They strolled on, their arms around one another, and Thomas felt a wave of sheer felicity sweep over him. "An English garden in the sunshine, and the woman I love," he said poetically. "What could be better?"

"A loaf of bread and a jug of wine. I'm getting hungry. Do you suppose we could get beer and cheese at the pub?"

Jacqueline's face was alight with a radiance the roses had not inspired. Thomas hugged her.

"You can have a barrel of beer if you want it."

"Let's not talk about barrels."

"If I can talk about them, you have no reason to object. Do you really think we'll find out anything in the village?"

"To tell you the truth, the thought of beer predominated when I agreed to go," Jacqueline said pensively. "But I suppose we have to check."

"You think Strangways is there?"

"I would be, if I were he. He is as obsessed by Richard as your friends; more obsessed, in a way, because his feelings are a sort of love-hate combination. He's been so abusive that his scholarly reputation hangs on Richard's villainy. Any discovery that supports Richard threatens Strangways. Yes, I would certainly be on hand if I had heard of a startling new document."

They had entered a belt of trees that protected the back of the gardens. The shade felt cool and refreshing. Thomas took his arm away so they could proceed single file.

"How do you know so much about Strangways?"

"Naturally I've read his articles. I don't walk into situations like this one without doing my homework."

"Ah. Wednesday afternoon, when you said you had to go to the hairdresser—"

"I merely implied that was my goal. I spent the afternoon at the British Museum."

"Where, to be sure, you have professional connections in the Reading Room. You are really the most. . . . If I may say so, your Freudian analysis of the unfortunate Strangways is a bit farfetched."

"Not at all," Jacqueline said coldly. "My professional duties necessitate contact with the weird world of historical scholarship. I know one man who is besotted with Mary, Queen of Scots. In his study at home there is a little shrine with a portrait of that appalling female draped in crimson velvet, with an eternal light and a white lily in a vase. Owing to the difficulty of procuring a constant supply of lilies on a professor's meager salary, the flower is plastic; but the sentiment is no less sickening."

"Anybody I know?" Thomas inquired, fascinated.

"You know him." Jacqueline grinned at him over her shoulder. "But my lips are sealed. I've never told anybody about your crush on Nefertiti, have I?"

"Everybody has a crush on Nefertiti at some point in his life," Thomas said. He could feel himself blushing, and changed the subject.

"Here's the fence. Ten seconds, did you say? One thousand, two thousand . . ."

He should have known better. Jacqueline was over the fence by the time he got to eight thousand. Thomas followed. Before Jacqueline could announce his time, he said quickly,

"You've torn your slacks."

"Cripes." Jacqueline tried to look over her shoulder, with a notable lack of success.

Thomas brushed at the seat of her pants and then announced mendaciously, "No, it's okay, just a streak of rust. Where did you acquire your stock of expletives? I haven't heard anyone say 'cripes' since I was eight years old."

"I'm trying to reform my vocabulary. The students

have a bad effect on me. The words sound foul enough coming from them, but from a lady of my years and dignity . . . Which way do we go?"

The path led along the fence and then wandered off into a hilly meadow decorated, as if deliberately, by black-and-white cows. Jacqueline began to sing. It was a maddening sound. Thomas wouldn't have minded if she had sung aloud, for she had a pleasant voice and the pastoral surroundings were appropriate for gentle harmony; but Jacqueline's singing was a kind of musical soliloquy, not an expression of well-being, and it issued as a low drone. Nor did Thomas find her choice of melodies soothing. She started with a snatch of the Mad Scene from *Lucia*, edited for untrained contralto, and went on to "Elinor Rigby" and that grisly memorial of old English murder, "Edward." Thomas was relieved when they finally reached the village and Jacqueline stopped muttering about drops of gore.

From his earlier visits Thomas remembered the Weldon Arms with pleasure, even if it had changed its name to flatter the current lord of the manor. It was an authentic fourteenth-century inn, and its former name, The Blue Boar, reminded Ricardians of their hero. Richard's badge of the white boar had furnished the inspiration for a number of inn signs during his brief reign; when the Tudors took over, sensible innkeepers hastily painted the boar azure in order to avoid offense.

Now he let out a hiss of exasperation as they turned the corner and saw the inn ahead. The narrow street was lined with cars and motor skooters. A thin blue veil of exhaust smoke dulled the brilliance of sunlight and flower gardens. Gaping tourists filled the gaps between vehicles, such as they were, and Thomas found himself trying to decide which nation could claim the least-attractive tourists.

Jacqueline jabbed him in the ribs as he studied a long-legged blonde damsel—Swedish, perhaps?—wearing a sleeveless low-cut open knit top.

"Don't become a dirty old man, Thomas, it's so boring. How are we going to get to the inn? The place is teeming."

"Let's go around to the private entrance," Thomas said. "I was introduced to Mr. Doakes last time I was here; maybe he'll remember me."

The harassed Doakes did not remember Thomas, but when the latter mentioned his name and Sir Richard's, the man's broad red face lost its worried frown.

"I'm sorry, sir, I truly am. I ought to 'ave known you. But you can see. . . ." He gestured toward the crowded street. "Not that I'm complaining, mind. It's good for trade. Come into the parlor, I keep that clear for my regulars. And this lady is . . .? A pleasure, Mrs. Kirby, I'm sure."

The inn parlor was a haven of peace and a gem of English architecture. The massive beams were genuine, though Thomas was a little suspicious of the copper pots strewn about. The small leaded windows muted the sunlight, so that the room was pleasantly shadowed. It smelled of ale and sausage and brass polish.

One of the regular customers was asleep in a corner. He was so old, so brownly withered, and so silent that Thomas wondered for a moment whether he was real. Jacqueline shared his qualms; when their host left to get them food and drink, she nudged Thomas and whispered, "Thomas,

I think he's stuffed. Mr. Doakes keeps him around to add atmosphere."

"Maybe he died just recently, and nobody noticed the difference."

Doakes returned with ale and home-baked bread and some of the excellent Wensleydale cheese. He seemed glad to get away from the uproar in the public bar; when Thomas asked him to join them, he accepted with alacrity.

"Forty years I've been 'ere, and every day I've missed old London," he said. "But now, when I see what the town is breeding up. . . ." He shook his head and applied himself to his modest pint. It did not cheer him. He continued gloomily, "With all respect to Sir Richard, it's 'is fault we've this crowd on our 'ands. All that nonsense up at the manor. . . ."

A grinding noise, like that of rusty gears, turned Thomas's head toward the shadowy corner where the elderly apparition sat. He started. A pair of evil blue eyes had opened in the mummified face, and a toothless mouth was emitting sounds. The lack of dentures and an incredible Yorkshire accent made the resultant speech unintelligible. Thomas turned to Doakes for enlightenment.

"Will says Sir Richard is the best master in the West Riding and 'e won't 'ear a word against 'im," Doakes translated. "All right, Will, all right, I'm of your opinion. Didn't Sir Richard send my own little grandchild to that 'ospital in London when she was ailing last year? But I still say it's no way for grown men and women to carry on. Fancy dress and playacting, that's bad enough, that is; but when it comes to pretending you're a dead man—well, all I can say is, it isn't 'olesome."

Apparently the aged Will agreed; the blue eyes had closed and the rusty jaws remained shut. Thomas exchanged a glance with Jacqueline and saw that she was thinking the same thing he was. The proceedings at Weldon house were not secret. No doubt the whole village knew what was going on.

Jacqueline finished her ale and stared pointedly at her empty glass. Thomas ordered another round. Under the influence of his own excellent brew, Doakes began to brighten.

"Ah, well," he said philosophically. "Sir Richard is a fine little man, for all his foolishness, and I wish 'im well. Here's to 'im, and the lady of 'is choice."

"Mrs. Ponsonby-Jones?" Thomas asked dubiously.

Old Will's mouth opened again. The sight was horribly reminiscent of Boris Karloff on the Late Late Show; from the black cavity came a series of sounds like a prolonged death rattle. Thomas would not have identified them as laughter if Doakes had not chuckled.

"The gentleman will 'ave 'is joke, Will. Not that the old —er—woman wouldn't like to be Lady Weldon, and the skinny old one too. Sir Richard's not that foolish. All of us will be glad to see Miss Liz as lady of the manor. She's a fine lass, for all 'er modern ideas."

"But . . ." Thomas began. He subsided as Jacqueline trod heavily on his foot. She was right; they were wasting time.

"Sir Richard sent me to ask for your help, Mr. Doakes," he said. "Someone broke into the house last night."

Doakes's grinning face sobered as Thomas explained. He shook his head.

"Now we can't 'ave that. Breaking and entering—that's against the law, that is."

He made no objection to fetching the hotel register and

going over it with Thomas. There were only six strangers resident in the inn, and Doakes's descriptions made it clear that none of them could be James Strangways. Further questioning elicited the information that no man of that description was renting a room in any of the cottages that accepted boarders. They thanked Doakes and rose to leave.

"Tell Sir Richard not to worry," said the host. "There'll be no more breaking in. We'll see to that."

Thomas glanced at old Will and was not surprised to see that the blue eyes were open and alert. He believed Doakes's promise. The village would close ranks when one of its own was threatened, and Thomas pitied the unwary reporter who ran afoul of any of them—even old Will. The very sight of him limping out of a dark doorway with his toothless mouth agape would set a nervous man screaming.

They were about to go out the door when old Will made his final pronouncement. The rolling "ooms" and "oops" filled the room like thunder. Doakes hesitated a moment before translating.

"He says the playacting is all to the good if it clears King Richard," he said finally. "He says King Richard never done it. And he says they'll all be watching, on Sunday, to see it proved that he never done it."

Old Will was mumbling furiously, and Thomas knew the old man was off in some imaginary world of his own. He wondered if that world was the same one in which Weldon spent part of his time. How could anyone believe for a moment that the dead past was really dead? It animated this semiliterate octogenarian as well as a group of supposedly sophisticated worldings. The thought was a little frightening.

Doakes ushered them out the back door into the street. He seemed embarrassed at Will's outburst; before closing the door he said under his breath, "You'll excuse old Will, sir and madam. He wanders a bit. . . . But then they're all strange on the subject of King Richard in these parts. I tell you, it isn't 'olesome!"

✣ 4 ✣

JACQUELINE was preoccupied and silent on the way back. When they reached the house, she went to change. The return trip over the fence proved that while her physical condition was excellent, white slacks were impractical for climbing rusty iron fences.

Thomas wandered into the gardens. He was full of bread and cheese and disinclined to face a horde of contentious Ricardians. Passing through the rose garden, he headed for an area he remembered from an earlier visit —a secluded paved courtyard whose mellow brick walls supported swags of ivy and trellised vines. There were stone benches, if he remembered correctly, and a fountain.

His memory was accurate, and the glory of late-summer flowers rewarded the effort it took to find the place. Seated on one of the benches were Liz and Frank.

Thomas hesitated in the gateway. It was an appropriate spot for a pair of lovers, but he had the impression that his arrival had interrupted a spat rather than a fond tête-à-tête. The warmth of Liz's greeting and Frank's brusque "hello" confirmed the impression. Thomas sat down be-

tween them—they were at opposite ends of the bench—
and tried to think of something to say. He was remembering the innkeeper's gossip about Weldon and the girl. It
made him self-conscious.

"Any luck?" Liz asked.

"No Strangways." Thomas told them what he had found
out.

"Hell and damnation." Frank said gloomily. "I didn't
really expect you'd come up with anything, but I
hoped . . ."

"There's nothing to worry about," Thomas said, with an
optimism he did not feel. "No one has been hurt. In fact,
the comedian, as Jacqueline calls him, has been rather
considerate."

"Hah," said Frank, fingering his scratches.

"Superficial," Liz said, looking at him contemptuously.
"You're right, Thomas. Rawdon is on his feet again."

"What was in his food?"

Liz giggled. She looked absolutely delightful.

"An emetic of some kind, apparently. Rawdon won't
say which one. The names that come to mind create
amusement rather than sympathy."

"So he, too, was more humiliated than hurt," Thomas
said. "As for me—"

"I think that was frightfully dangerous," Liz said.
Thomas thought what a charming, sympathetic girl she
was. "Surely you'd have been in bad shape if you hadn't
been found right away."

"But I was found right away. Everyone knew we were
going to the village, and Jacqueline is not the patient type.
When I didn't appear on schedule, the joker could assume
she would go looking for me."

"And how did she know where to look?" Liz inquired.

"Wilkes saw me heading for the nether regions."
Thomas said, remembering the explanation Jacqueline
had given as they returned from the cellars. "But it was
partly intuition, I suppose. After Frank's encounter . . ."
He broke off with a gasp. "Oh, now, you can't suspect
Jacqueline. She's a stranger—"

'Precisely. She's the only newcomer in our midst and
the only one who isn't dedicated to the cause. And I imagine she has a rather weird sense of humor."

Thomas sputtered. Frank burst out laughing.

"Come off it, Liz. You're accustomed to having every
damned male in the crowd flap his wings and crow as you
walk past. Now you have a bit of competition."

Liz glared at him. Frank evidently felt he had gone too
far. He added quickly, "Jacqueline isn't the only
stranger."

"O'Hagan," Thomas said thoughtfully. "Hadn't any of
you met him before?"

"No," Liz said. "I must admit he's odd. Maybe he has a
few screws loose."

"It seems to me," Frank said, "that the most important
thing is to forestall any further accidents. If we can't identify the comedian, perhaps we can anticipate his next
move."

"Good," Thomas said approvingly. "So far he seems to
be following the Tudor legend. So the next victim should
be—"

"Lord Hastings," said Frank. "Who is, of course, our
popular idol of stage and screen."

Liz had been inspecting the foxgloves with what
seemed to Thomas sinister interest. Now she turned.
"And you are looking forward to that, aren't you?"

"Why not?" Frank looked defiant. "I've been made a

fool of; allow me to enjoy watching someone else deflated. If anybody asked for deflation—"

They glowered at one another, and Thomas felt a sentimental amusement. It had been many years since he had engaged in a battle of words with a pretty girl. . . . His debates with Jacqueline were hardly in the same category.

"The point is not to enjoy Philip's humiliation but to catch the miscreant," he said mildly. "If you are right, then all we have to do is guard Philip."

"Right," Frank said reluctantly. "Don't worry, Thomas; I'm not foolish enough to neglect my obvious duty simply because—"

"You're jealous," Liz said. "You accuse me of jealousy; why, you're livid with it! Phil is handsome and famous and talented and confident—"

"And I'm not." Frank stood up. His face was red but there was dignity in his anger, and in his control of it. "All right, Liz, that's all I'm going to take today. Find yourself another whipping boy." He stalked out of the garden.

When he had gone, Liz seemed to droop. She gave Thomas a glance in which defiance and misery were equally mixed, and turned back to the foxgloves. "You think I'm frightful, don't you?"

"Of course not. I think you're worried. But you ladies don't have any cause for concern. Not even his enemies accused Richard of murdering women."

"Except his wife." Liz turned. She was smiling faintly. "And that is my darling mum. How do you suppose your comedian plans to counterfeit consumption?"

"It will be poison, if our boy is following the Tudor myth," Thomas said uneasily. "Your mother is not a young woman, my dear. I don't like the idea of someone playing tricks on her."

Liz smiled. She rose and held out her hand to pull Thomas to his feet.

"You really are a darling. Come along, Thomas, the afternoon meeting will be starting shortly. We mustn't miss it. Diccon has strictly forbidden discussion of our mystery; he says we've wasted enough time already."

"So we're to hear Frank rehashing the murder of the princes," Thomas said, falling in step beside her.

"And Lady Isobel reading her new poem—if time permits."

"Time probably won't permit," Thomas said, cheered by the thought. "We're two meetings behind schedule now. All the same, Liz, are you certain about Hastings being the next victim? Haven't the Tudor slanderers implied Richard murdered Edward the Fourth?"

"Not even Sir Thomas More would be that absurd." Liz frowned thoughtfully. She looked very pretty when she frowned. Thomas was tempted to put his arm around her, but thought better of it.

"Unless," Liz went on, "one might claim that Richard was indirectly guilty of Edward's death because he made no attempt to dissuade him from the debauchery that hastened his end."

"Beautiful," Thomas said, laughing. "I'm surprised More didn't think of that one. Remember his statement that Richard was responsible for Clarence's execution, although he protested publicly against it, but that he didn't really protest as loudly as he might have done, and so probably didn't mean it?"

"This isn't getting us anywhere, Thomas."

"No. But we will have to watch Philip closely."

"That," said Liz, "I can do."

II

Earlier, Thomas had found the Ricardians exasperatingly emotional. He now found himself in the inconsistent position of deploring a demonstration of British phlegm. The afternoon meeting was proceeding according to schedule, and so far no one had referred to the unfortunate tricks.

However, as he glanced around the room, Thomas saw that the mystery had left its marks. The effect showed in flushed faces and glittering eyes, in the rector's troubled frown and in Rawdon's sickly pallor. It showed most plainly in Philip. The hard, handsome face was calm as he followed Weldon's introductory remarks. The actor's long, flexible hands were relaxed. But one foot tapped in a restless rhythm on the carpeted floor.

They were meeting in the library, since the Great Hall was being decorated for the evening's festivities. Nervously Thomas rehearsed in his mind the steps of the dance he had been practicing. Then he forced himself to pay attention to the proceedings.

Weldon looked more like his hero than ever. There was only one sign of nervousness, and that was a gesture he might have borrowed from Richard III, whose portrait showed him fingering a ring on one hand—a habit mentioned by historians. In the portrait Richard wore three rings on his right hand—a modest collection for a man of his clothes-conscious era. Weldon wore only one; he kept twisting it and pushing it up and down as he talked.

His remarks included a welcome to the distinguished American visitor, who squeaked an acknowledgment, and a hint of the joys in store for the evening. Weldon ended by introducing the first speaker, and Frank walked up to the temporary rostrum.

Thomas had not expected to do so, but he found Frank's talk fairly interesting. The young man had a logical mind, in spite of his legal training. Even the bruises on his unhandsome face did not detract from his poise, and his low voice, with its beautifully modulated vowels, was a pleasure to hear.

Thomas glanced at Jacqueline. He suspected she was more sympathetic to Richard than she admitted; but it would be like her to take the negative side out of sheer perversity. And she knew quite a bit about the subject. That was another of her irritating qualities, Thomas thought, trying to harden his heart against the effect of the elegant profile framed in ruddy hair. If she would just admit she knew, instead of pretending girlish ignorance and then walloping the unwitting victim with a cartload of specialized data. . . .

Frank took the conventional—among Ricardians— view that the real murderer of the princes was Henry VII. He recalled Henry's inexplicable failure to discover the fate of the boys after he entered London, and summarized the inconsistencies in More's story of the confession. He pointed out that Richard's behavior was equally illogical if he was guilty of the crime. As England's grim history proved, a deposed monarch was often as good as dead; but the bodies of other murdered kings had been publicly displayed so that there could be no doubt of their deaths. If Richard wanted to prevent rebellions in favor of his nephews, he had to make sure they were known to be dead.

As Frank went on, Thomas found his attention straying

from the speaker to Sir Richard. Weldon's hands were not still for a moment; the ring moved up and down, around and around. There was a queer little smile on his face as he listened to the lecture.

With a sudden thrill Thomas remembered the letter. The fantastic events of the past twenty-four hours had put it out of his mind, and yet it was the raison d'être of the whole weekend. What was in that letter? Was it the cause of Weldon's secretive smile?

If so, the rector did not share Weldon's feelings; he was sober and preoccupied, nodding absently from time to time as Frank made a point. So far as Thomas knew, Ellis was the only other member of the group who had seen the letter. That wasn't right. The committee should have its chance before the public fanfare began. Wasn't that why they were here? Thomas wondered if the others, like himself, had been so worried about the unpleasant jokes that they had forgotten the purpose of the meeting. He promised himself that he would corner Weldon as soon as the session ended.

He had to contain himself while the doctor spoke on medieval medicine and Percy read a pompous long-winded paper on the education of a boy of noble rank in the fifteenth century. As the afternoon wore on, the room began to darken. The sun had vanished behind the rain clouds Jacqueline had predicted earlier. A cool wind came through the open windows, and Thomas fidgeted impatiently. A burst of applause brought him out of his brown study. Percy had finished and his fond mama was clapping. Thunder rolled in ominous echo as Sir Richard brought his gavel down, ending the meeting.

Thomas caught up with his host at the library door and drew him aside. The others were heading for their rooms to prepare for the banquet. Jacqueline lingered, but Thomas scowled at her and made shooing motions with his hand. He wanted to tackle Sir Richard alone. For a wonder, Jacqueline obeyed.

The interview was not satisfactory. Weldon was vague. Of course he meant to show the letter to his colleagues. There had been so many distractions. . . . Tonight? Possibly. . . . They would discuss it later. Would Thomas excuse him? He had to consult with Wilkes about the arrangements for the banquet. . . .

Weldon slid away, smiling sweetly. Thomas swore. He felt the need of something to calm his nerves, so he rang and ordered a drink. It was brought by one of the footmen; Wilkes was evidently busy. Carrying his glass, Thomas went upstairs.

He took off his coat, tie, and shoes, and settled himself comfortably on the bed with a copy of Sir Thomas More. Rain hissed softly against the window; drawn draperies and an excellent reading light gave a warm, enclosed feeling to the room. The slanders of Sir Thomas exacerbate the feelings of Ricardians, but his prose is not particularly stimulating. Thomas's eyelids drooped. . . .

He was awakened by a tap on the door. He fumbled for the book, with the unreasonable sense of guilt people feel when they are caught sleeping during the day.

Jacqueline slipped into the room. She was wearing a dark-green housecoat that matched her eyes. Thomas sat up. He was no longer sleepy, but one look at Jacqueline's face told him that his hope was in vain.

"I came for a chat," she said, sitting down in an armchair. "What are you reading? Oh, Sir Thomas More. Or do you follow the school that claims Morton wrote the book?"

Thomas sighed. Really, Jacqueline's expertise was very exasperating.

"Bishop Morton was one of Richard's bitterest enemies. More undoubtedly got some of his information from the old wretch, but . . . no, I think More wrote it. What does that prove? More may be a saint but he's not canonically infallible. Damn it, it's a terrible book! Full of lies, innuendos, dirty—"

"You people are such masochists," Jacqueline said. "Why do you read it if it infuriates you so much?"

"I don't know. Maybe it's incredulity; I can't believe an intellectual like More could produce such stuff. He's a master of doublethink. Listen to this:

'He slew with his own hands king Henry the sixth, being prisoner in the Tower, *as men constantly say,* and that without commandment or knowledge of the king, which would undoubtedly if he had intended that thing, *have appointed that butcherly office to some other* than his own brother.*"

Thomas's tone italicized the phrases. He added, with mounting indignation, "Pure rumor, in other words. 'Men say!' And did you get that incredible piece of logic in the last part? If the king had ordered Henry to be killed, he wouldn't have sent his own brother to do the deed; but men say Richard did it, so therefore it must have been done without Edward's knowledge! The book is full of that sort of thing. Here . . ."

"You don't have to convince me. I agree with you."

"Here, where he says . . ." Thomas put the book down. "If you agree, why are you being so obnoxious about Richard? Want to join the society?"

Jacqueline smiled. She stretched lazily; the long, wide

sleeves fell away from her arms. Clasping her hands behind her head, she wriggled down into the chair.

"I'm not being obnoxious, just logical. You can't clear Richard of the boys' death any more than you can convict him. There is no proof. It is incomprehensible to me that any historian can take More's *Richard* seriously; or rather, it would be incomprehensible if I didn't know historians as I—Thomas, you aren't listening."

"Why don't you come over here and get comfortable?" Thomas suggested.

"I'm very comfortable right here."

"I'm not."

Jacqueline lowered her arms and folded her hands primly in her lap. "Finish your drink," she said in a kindly voice. "No, Thomas, stay right where you are. I refuse to engage in dalliance—if that is the phrase—during an English country weekend. How conventional! And Percy is probably listening at the door."

Thomas glanced nervously at the door. He didn't take the suggestion seriously enough to get up and look, but it dampened his ardor. Reaching for his glass, he said in resigned tones, "Well, at least you have an open mind. I still think there is serious doubt about Richard's guilt."

"You don't really believe Henry the Seventh—"

"Yes, I do. I think that during the summer of 1483 the boys were removed from the Tower to a remote northern castle. That's why we don't hear any more of them in the contemporary annals, which were written by Londoners."

Enthusiasm made Thomas's eyes shine and his face glow. Jacqueline's eagle eye softened as she watched him, but Thomas was oblivious. He went on,

"All the anomalies are resolved by the assumption that

Richard was innocent. Sir James Tyrrell did murder the boys—in 1485, at the command of Henry the Seventh, not Richard the Third. Twenty years later, after Tyrrell was safely dead, Henry put out the 'confession,' altering the facts to fit the assumption of Richard's guilt. He didn't do it very skillfully; the story, as it has come down to us, is inconsistent throughout. But by that time there was no one alive who could or would challenge Henry's version. Elizabeth Woodville, the boys' mother, was dead—"

"The boys' sister was still alive," Jacqueline interrupted. "Henry's queen, Elizabeth of York."

"Henry's queen, and the mother of the heir. What could she do, even if she knew the truth? I've always suspected Elizabeth of York was not the paragon of virtue the Tudor historians described. There is an old story that she took an active part in the conspiracy against Richard, and wrote personally to Henry Tudor promising to marry him if he was successful. She didn't love Henry; she'd never even met him, and by all accounts he was a particularly unlovable character. She wanted revenge—revenge against Richard, who had cast her family down from its high place, and publicly humiliated her by announcing he had no intention of marrying her. I think she was in love with Richard, before he rejected her. *He* was capable of inspiring love; one old woman, who had known him personally, described him as the handsomest man in the room, after his brother Edward—"

Jacqueline stood up.

"You talk about them as if they only died last week," she said sharply. "It's unnerving, Thomas."

The room was very still. Only the rustle of rain against the window broke the silence.

"It's only a game, Jacqueline," Thomas said, after a moment. "An intellectual game, slightly absurd, perhaps, but harmless."

"Not so harmless. You people are maddening. You sit around debating five-hundred-year-old murders while a mad comedian is in your midst. Have you forgotten what happened to you this morning?"

"No, and I haven't forgotten the letter, either." Thomas told her of his talk with Weldon. "He's acting damned peculiarly," he concluded. "I can't figure out what's bugging him."

"Can't you?"

"Oh, well, he's worried about his precious letter. Nothing else seems to matter to him. I'm more concerned about the jokes. You know Philip is next on the list?"

Jacqueline nodded.

"I just stopped by to visit him."

"You went to his room?" Thomas sat up. "Really, Jacqueline. . . ."

"You didn't object to my coming here." A glint of some indefinable emotion warmed Jacqueline's green eyes. "He's on the alert. I hadn't finished knocking before he had the door open and both hands wrapped around my throat. They didn't stay there," she added thoughtfully.

Thomas decided not to pursue the subject. "Well, I'm glad he's expecting trouble. Maybe he'll catch the joker."

"Or vice versa."

"Stop giving out mysterious hints," Thomas snapped. "Is there something you want me to do? What can we do? Shall we tackle Sir Richard once more again about the letter?"

"No. I don't think the letter is important now." Jacqueline drifted toward the door. "I've got to get dressed."

"What in?" Thomas asked curiously.

"Just a little thing I whipped up." Jacqueline turned her head and smiled at him over her shoulder. "If I do join the society, Thomas, I'll join the American branch."

Whereupon she departed, leaving Thomas to ponder this most mysterious hint of all. After some minutes of fruitless cogitation he rang for another whiskey and soda.

Suitably refreshed, he turned to the matter of his costume. He had tried it on before, so he knew its intricacies, which were not many. There were no points to be tied—how the Hades did one tie a point, anyway?—no elaborate ruffs to be adjusted or tights to be smoothed over the legs. The outfit was surprisingly comfortable. Giving his fur-trimmed skirts a tentative kick, Thomas wondered why women were so determined to get into trousers. Skirts gave a feeling of freedom, a lack of constriction. . . . He tripped, caught hold of a chair, and untangled his shoe from the hem of the garment. Of course it was rather difficult to *do* anything in skirts. They were suitable only for a leisured progress, a lounging, deliberate pace. The men of the fifteenth century didn't go to war in their elaborate robes. Romans wore the toga only on state occasions.

Meditating on costume, a subject he knew very little about, Thomas draped a heavy gold chain across his shoulders and studied the effect. Very nice. Too bad that men of his generation couldn't wear jewelry; it was a human impulse to like glitter and bright jewels. Only in the past century had men been deprived of their peacock habits and forced into somber blacks and grays. Pepys had gloated over his gold-trimmed cloak; the cavaliers had swaggered in plumes and velvet, in lace collars and crimson satin breeches.

Thomas added another chain, studied his reflection

complacently, and went on reassuring himself. Tutankhamen's jewel boxes had bulged. Roman generals wore golden armor. D'Artagnan flaunted the queen's diamond ring and Porthos his embroidered cloak; male dress uniform, even now, sparkled and shone and dazzled the eye with primary colors. Maybe, Thomas thought musingly, that was what was wrong with the older generation today. Repressing their natural tendencies in order to conform to some neurotic notion of propriety. . . . Thomas put rings on six of his ten fingers and viewed the posturing image in the mirror with complete satisfaction.

From the shadowy depths the Duke of Clarence looked back at him. Long fair hair flowed from under a gilt coronet. Jewels winked in miniature bursts of color. Velvet smoldered richly; ermined bands stood out like streaks of snow. One ringed hand rested lightly on the hilt of a jeweled dagger.

Thomas felt a small shock. He had not been aware of reaching for the dagger. Odd, how atavistic memories lingered. The hilt had felt right, somehow.

The dagger was a compromise between the sword Thomas secretly yearned to wear and his knowledge that such a weapon would have been inappropriate with court costume. He didn't think the dagger was out of character. The Duke of Clarence had been a sneaky devil, who suffered—with justification—from feelings of persecution.

The first warning bell echoed down the corridor. Thomas adjusted his coronet and smoothed the long flaxen locks that fell to his shoulders. The wig was the only part of the costume that made him self-conscious, but it would have spoiled the effect to omit it. He turned from the mirror. He had ten more minutes before the next bell, which would summon the committee to cocktails in the drawing room, but he did not linger. This period of time was potentially dangerous, for the guests had to pass along the mazelike corridors. Perhaps Jacqueline had been hinting, in her oblique fashion, that Philip could do with an escort.

Thomas peeked out into the corridor. It was deserted. Picking up his skirts, he went to Philip's room and knocked on the door.

It was not until he felt the prick of a sword point at the base of his throat that he realized Philip might misinterpret his motives.

"Hey," he croaked, looking down the shining blade at Philip's grim face. "It's only me."

"Oddly enough, that doesn't reassure me." Philip stepped back a pace, but the sword remained in position. "Come in, if you like. Sit down over there."

Walking very lightly, Thomas crossed the room and took the indicated chair. He smiled. "It's only me," he repeated.

Philip lowered his point. He was wearing a costume similar to the one he had worn the day before, but even more striking. His doublet of black velvet was trimmed with ermine and had enormous padded sleeves. Across his broad chest hung a heavy chain of silver suns and roses— the Yorkist collar. Black and silver made a somber dress, Hamletian rather than Richardian; Frank had probably borrowed it from a colleague's theatrical wardrobe. The actor's coloring echoed the cold shades. His silver-gilt hair shone pallidly, and his gray eyes were as hard as the steel of the sword blade.

"I didn't recognize you at first," he admitted. "Where the hell did you get that wig?"

"Costumer's in London." Thomas adjusted his coronet,

which had slipped sideways. "Don't you like it?"

"Absolutely love it, dear boy," Philip said viciously.

Thomas leaned back in the chair, but he was not feeling happy. The other man was not merely tense; he was a mass of jangled nerves.

"What are you worried about?" Thomas asked. "The jokes are probably finished. They were easy to arrange when no one was suspicious, but now that we've been alerted to the danger, the unknown can't hope to catch you off guard. You can handle yourself pretty well, even without that sword. And there's no cause for alarm. At worst, just a joke; a little embarrassing, maybe, but . . ."

His voice died as he saw the other man's eyes.

He could not entirely blame himself. It had been a long time since he had been that young. Maybe he had never been that young; an average bumpkin, with no particular vanities, he had taken the inevitable jokes of his contemporaries with equanimity. But the prickly years of adolescence are always painful. It is a period of mental imbalance; every glance silently criticizes you, every whisper concerns your secret weaknesses.

But, Thomas reminded himself, you grow out of it. You learn, with mingled relief and chagrin, that people are too absorbed in themselves to care much about you; you discover that you are no more and no less comical than any other man. Your doings are just as trivial in the vast web of the universe, and the only way to endure your own insignificance is to laugh at it before the last great joke is played upon you.

This boy had never learned any of these things. He was still a boy, whatever his actual age, and his acquired facade was as smooth and as brittle as an eggshell. He could suffer pain, but he could not endure himiliation.

The moment of communication had been mutual. Phil looked away. He straightened up, lowering his blade. He knew his trade; even when he was intensely preoccupied his movements were graceful and economical.

"Let's have a drink."

"I've already had one."

"So have I. I'm about to have another."

Sheathing his sword, he crossed to the bureau, took out a bottle, and splashed liquid lavishly into a glass.

"I know it's ill-bred to carry one's own booze," he said sarcastically, handing the glass to Thomas. "But I'm not an aristocrat by birth, and it unnerves me to have servants popping in and out. Cheers."

He raised the bottle to his lips and kept it there so long that Thomas was moved to remonstrate. "Take it easy. If our mystery man is gunning for you, you'll need all your wits about you."

Philip lowered the bottle—but only, Thomas thought, because he needed to breathe. The theatrical profession was not noted for sobriety, but surely, in this case, getting drunk was contraindicated. Philip was no fool. . . .

And maybe he wasn't worried, for the best of all possible reasons. The man was an actor, Thomas reminded himself. The display of nerves could be pretense. If Philip was the joker, he could drink himself insensible, knowing himself to be safe.

Thomas drank. He had been born with a constitutionally weak head and ordinarily was careful about imbibing, but now he felt the need to steady his nerves.

"Did Jacqueline send you along to protect me?" Philip asked suddenly.

"What makes you think that?"

"She read me a long lecture about drinking." Philip

smiled. "That is quite a woman, Thomas."

The smile and the narrowed eyes were offensive, but Thomas refused to rise to the bait. After a moment Philip went on,

"Yes. A shrewd and sexy woman. She makes Liz look like a scrappy schoolgirl."

"Well, I wouldn't—"

"Not that I give a damn about the wench."

"You have been rather—"

"Oh, well, one has to keep one's hand in. Give the girl a thrill. That poor stick she's engaged to—can't imagine what she sees in him."

Thomas smiled to himself. The stock phrase almost constituted a declaration of love. Then the smile faded as he contemplated Philip's classic profile. The pose was probably unconscious, but the words . . . You couldn't believe a thing the man said.

"No," he snapped, as Philip reached for the bottle. "Leave that alone, you've had enough. Frank's a pleasant-enough lad. Why don't you lay off him?"

"Oh, he won't last," Philip said. "Not with Sir Richard the Third in the running. Liz would never have accepted Honest Frank if Mum hadn't been so dead set against him."

"Why should Mrs. Ponsonby-Jones be against it? I should think Frank would be considered a good match."

"Ho," Philip said derisively. "He's as poor as the proverbial church mouse, old boy. And not well thought of by his firm. There was some talk of a forged check while he was at Oxford. . . ."

"Where did you pick up garbage like that?"

Philip smiled. "I can tell you equally jolly tidbits about the others. Isobel is a lush, of course. She'll end up in a

Haven for Alcoholics one day. And she'll continue writing her ghastly books; her readers will never know the difference. You know about Sir General 'Bloody' Kent, I suppose; they let him retire, to save the good name of the service, but it he hadn't done so he'd have ended up in the dock. One of his junior officers is still rather badly scarred. . . ."

Thomas exclaimed in horror. Philip went on, with growing relish. "Dear old Mum is a gambler. She's heavily in debt. Her son is peculiar, to say the least. Rawdon has killed half a dozen patients since he got on this natural-food-kick, by prescribing wheat germ instead of penicillin—"

"And you?" Thomas inquired drily. Philip was baiting him, of course, and doing a good job of it. Face and voice were trained to carry conviction.

"Why should I incriminate myself? Ask Fearless Frank; I expect he has my dossier at his fingertips."

The bell rang before Thomas could think of an appropriate reply. He rose, wary of his skirts, and followed Philip out. The actor's face was as bland as butter. Thomas wondered how many of the scurrilous stories were true. He also regretted his virtuous interruption. It would have been interesting to hear what Philip had on the saintly-looking rector.

At the head of the stairs Philip stopped, catching his breath. There were no electric lights below. The hallway was dark except for the pale flare of candles. Across the polished floor a figure moved with the smooth silence of a ghost. It wore robes of apple green, trimmed with silver. The long gauzy veil lifted like a cloud from the tip of the tall cap.

Liz looked up and laughed at their startled faces. She

sank to the floor in a low curtsy as the two men descended the staircase. Thomas replied with a bow that in his opinion didn't compare too unfavorably with Philip's courtly gesture. It was easier to play the game in semidarkness. Thomas was no longer self-conscious, but he found it increasingly difficult to keep track of which century he was living in.

The drawing room was also lit by candles. Sir Richard had a certain flare for the theatrical. He was King Richard to the life as he raised a tall beaker to greet the newcomers—Richard as he might have been in the happy days when he lorded it over the north, before the deaths of brother, son, and wife. On his smooth brown head he wore a circlet of gold; and Thomas was reminded of the famous story of the crown plucked from the thornbush after the Battle of Bosworth. Richard had worn it into battle, disdaining the warnings of his friends that he would thus be marked out for the fiercest attacks of his enemies.

Thomas forgot Bosworth as the smiling host handed him a goblet—a high, carved beaker of gold flashing with fake jewels. Or were they fakes? Thomas shrugged. He took a hearty swallow, and almost choked. Weldon was going all out for authenticity. The drink was not gin or Scotch or brandy, but a heady mixture of spiced wine.

Someone smacked him on the back—a misguided gesture that brought on the fit of coughing he had thus far managed to avoid. When Thomas had cleared his streaming eyes, he saw Kent grinning at him. The bronzed soldier was the only one in the group who was not wearing a wig or long hair. Thomas saw him, not as the eventually ineffectual Buckingham, but as the product of an era far removed from the fifteenth century. Kent's very features resembled those of certain hawk-nosed Roman busts.

"Take it slowly," Kent warned, as Thomas raised his cup. "It tastes like treacle gone bad, but it's powerful stuff."

Thomas ignored him and drank again. Once you got used to it, the stuff wasn't half bad.

When he lowered the goblet, Kent had gone. Thomas blinked at the vacant space. Someone moved in to fill it. A white moustache . . . O'Hagan. Thomas studied the moustache. Amazing appendage, he thought; you don't see a face at all, you just see a moustache.

"Who're you?" he asked amiably. "I mean, I know who you are. Glad to see you. Who're you s'posed to be?"

O'Hagan was wearing a nondescript garment that might have passed as a medieval robe. Thomas rather suspected it was the man's bathrobe, but that was none of his business.

"Oh, I don't have a part," O'Hagan said. He started to walk away, but Thomas grabbed his arm.

"You must be somebody," he insisted. "Everybody's somebody."

He waved his goblet. There was a soft splashing sound and Thomas glanced around to see Wilkes refilling his glass. The sight almost sobered him. Wilkes was wearing a doublet and hose in Gloucester's livery colors, white and red. Richard's badge, the white boar, was embroidered on the left breast of the doublet. In his normal attire the butler's air of dignity overcame his physical deficiencies; Thomas now observed, with pained surprise, that Wilkes was bowlegged as well as spindle-shanked. The dignity was gone too. Wilkes's narrow shoulders slumped, but his face wore an expression of grim endurance.

"Thank you, Wilkes," Thomas said sympathetically.

Wilkes bowed his head.

"Thank *you,* your Grace."

Thomas drank.

"Amazing stuff," he remarked to O'Hagan, who had emerged from a refreshing dip into his own goblet.

"It would be a sensation at an office Christmas party," O'Hagan agreed. He giggled.

"No, but le'ssee," Thomas insisted. "You gotta be somebody. Wanna be Lord Stanley?"

"All you've got left are the unsympathetic parts," O'Hagan complained. "Stanley was a lousy traitor. Even I—I mean, nobody thinks much of him."

This seemed reasonable to Thomas, who had emptied his glass.

"You can be Lovel," he offered generously. "Richard's bes' friend."

"He met a sticky end, too. No, I think I'll be Henry the Seventh. At least he survived Richard."

He moved away. Thomas watched him critically. The man was drunk. He was swaying.

The whole room was swaying.

Thomas shook his head at Wilkes, who was advancing upon him with a full pitcher and a look of concentrated malevolence. He went to Weldon.

"Wonderful party," Thomas said. "But aren't you asking for it, Dick?"

"What d'you mean?"

"Darkness," Thomas said. "Intoxicating liquors. Perfect for the comedian."

"Nonsense," Weldon said shortly. "There will be no more jokes."

"How do you know?"

"It was Percy, of course. Who else could it be? I gave

the boy a lecture. He won't dare go on."

"But Percy couldn't—"

"Use your head, Thomas. None of the tricks required any particular physical strength—except perhaps the one played on you. But with a pulley arrangement of some sort, using the hooks in the ceiling of the wine cellar, a child could have managed that as well. No, it was Percy. The boy isn't . . . We've had trouble with him before this."

"I'm sorry," Thomas said.

"Don't be sorry. Don't let regret spoil this." Weldon faced him squarely. He said softly, "This is important to me, Thomas. More important than you realize."

The red glow in his eyes might have been reflected firelight. To Thomas it looked like the glow of fanaticism.

"What's important?" he asked. "A reconstruction of a medieval banquet, or—"

"Richard." The glow became a steady light. "Richard's good name. Tomorrow is important, Thomas. I won't let anything interfere with what is going to happen. Anything! If I told you—"

He broke off. Lady Isobel had arrived.

Her costume was even more elaborate than the one she had worn the previous day, a black gown that blended with the shadows and left the wearer's powdered bust and face hanging in midair. The woman looked horrible like a waxen effigy. The long flaxen hair streaming over her shoulders was as dry as an untended wig. The thin lips were set in a smirk.

"My lords and lieges," exclaimed Lady Isobel. She curtsied. There was a sharp cracking sound. Thomas was reminded of dry bones snapping.

Thomas reached for a glass—any glass, he didn't care whose. Damn it, the charades were becoming unnerving.

He began to understand the old obsession about possession, the danger of opening one's mind to invasion by the dead. He had a hideous vision of the group yielding to their various alter egos and wallowing in the treachery and blood that had marked the end of the fifteenth century. Personally he didn't feel the slightest empathy with the unpleasant Duke of Clarence, but . . . He put his beaker back, scarcely tasted. Possession was as a superstition, but there was danger in identifying too strongly with another personality.

Lady Isobel made the circuit of the room, exchanging archaic greetings and allowing the men to kiss her hand. Thomas told himself he wouldn't kiss it, but when the woman greeted him he found he had to. It was right under his nose.

He got a whiff of mixed spirits that momentarily stupefied him as Lady Isobel laughed gaily up into his face.

"Dear brother Clarence," she chirped.

"Ah, yes," Thomas mumbled. "Elizabeth."

"Your Grace, if you please. Elizabeth was always on her dignity, remember? Oh, isn't this fun? Have some more malmsey, Clarence!"

"Fun," Thomas said hollowly.

The bony fingers, still clinging to his, suddenly contracted. The long nails dug in like claws. Thomas turned.

Jacqueline stood in the doorway.

Thomas's second reaction was one of amusement. Jacqueline had upstaged the other women and made the best entrance of all. His initial reaction could not have been expressed in words. It was a long, shaken breath of pure lechery.

Of course he had warned Jacqueline, in London, that they would be wearing costume. This gown had never been wrenched from a costumer's musty racks; it was a sweeping, full-sleeved garment of ivory and gold threads. In fact, it was no more medieval than any of the other "at home" outfits popular for parties, but Jacqueline wore it royally. It was cut very low in front, and the evocative light that had picked out Lady Isobel's sharp bones made warm and pleasing contrasts with Jacqueline's curves. The real glory, however, was her hair. Thomas had never seen it unbound. It rippled in a coppery stream over her shoulders almost to her waist.

He watched while Jacqueline advanced on the group consisting of the rector, the doctor, and O'Hagan. She cut the latter neatly out of the group, removed him to a cozy sofa near the window, and sat down beside him.

Thomas was aroused from thoughts that did not become him by Weldon's impatient exclamation. "Where are Percy and his mother? It's late; we must begin."

Mrs. Ponsonby-Jones may have delayed her entrance in order to be the last to appear, but something had happened to distract her. She trotted into the room without pausing to strike a pose.

"Where is Percy? Liz, have you seen your brother?"

Liz turned

"No, I came down some time ago."

"He's not in his room," said Percy's mother.

Jacqueline stood up and began to run. She crossed the room doing a solid six miles an hour, and vanished out the door.

It was a ludicrous sight, but Thomas was not amused. He was still hypnotized by history. Jacqueline's streaming hair and pale face, her golden gown conjured up visions out of England's past—visions of queens and royal ladies fleeing for their lives. Catherine Howard, Henry VIII's next-to-last wife, whose wailing ghost is still seen rushing down the corridors of Hampton Court; Anne Boleyn, Mary Queen of Scots, Lady Jane Grey. All Tudor victims . . .

Something snapped into place in his mind with a horrible click. He leaped up and followed Jacqueline. Liz and Frank reached the door at the same time. Their faces were shaped into the same expression of pallid fear.

"Where?" Frank asked. "The cellars . . ."

Thomas saw Jacqueline taking the stairs two at a time. Her skirts were raised to her knees.

"Upstairs," he grunted, and shoved past the others.

Jacqueline didn't bother investigating the boy's room; she looked in the other bedrooms. Thomas had never realized the sheer size of Weldon House until that time. It was nightmarish. The doors seemed to go on forever, down one unending corridor after another.

"How the hell many doors are there in this museum?" Jacqueline wailed, opening another door.

She hardly paused; but there was a split second's hesitation before she flung herself across the threshold. Thomas reached the door in time to see what was within.

The figure sprawled on the bed was Percy; there was no mistaking that gross shape. The face was hidden by a fat white pillow.

"Smothered in the Tower" someone behind him was babbling. Thomas could not identify the voice; it was shrill with horror. "Smothered between two feather beds!"

✢ 5 ✢

IN the split-second pause between discovery and action, Thomas's ingenious imagination presented him with a series of horrific pictures. It was a wasted effort. When Jacqueline snatched the pillow away, he saw Percy's familiar pink face, open mouthed and wet-lipped; the lips vibrated perceptibly to the sound of Percy's regular breathing.

Along the corridor came the pounding of feet. Not even maternal love could drive Mrs. Ponsonby-Jones's heavy frame beyond a certain rate of speed; she was the last to arrive. The staring onlookers in the doorway staggered back as she thrust through them. Catching sight of the pillow in Jacqueline's hand and the outstretched feet of her son, she gave a heartrending cry. She flung herself onto the bed. The springs squealed and Percy's relaxed body bounced before she gathered it into her arms.

It took considerable time to convince the woman that Percy was alive and well. Percy's head drooped over her arm; his mouth had sagged into an idiotic grin.

"He's drunk," Thomas said.

"No. Drugged, though, I think. Mrs. Ponsonby-Jones, if you would let the doctor have a look at him . . ."

Rawdon was on the other side of the bed, trying to get at his patient. It took Jacqueline's and Thomas's combined efforts to pry the distracted mother from her son, and they had to wrestle with her again when the doctor, after peering into Percy's eye, administered a few hearty slaps. The next time he lifted the boy's lid, it stayed up. The expression of the single blue eye boded no good for the slapper.

Mrs. Ponsonby-Jones was removed; she was only a hindrance. The others set about the work of restoration, and Thomas, for one, enjoyed it. Percy's howls, when he was thrust into a cold shower, warmed the cockles of his heart. The boy emerged dripping and blue, but by then he was sufficiently restored to regain his natural curiosity.

"You mean I was doped?" he inquired, through chattering teeth. "Really doped? How marvelous!"

Thomas left the boy to the tender mercies of the doctor and Weldon and returned to the drawing room, where the others had reassembled. Joining Jacqueline, who was setting with Liz, he said, "Percy is himself again. It must have been a mild dose."

"No harm done except to our nerves," Jacqueline agreed. That her nerves were indeed affected Thomas deduced by the presence of the purse—large, white, and bulging. She must have gone to her room to fetch it as a child reaches for a furry animal in time of stress. She lifted it to her lap and began to burrow in it with both hands.

"Do you think he took the stuff himself?" she inquired.

Shocked, Thomas silently indicated the presence of the

boy's sister. Liz looked at him. She was dry-eyed and un-
naturally calm.

"He might have done," she said. "He has a bottle of
tranquilizers."

There was a short, uncomfortable silence. Jacqueline
continued to burrow. Finally she came up with a battered
pack of cigarettes.

"This is the tenth time I've failed to quit smoking," she
said, as Thomas took a lighter from the table. "Liz just told
me about the tranquilizers."

"Mother keeps pressing them on him," the girl said in
the same expressionless voice. "She think's he's nervy and
sensitive. I know he's a little horror, but. . ."

"It's too fashionable these days to blame everything on
poor old Mum," Jacqueline said, blowing out a neatly
rounded smoke ring. "That doesn't mean she isn't sometimes culpable. But you're all right."

Her tone was matter-of-fact. The girl's face lost some of
its pallor. She managed a faint smile.

"I'm okay, you're okay," she said. "Sometimes I'm not
altogether sure of that."

She got up and crossed the room to the fireplace, where
Frank was standing. He put his arm around her and she
leaned against him.

"Well?" Thomas asked.

Jacqueline blew out another smoke ring. The first one
had been a fluke; this attempt resembled a mashed dough-
nut. Jacqueline's eyes narrowed in annoyance. She tried
again, producing a gusty blob with no discernible shape.

"The boy might have drugged himself," she said. "But
that isn't the most interesting thing about this last inci-
dent."

"What is?" Thomas inquired resignedly.

"You were terrified, weren't you?"

"You're damned right I was, and I'm not ashamed to admit it. Percy is an obnoxious brat, but I don't want to see him—"

He broke off, staring at Jacqueline. She looked more enigmatic than usual, thanks to the veil of smoke that obscured her features like the vapor surrounding the pythoness.

"You were scared too," Thomas said. "Like the rest of us, you expected a catastrophe. And the interesting question is—why did we?"

"Precisely. No one has been hurt or seriously injured. Percy's absence could have been explained in a number of harmless ways. Yet the moment his mother announced he was not in his room, we panicked."

"The triumph of instinct over reason," Thomas said. "God knows the atmosphere around here is thick enough. Darkness, rain, the mournful sighing of the wind, and all that sort of thing—not to mention the shades of dead kings and queens gliding through shadowy halls. We're haunted by the memories of old murders. But it's more than that, isn't it?"

"How poetic." But Jacqueline's tone was affectionate; she smiled at him in a way that made his head spin. Or possibly, Thomas told himself, it was the wine.

"I know what worries me," he said, "and it isn't the atmosphere. The joker has taken care not to injury anyone seriously, but what if something goes wrong? What if he picks on someone with a weak heart or an unusual susceptibility to a drug?"

Jacqueline nodded. There wasn't time for her to comment; they were joined by the doctor, who had completed his ministrations.

"Is Percy all right?" Thomas asked.

Rawdon nodded. His gilt crown bobbed, and he made a grab for it.

"I keep forgetting the damned thing," he complained, looking as gloomy and cadaverous as Henry VI probably had looked most of the time. "Apparently the drug was in some vile fruit drink the boy habitually consumes. Did you see his room? Stocked like a shop! Biscuits, sweets—even the fruit is deadly unless it was organically grown, which is unlikely. Insecticides—"

"It would have been easy for someone to drug him, then," Jacqueline interrupted the diatribe.

"Oh, quite. The unfortunate boy never stops eating. If I had him under my care—"

Thomas had heard enough.

"I wonder what's going to happen now. Will Dick want to go on with the banquet?"

Weldon answered the question himself. He appeared in the doorway with his arm around the shoulders of a swaggering Percy.

"Here we are," he said. "Ready to take up where we were—er—interrupted. Mrs. Ponsonby-Jones will join us later on."

For a moment Thomas didn't think Weldon was going to get away with it. The room rang with unspoken questions. But Weldon stood firm, his dark eyes challenging; and no one spoke.

Liz was the first to respond. Like someone in a trance she walked forward, and Sir Richard moved to meet her. He offered her his arm, in the old courtly gesture; she placed her hand on his. The candles flickered in a sudden gust of wind; the two slight figures, robed and crowned, seemed to flicker too, like the unsubstantial fabric of a dream.

Thomas heard a voice remark softly.

"Stands the wind in that quarter? 'Nay, do not pause; for I did kill King Henry, But 'twas thy beauty that provoked me. Nay, now dispatch; 'twas I that stabb'd young Edward, But 'twas thy heavenly face that set me on.' "

The voice was Philip's, of course. Thomas turned. "I hope your quotation does not constitute an accusation."

"Did you see Weldon's face when she took his hand?" The actor's face was covered with a faint sheen of perspiration.

"Don't be ridiculous," Thomas said shortly. "At any rate, you're in the clear. The comedian appears to have skipped you. I'm inclined to agree with Sir Richard. It was Percy."

"After this last episode?" The lines in Philip's forehead smoothed out. "Yes, I see. A typically juvenile attempt to remove suspicion from himself."

"Sir Richard lectured him—accused him of perpetrating the tricks. This would be a predictable reaction."

"I wish I believed it," Philip muttered. "I can deal with Percy."

"Come along," Thomas said. "To the feast! Begone, dull care!"

Philip laughed hollowly.

II

The Great Hall was alive with ruddy, shifting light. A fire roared in the hearth, and along the wall torches set in iron brackets sent up streams of orange flame. The long table on the dais was covered with snowy linen. The floor was strewn with rushes; they were semi-dry and rustled underfoot, giving out a sweet scent as the herbs and flowers among them were crushed by the feet of the guests. Along the walls, stiff as statues, stood rows of servants in full medieval costume. Thomas was reassured to see the snout of a portable fire extinguisher poking out from under a tapestry. It was still raining outside, but Weldon was taking no chances.

Weldon led his lady into the Hall as a blare of trumpets assailed the ears of the guests. Waiting for them near the dais was the stoical figure of Wilkes, in the uncongenial role of the medieval marshal. With his small gilt baton he indicated the chairs each diner was to occupy. As Weldon took his place, the trumpets died. Thomas let out a breath of relief. The musicians did not lack ardor, but at least one of them had to be tone deaf as well as untrained.

The unfortunate Wilkes now reappeared in the role of the medieval butler, the mandatory white napkin draped around his neck. Thomas watched with amusement as he poured wine into the cover of Weldon's cup and raised it to his own lips. He hoped the butler didn't have to go through the rest of the taster's ritual; it would take forever, if he dipped into every dish.

Weldon had tactfully dispensed with the massive salt-cellar that separated the nobles from the nonentities at a medieval table. Thomas found himself seated between Frank and Rawdon. Liz was some distance away, between the rector and Philip. Frank's expression made it clear that he did not approve of this arrangement.

Thomas took a heady swallow of wine and slapped the younger man on the back.

"Cheer up," he said expansively. "Enjoy. Dick has gone all out on this affair."

"Yes, but that damned actor—"

"He hasn't got a chance," Thomas said. He finished his wine.

Frank's dark hair brushed the back of his collar and waved over his ears. His expression was lugubrious and he was sweating. The Hall was already uncomfortably hot, and the fire was roaring like a blast furnace.

"You know something?" he asked.

"Where's your crown?" Thomas demanded. "You oughta have—"

"It kept falling off."

"So does mine. But you're a prince. You oughta have—"

"You know something?"

"No, what?"

"You're drunk," Frank said seriously. "And I'm getting drunk. And I mean to get a lot more . . ." He stopped, his eyes widening. "Good Lord," he said.

Thomas read his lips. He couldn't hear a thing except the off-key bray of trumpets. The door of the Hall opened. Through it came the vision that had astounded Frank.

It might be described as a bevy of serving wenches. Thomas assumed they were village girls; surely the house didn't have a staff of this size. Kirtled and laced and buskined to a dizzying degree, they were having a hard time controlling their laughter, as their red faces and popping eyes showed. They carried platters and bowls and flagons. As the procession entered, it divided, and down the center marched two stalwart village lads wearing baggy tights and long wigs. Between them they supported a mammoth platter on which sat a swan in full feather.

Thomas knew the swan was safely dead and roasted, its feathers restored to present a replica of life. The idea repelled him, although he knew such frivolities had been common at medieval banquets. He reached for the goblet, which one of the servants had just refilled.

Medieval diet suggests a group of lowly peasants munching stale black bread, or Henry VIII chomping on a leg of lamb while the fat drips down his front. In fact, the *haute cuisine* of the fifteenth century was extremely elaborate. Thomas let out a low whistle of approval after he tasted the soup that constituted the first course. Wilkes was dissecting the swan at a serving table—"plucking" might be a more accurate word—and his fleshy nose indicated what he thought of the task. Thomas did not watch.

Frank was not so appreciative. "What in God's name . . ." he began, indicating the thick liquid in his bowl.

"Blandissory," Thomas said, dipping into the brew again. "Made of beef broth, almonds, and sweet wine boiled together as a base and strained; then you add capon, ground in a mortar—I suppose they would use a blender today—tempered with milk of almonds and sugar. Add blanched almonds. . . ." He lifted his spoon and studied the nut peeping coyly out of the soup before putting the spoon in his mouth. It was impossible to sip blandissory genteelly from the spoon; the almonds got caught in your teeth.

"Too sweet," said Frank grumpily. "Give me a nice clear consommé."

Nobody did. By the end of the first course, even Thomas's stomach was beginning to feel the strain.

The everyday fare for a lordly household usually involved two separate courses, each consisting of three or four dishes. Picking jadedly at swan, Thomas thought with consternation of one famous medieval banquet that had included sixty separate dishes. Surely Weldon wouldn't try to outdo that feast.

The subtlety that ended the first course—which had included three other dishes of meat and fish in addition to soup and swan—was a masterpeice. It was borne in by the same grinning footmen who had opened the ball with the swan. A concoction of spun sugar and egg white, it had been formed by some Michelangelo of a chef into a representation of Sampson pulling down the pillars of the Temple.

The second course came in with a frumenty of venison. The meat, cut in strips, floated in a stewy soup made of wheat boiled in milk, egg yolks, sugar, and salt. Thomas started to describe the ingredients to Frank, but was stopped by a long, agonized expletive.

"I can't stand this," Frank muttered. "I'd sell my soul for a chunk of rare beef."

"They used spices a lot," said Thomas, who was getting his second wind, gastronomically speaking. "This next dish is ground meat—pork, probably—mixed with about a dozen spices and then baked in a pastry shell—called a coffin, if that interests you."

Frank groaned.

Thomas added, "I hope Weldon doesn't go berserk and offer us a cockatrice. They cooked a capon and a suckling pig and cut them in half; then they sewed the front part of the chicken onto the back part of the pig and the front part of the—"

"Good God," said Frank.

The entertainment—jugglers, dancers, music—which ordinarily accompanied a banquet did not appear. Apparently Weldon had anticipated that his guests would be too fascinated by the exotic food to concentrate on anything else, except possibly Ricardian gossip. Thomas found plenty of entertainment in watching his colleagues' reactions to the food.

The doctor, on Thomas's left, was having fits. He dined mainly on bread, and kept up a running commentary about what the food was doing to the collective stomachs of the group. Thomas had to admit he had a point. Everything was spiced and seasoned and sauced, and the heavy sweet wine—malmsey, by any chance?—made digestion even more perilous. He barely touched his junket of rosewater and cream and sighed with relief when the subtlety signalizing the end of the second course was borne in. The spun-sugar replica of Middleham Castle wobbled dangerously on the sturdy shoulders of the serving men. Thomas deduced that the kitchen staff had been indulging in malmsey too.

He waited apprehensively for a possible third course, but Weldon had the proper respect for effete modern appetites. The servitors passed around with basins of scented rosewater and napkins. Then the guests all settled back expectantly as Weldon rose.

Somewhere between the soup and the last subtlety, Mrs. Ponsonby-Jones had taken her place beside Weldon. No one less resembled the pale, consumptive Queen Anne; the woman's square face was ruddy with gratified pride and her bulk overflowed the chair. Apparently her *crise de nerves* had passed. Looking at Percy, Thomas agreed that there was no cause for concern—except for the dangers of gluttony. Percy shone like a greased pink pig from his hair to his third chin.

For security reasons, Weldon explained, he had decided to dispense with hired entertainment. The villagers who had assisted with the serving all were known to Weldon and the servants. Unfortunately none of them were adept in the skills of music and dance—with the exception of Tom Belden and his son, young Tom, whose performances on the trumpet had added so much to the spirit of the evening.

Therefore, Weldon continued, he had decided it would be safer, and more intimate, if they entertained themselves. He regretted the necessity of a phonograph for certain parts of the evening, but they would just have to pretend the music came from a group of live minstrels in the musicians' gallery. So, let the joy begin! They would start—he glanced at Lady Isobel, who was holding a sheaf of papers like a club—with the literary treat postponed from an earlier session.

Lady Isobel rose. Her expression was one of intense piety. Under the shield of the long damask tablecloth Thomas slid his feet out of his shoes and prepared, if possible, to sleep with his eyes open. It was clever of Weldon to bring on Lady Isobel now; their critical sense drugged with food and wine, the listeners would not suffer quite so intensely.

> *"The sun shone bright, the sky was fair,*
> *The birds did sweetly sing,*
> *Across the green of Bosworth Field,*
> *There rode the brave young king."*

The verses would have been barely endurable if they had come from a sentimental nine-year-old girl. From the gaunt old woman they were absolutely embarrassing. Liz might have been joking when she claimed to have a crush on Richard of Gloucester (was she joking, though?), but

Lady Isobel really did. Her voice was low and charged with passion; it quivered as her emotion mounted. Thomas focused his attention on Jacqueline. Her expression of outraged disbelief was almost funny enough to make up for the poem. Despite all his efforts an occasional stanza got through to his brain.

> "Boldly he mounted his great white steed,
> He gazed upon the sky,
> His slender hands took up the reins
> And a tear stood in his eye.
>
> He brushed it back with a mailed hand,
> 'We ride to battle,' he said.
> 'I'll live a king or die a king,
> And I'll have the Tudor's head.' "

Thomas slid further down in his chair. A kindly man, he never enjoyed watching people make fools of themselves. This was worse than the piano recitals of his friends' untalented children. Slender hands and tear-filled eyes . . ."I doubt if he cried much," said Jacqueline's caustic voice in his inner ear.

Fortunately the last verses were more or less inaudible. Richard's gallant death—the word "gallant" appeared pretty often in the work—moved Lady Isobel to gulps and unintelligibility.

Even Weldon looked shaken when the distraught poet dropped into her chair, resembling not so much a drooping lily as a wilted stalk of crabgrass.

"No applause, please," he said, as the other guests eyed one another with varying emotions. "It would be quite inappropriate after that . . . that . . . er. My dear Isobel, take some wine."

Lady Isobel had taken too much wine already, Thomas thought. She complied, however, and smiled wanly as Weldon patted her on the shoulder.

"The muse," she murmured. "Such a hard taskmistress . . . It takes such a lot out of one, Richard."

"I know," said Weldon. "It does indeed. . . ."

The next performer was Liz, who sang several medieval ballads in a pleasant, if undistinguished, voice. The only ones Thomas recognized were Dufay's *"Adieu, m'a-mour,"* and a religious song by Dunstable. Liz then announced that she would scream if anyone asked for "Summer Is Icumen in" or "Greensleeves." The rector, who had been about to request the latter, closed his mouth and looked confused.

After the doctor had given a demonstration of how to put on a suit of armor—from which he had to be removed by two of the burlier servants—Philip took the center of the stage. It was an unfortunate choice of entertainment; the mood of the gathering was uncertain to begin with, and the two soliloquies from *Richard III* did not lighten it. The first, the opening "Now is the winter of our discontent" was a bit of sparkling black humor; but then Philip went on to Richard's agonized speech on the eve of Bosworth. All of them knew the setting: Richard, snatching a few hours' sleep before the morrow's battle, is visited by the specters of his victims, all mouthing the same curse, "Despair, and die!"

Philip became the twisted, tormented villain of Shakespeare's play. His voice rang all the changes of human passion—defiance, terror, remorse. It dropped to a ringing whisper on the final lines:

"I shall despair. There is no creature loves me;
And if I die, no soul will pity me:
Nay, wherefore should they, since that I myself
Find in myself no pity to myself?"

The spellbound audience paid the performer the supreme tribute of silence even after he had straightened up and shed his player's skin. He strolled nonchalantly back to his place at the table; and Thomas saw Liz shrink back as he seated himself beside her. He didn't blame the girl. It had been too good a performance to be wholly comfortable.

Weldon gestured; and from the darkness of the gallery, pipes and drums burst forth in a dance tune. The diners rose; all of them had practiced medieval dancing. Thomas heaved himself out of his chair, although he was dubious about his ability to move, much less tread an airy measure. As he moved gingerly away from the table, Kent plucked at his sleeve.

"Feeling queasy?"

"Well . . ."

"Me too. Come along. I know what we need."

Thomas followed him out into the corridor. The candles were burning low. He wondered what time it was. The party could go on till dawn if the participants held out.

Kent led him to the dining room and a row of decanters on the sideboard. He poured a stiff jolt of brandy and offered it to Thomas.

Thomas drank. There was a moment in which matters hung in the balance. Then the upheaval settled, and he sighed deeply.

"Thanks. I needed that."

"Brandy will cure anything," Kent said, following his

own advice. "I don't like doctors. Never need 'em."

Thomas was inclined to agree. His head felt absolutely clear as they went back to the Hall; but for some odd reason the rest of the evening became kaleidoscopic. He would be conversing with someone in a coherent manner; then the room would spin around and he would be elsewhere, with other people. At the time this situation seemed perfectly normal.

During one of these episodes he found himself with O'Hagan, who was singing "The Maple Leaf Forever." Thomas expressed mild surprise at the choice of song; O'Hagan explained that he was singing the Canadian anthem because he couldn't manage the high notes of "The Star-Spangled Banner." Thomas found this logical, but was moved to demonstrate his own patriotism and tenor voice. He sang all three verses of "The Star-Spangled Banner." O'Hagan continued to sing "The Maple Leaf Forever." He only knew one verse, so he sang that one over and over, while he and Thomas nodded at one another in mutual approbation.

A shift in scene found Thomas discussing Buckingham's rebellion with Philip and Kent. After enthusiastically supporting Richard's takeover of the throne, Buckingham had retired to his castle in Wales,and then had returned at the head of a hostile army. Some Ricardians believed Buckingham was responsible for the death of the young princes, as the first step in his own climb to the throne.

Thomas doubted the theory and said so. Kent, who was playing Buckingham, took the criticism personally. He left, snorting with rage. Unperturbed, Thomas turned to Philip. "Man's drunk," he said seriously. " 'Magine getting so excited about a rational dishcushion. You see my point, don't you?"

"I'm sick of the whole business," Philip said. His face was flushed.

Thomas peered at him.

"Ah," he said. "Ah. Still nervous, my friend? Don't be. Got it all figured out. See, Richard didn't exactly murder Hastings, exactly. It was an exic—an extic—a legal killing. Treasons. Not like the l'il princes. Not that Richard killed the princes, mind you, but if somebody is picking on Richard's victims, then the fellows who were sexecu—I mean, they had their heads chopped off . . . those fellow don't count. You see my point, don't you? I mean . . ."

"For God's sake," said Philip, between his splendid white teeth, "I am getting so bloody sick and tired of all you bloody fools holding my hand. I am not nervous!"

The room turned upside down. Thomas next found himself dancing with Lady Isobel. This seemed such an unlikely activity for him to have chosen that he stumbled over the rushes, which had gotten trampled into heaps. Lady Isobel held him up with an unexpectedly strong arm, and giggled at him. She said something about butts of malmsey. Thomas glowered at her and then realized she was indicating the brimming bowl on the dining table.

"Oh, no," said Thomas vigorously. "Not me. Not that stuff. Gotta keep a clear head. Not get drunk."

The next scene was the dining room. Thomas put down an empty glass and wandered back to the Hall. The music was still going full blast, and Sir Richard was performing a country dance with Mrs. Ponsonby-Jones. The big woman was surprisingly light on her feet; her crimson skirts swirled as she moved. Sir Richard's crown had slipped over one eye.

Thomas looked for a partner and found none. He felt like dancing, so he did—an energetic solo, with high jumps and vigorous arm gestures. He considered another trip to the dining room and decided against it. He was feeling splendid. Arms clasped behind him, he began to stroll around the room. The hangings and potted plants placed at strategic intervals made convenient nooks that contained benches and chairs on which tired dancers might rest. Several of the alcoves were inhabited, not by dallying lovers, but by contentious Ricardians. The rector, perched on a high stool with his slippered feet dangling, was discussing the precontract of Edward IV.

"A precontract was as legally binding as marriage," he said, shaking his finger at the doctor. Rawdon looked bored, as well he might; this topic was almost as familiar as the murder of the princes.

"I know," he said testily. "That is not the question. The question is, did such a precontract really exist? It was officially recognized by Parliament, and Henry Tudor's determined efforts to suppress that decree indicates . . ."

Thomas moved on. In the next niche, Philip and Liz were sitting side by side. For a moment Thomas thought he was getting confused. The topic of conversation was the same, although the people were different.

"Why would Henry want to suppress *Titulus Regius* unless it was true?" Philip demanded.

Liz nodded. Her eyes were shining. Thomas wondered how Philip could go on talking with a face like that six inches from his. Like the others, Philip was crackers on the subject of Richard the Third.

"Then there is the question of the Bishop of Bath and Wells," Philip continued. "Edward the Fourth imprisoned him and so did Henry the Seventh, after he took the throne. That suggests the old boy had knowledge dangerous to both men, and what could it have been but the truth—that Edward was never legally married to his queen."

"Clarence probably knew about it too," Thomas said. "He had his eye on the throne, and . . ."

Nobody seemed to be listening to him, so he moved on. In a corner behind a rubber plant he found Frank, alone. Thomas put his head around the rubber plant.

"Clarence probably knew about it too," he said. "He had his eye on the throne. . . ."

"Oh, it's you," Frank said unenthusiastically. "What the hell are you talking about?"

"The precontract," said Thomas, surprised. "Isn't that what we've been talking about?"

"We haven't been talking. And if you are planning to discuss Richard the Third or any of his kin, don't."

"If that's the way you feel, I'm leaving," said Thomas.

"Do."

Thomas moved on. He wasn't angry with Frank; the poor guy was probably brooding about his fiancée's tête à tête with Phil. Not that there was anything to brood about; the conversation could hardly have been less romantic.

By an oblique train of reasoning this reminded Thomas that he hadn't seen anything of Jacqueline for some time. He began to look for her. The torches were burning low, and he was feeling drowsy; it was only by chance that he saw the shimmer of a golden skirt in a shadowy corner. He wandered over.

Jacqueline was not alone. She was not aware of his approach, not even when Thomas leaned forward, squinting, to make sure of his quarry. The red-gold hair flowed down over Jacqueline's shoulder and over the arm of the man who . . .

"Hey!" said Thomas indignantly. It was bad enough to find Jacqueline in a dark corner with a man. That the man was identifiable by his snowy hair as O'Hagan made matters worse. The white rabbit had been snared by the fox, and Thomas wondered why the fox had bothered. There was something very funny going on. . . .

"Hey!" he repeated. The first exclamation had apparently gone unheard. This one had the desired effect. Jacqueline pulled away. Thomas stared in consternation. The alcove was dark, but there was no mistake; the rabbit's face stared back at him, pale and moustacheless. The moustache . . . the moustache was . . .

Jacqueline raised a hand and peeled the luxuriant appendage from her cheek.

"Oh, Thomas," she said casually. "Would you mind . . ."

Drunk or sober, Thomas told himself, he had a mind that worked like a steel trap. The pieces of the puzzle fell together with a resounding click; growling joyfully, Thomas leaped at O'Hagan and got a punch on the nose that sent him sprawling on his back. He wallowed among the rushes.

"That's enough of that," Jacqueline said icily. "Both of you stop it this instant."

The lights went on in a blinding flash. Whether by design or accident—Thomas suspected the former—the romantic pair had met in the area where the main switches were located.

Her hand still on the switch, Jacqueline studied Thomas with twitching lips.

"Have some hay," she quoted, rather freely. "It's especially good when you feel faint."

Thomas began to pluck dried rushes from his wig. His eyes were glued to O'Hagan; he was finding the truth hard to believe. From other parts of the hall people converged on the trio.

"Strangways," said Thomas. "I'll be *eternally* damned if it isn't James Strangways."

There could be no doubt; the face now bared to the world by the removal of the moustache was unquestionably that of the man whose photograph Thomas had seen on the back of his biography of Edward IV. The dark hair was now pure white, and there were a few more wrinkles around the eyes and the wide, mobile mouth, but the features were the same. The moustache had not been the only disguise; there was no trace of the blinking rodent in Strangeways's look now. He even looked taller. Jacqueline's hand rested on his arm, and Thomas sensed that if it had not been for this mild restraint, Strangways would have vaulted his fallen form and fled.

If he had meditated flight, it was now too late. They were surrounded by a circle of staring faces, on some of which comprehension and outrage had begun to replace bewilderment.

Frank was the first to speak.

"My God," he said.

Lady Isobel plucked at his arm.

"What is it? What is happening?"

"Mr. O'Hagan has lost his moustache," said Mrs. Ponsonby-Jones. "That is very strange." She glared at Jacqueline, as if blaming her for the shaving of O'Hagan.

Percy burst into a high-pitched giggle. "Mum, you are stupid. This isn't Mr. O'Hagan. Don't you recognize him? I do! I suspected all along—"

"Be quiet," Weldon said. The tone quieted Percy; he glanced at Weldon in shocked surprise. Sir Richard's self-control was more impressive than ever. Even the tipsy crown didn't mar his dignity, and Strangways, who had been smiling, lowered his eyes under Weldon's gaze.

"I also recognize you, Mr. Strangways," Weldon said. "Your behavior surprises me, I confess. I had considered you mistaken, but not unprincipled."

"I owe you an apology," Strangways admitted. "Very bad form—isn't that the correct phrase? But I assure, you, deceiving you about my identity was the only way in which I have abused your hospitality."

His voice was several shades deeper than O'Hagan's had been.

"But how did you manage it?" Thomas demanded. "What have you done with the real O'Hagan? Is there a real O'Hagan?"

"Oh, yes, he's real. He's the jackass who took over the American society after they threw me out for heresy." Strangways smiled. His front teeth were a trifle prominent, but the effect was now rather canine than rodent. "I still have a few friends in the society; they keep me informed, so I knew when O'Hagan was due to arrive. It was easy to cut him out of the crowd at the airport; I knew what he looked like, and young Frank didn't. I pointed him out to a friend of mine—he wouldn't have gone quietly with me—and my pal smuggled him away to London, where he is now hiding. The man's a bundle of neuroses; he thinks the meeting has been postponed, and that every reporter in England is in pursuit of him. Meanwhile, I stuck on my moustache and my name tag—I thought that was a particularly good touch—and caught Frank's wandering eye. Simple."

Although he demonstrated some embarrassment at being caught, Thomas thought this emotion was subordinate. He was having a hard time keeping his mouth straight, and he was standing very close to Jacqueline.

Thomas transferred his accusing stare to that lady.

"How long have you known about this?"

"I suspected it some time ago," Jacqueline said. "There is an aura, is there not?—a subtle outflow of masculine energies—no true woman could ignore its emenations. I felt it . . . here. . . ." She clasped her hands over her heaving bosom and grinned at Lady Isobel. Then her voice changed. "I thought it peculiar that Mr. O'Hagan denied knowing Strangways, when both of them had been associated with the American society. That wasn't necessarily damning evidence; but surely it was obvious that if you were harboring a cuckoo in the nest, it had to be Mr. O'Hagan. He is the only person who is not known by sight to any of you. The moustache was too good to be true; his other features are unmistakably those of the man in the photograph. If you are trying to identify someone, you look at the facial bones—nose, jaw and cheekbones, the setting of the eyes."

"Most people don't, though," Strangways said coolly.

"His hair . . ." Thomas began.

"Turned white overnight when I learned the terrible truth about Richard the Third," said Strangways.

He ducked, suddenly, as a fist brushed his jaw. Thomas, now completely sober, grabbed Kent just in time to prevent a second attack. The general's face was purple with rage. His arm felt like a steel bar, and he did not subside until Frank had added his weight to Thomas's. Kent began to swear. He was panting so hard that most of the words were obscured, but a few of the riper military adjectives came through intact; Lady Isobel squealed and put her hands over her shell-like ears.

"Let me at the bastard," Kent said, still wheezing. "Just let me knock that superior smile off his treacherous face. After all he's done to you . . . and you . . ." His head bobbed from one side to the other, indicating Thomas and Frank, who were still holding him.

Frank looked at Thomas. The younger man's cheeks were flushed and his eyes shone with amusement.

"Now then," he said soothingly. "No harm's been done. Actually, I'm rather relieved to find that Mr. Strangways is our mysterious comedian. It makes the whole thing less disturbing."

Again his eyes met those of Thomas, and the latter nodded vigorously. "Quite right, Frank. If you and I don't choose to chastise Mr. Strangways, I don't see why anyone else should be vindictive. Let's all cool off and talk rationally."

Strangways was no longer smiling. "Just a minute," he said. "There's no reason why you should take my word for it, but for your own sakes you had better do so. I didn't play those damned jokes."

Against his will Thomas found the avowal convincing. He was still trying to adjust to the transformation. He found Mr. Hyde much more attractive than the former personality. Strangways looked younger and tougher than the false O'Hagan; his eyes were direct and honest.

Then Strangways spoiled the effect by adding, "I don't need to make fools of you. You're about to do it with no help from me."

Another roar from Kent alerted Thomas; he wound

both arms about the general's writhing body.

Then Weldon's voice cut through the uproar like the lash of a whip.

"Stop it! We've had enough of this, Kent," he said. "Let him go, Thomas. Let go, I say."

Thomas did so. Kent stood still, his color fading.

"Now,"Weldon went on, "let us disprove Mr. Strangway's opinion of us by acting rationally. I don't mean to hold an inquest into the jokes—if you want to call them that. Unless Mr. Strangways can prove an alibi . . ."

Strangways was more cowed by his icy courtesy than he had been by Kent's attempted assault. He shook his head. "How can I? Everyone was coming and going."

"Precisely. The same thing applies to the rest of us," Weldon continued with scrupulous fairness. "Since, as Frank says, no harm was done, I propose to forget what has happened. A more pertinent question is—what do we do with Mr. Strangways?"

"Throw him out," Kent growled. "Kick him out the doors."

"It is one thirty in the morning," Weldon said. "There is not a room to be had in the village, and it is beginning to rain again. Because Mr. Strangways has behaved badly is no reason why I should emulate him."

"Imprison the miscreant," said Mrs. Ponsonby-Jones angrily. "Fling him into a dungeon!"

"Don't be absurd," Liz said sharply. She moved forward, her green skirts swaying, and eyed Strangways with cool appraisal. "Perhaps you'd like us to load him with rusty chains, Mother. After that banquet, dry bread and water would be superfluous."

The rector coughed. "We can hardly imprison the gentleman," he said. His mild voice was shocked. "That would be violating the law. The police—"

There was an immediate, unanimous murmur of negation. Strangways smiled. "I'm perfectly willing to face the police," he said.

"You would be." Philip pushed forward. "Padre, think again. I'm the last man to object to publicity, but if we want to make thorough asses of ourselves for the benefit of the newspaper-reading public of the world, the surest way is to call the police in."

"Quite right, quite right," the doctor said. "It must not get out. Dignity . . . reputations . . ."

Strangways looked at Philip. The two men were the same height; their eyes met like blades crossing.

"Hearing you was a privilege," Strangways said. "I may regret my lack of manners, but I don't regret having had the chance to hear your Richard."

Philip made an impatient gesture.

"These exchanges of courtesy bore me," he said curtly. "Sir Richard, I agree that we can't convict Mr. Strangways without proof; but surely you aren't going to allow him to be present tomorrow?"

"No, no. Mr. Strangways will leave in the morning. For the present, I fear he will have to endure my company."

"But . . ." Kent began.

"I've been anxious to talk with him," Weldon went on; and Thomas was amazed to see the familiar gentle glow of Ricardian passion warm the little peer's face. "I feel sure I can convince him of his errors."

Strangways laughed. He turned to Jacqueline, who had been oddly silent. "If I can't have your company, my dear, Sir Richard's is next best. A duel of wits, eh? We'll see who convinces whom."

He stepped forward. Weldon took him by the arm, as

he might have done with any of his friends. As they walked away, Weldon was already talking.

"There'll always be an England," said Jacqueline, staring after them.

III

Instead of breaking up after the Great Discovery, the party revived. The event had sobered most of the guests; they took immediate steps to remedy this distressing development. Frank made a beeline for the punch bowl. Kent stood gnawing his lower lip.

"What about a drink?" Thomas asked him.

Kent looked up. He was playing with the jeweled dagger at his belt, and the look on his face chilled Thomas.

"Look here, General," he began.

"Oh, it's all right," Kent cut in. "If Dick wants to play the gallant fool, that's up to him. Richard forgave *his* enemies, didn't he? Yes, I'll have a drink—but not that foul brew in the bowl. I need some brandy to take the bad taste out of my mouth. Coming, Rawdon?"

He stamped off, followed by the doctor and Mr. Ellis. Lady Isobel and Mrs. Ponsonby-Jones had struck up a temporary alliance, to express their ladylike disapproval of the whole transaction. Arm in arm, they advanced on the punchbowl. Jacqueline stood like a statue, her eyes slightly crossed, communing with something invisible.

Thomas turned to Philip.

"Oh, what a rogue and peasant slave am I," he said, smiling. "Kent thinks I ought to challenge Strangways, or something."

"Wrong play, right interpretation," Philip said. "There's nothing wrong with the general except that he's out of place in a civilized society. He'd have been first rate in the fifteenth century."

The actor looked more cheerful than he had for hours. Thomas didn't have to search far for the reason. Deny it though he might, Strangways was the obvious candidate for the part of the comedian, and he wouldn't be fool enough to try another trick now that he had been unmasked. Philip was relieved of his worst fear—humiliation.

"Let's all have a drink," he said. "Come along, Liz . . . Jacqueline. . . ."

The four of them went toward the dais. As they approached the table, Frank lifted his cup in a mock toast.

"This is a slight improvement over the last batch,"he said cheerfully.

"It could hardly be worse," Philip said. He filled a cup and offered it to Jacqueline, who refused, and then served the others.

Across the room Thomas saw Weldon and Strangways seated on a bench in one of the alcoves. Their heads were together; Weldon gestured animatedly as he talked. Something stirred the branches of the plant next to them.

"Look at that," Thomas said, nudging Jacqueline. "It's Percy, eavesdropping on the debate."

"What does he expect to overhear?" Frank asked, perplexed.

"It isn't what you hear, it's how," Philip said. "When you're young you think adult conversation is loaded with forbidden secrets. Didn't you ever eavesdrop, Frank, my lad?"

"No," Frank said.

"The little paragon," Philip murmured. He reached for the dipper, jostling Frank.

"Let's dance," Liz said quickly.

Frank gave the other man a black look, but went with her. Philip drained his second cup with the air of a man who drinks for a set purpose, and filled it again.

"Thomas," said Jacqueline. "You haven't danced with me yet."

Thomas was delighted to oblige. Neither of them tried to follow the rhythm of the jigging, bouncing medieval dance. They moved languidly about the floor; after a while Thomas began to hum "Stardust." It was a delicious, relaxing interval, except for one small irritation. . . .

A hard, lumpy object banged rhythmically against his hip.

"Do you have to carry that purse even when you . . ." A thought struck him and he stopped in his tracks. "What did you do with it when you were hugging Strangways?" he asked, with genuine curiosity.

"Hugging?" Jacqueline repeated. She laughed softly.

"Never mind," Thomas mumbled against her hair.

"Now, Thomas, don't do . . . We're right out in the middle of the floor; everybody can see us."

"I don't care," Thomas repeated. "Unless you want to go someplace more private?"

"Not now," Jacqueline said, with another soft laugh. "I adore you, Thomas, but you are not completely sober, and I want a man's complete attention when I—'hug' was the word, wasn't it?"

"Like this," Thomas said, demonstrating. "Perfectly good word—so far as it goes." He began to hum "Stardust" again.

When he next became aware of his surroundings, it was dark. It was cold. It was wet. Something kept falling on his head. Raindrops? Someone's lawn sprinkler? Niagara Falls?

Where the hell was he?

"Stand still," said a voice, as he struggled blindly. "Please, Thomas, for God's sake, don't fall down! I'll never get you up. . . ."

She slapped him. The outrage of the act woke Thomas more effectively than the pain. He reached out, snarling. Jacqueline got in several more hard smacks before he located her wrists. He was awake by then, and fighting mad. He shook her.

"What the hell are you doing?"

Jacqueline, always an excellent tactician, collapsed like a folding umbrella, and Thomas caught her in his arms.

He was standing on the terrace outside the Hall, with rain streaming down his face and—no doubt—ruining his rented wig. The light from the nearest window stretched out across the flagstones like a fiery pathway to Hell. Biblical and Miltonian images swam through Thomas's brain, assisted by the demoralizing warmth of the body he clasped.

The body turned rigid and shoved at his chest with both hands. "Are you awake now, or shall I slug you again?" Jacqueline inquired.

"I'm awake . . . I think." Thomas shook his head. "What happened? How did we get out here?"

"We came out for some fresh air—the phrase was yours. There are some garden chairs, if you recall, under a roofed section of the terrace. We sat there for a while. I remember thinking," said Jacqueline remotely, "that you were not at your best. I admit to becoming mildly vexed when you started snoring. But then, when I tried to wake you, and couldn't . . ."

"So you dragged me out into the deluge. 'Greater love than this . . .' I hope your dress isn't ruined."

"It's drip-dry. Thomas, you aren't concentrating. I don't think you were drunk."

"Oh, oh," said Thomas.

"Yes. Are you okay now?"

"Let's go."

When they reentered the Hall, Thomas understood why the beam of light had been ruddily red. Someone had turned out the electric lights. The torches were burning low. In the soft, hellish glow they searched the darkening Hall.

Thomas stumbled over the first body. It lay on its back in the middle of the dance floor, and even in that position it presented a formidable obstacle. Mrs. Ponsonby-Jones snored. Her expression was as affable as Thomas had ever seen it.

"She's all right." Jacqueline tugged at him as he bent over for a closer look. "She wouldn't be snoring like that if she were . . . Where are the others?"

In the great chair of state that Weldon had occupied they found Liz, curled up like a sleepy child. Her head was pillowed on her arms and her brown hair tumbled over the curved armrest.

Percy was still behind the rubber plant. He snored even louder than his mother.

The Hall had no other occupants. They searched all the alcoves before heading for the door. Jacqueline paused for a moment to switch on the lights. In the bright glare the place looked ghastly. Thomas squinted at the heap of crimson velvet in the middle of the floor, the trampled rushes, the smoldering torches.

"The last act of *Hamlet,*" he muttered. " 'Give me the cup—there's yet some poison left. . . .' "

"Good old Shakespeare," said Jacqueline. "A *bon mot* for every occasion."

She led the way to the dining room, where they found the doctor taking his forty winks. He stirred and mumbled when Jacqueline poked him.

"Brandy," she said. "I suppose that was drugged too. Come on, let's see how many of them made it upstairs."

Kent was the only one of the crowd who had gone to bed in the conventional fashion. His clothes were piled neatly on a chair, and Thomas was pained to observe that he wore bright-striped pajamas. He did not stir, even when Jacqueline callously switched on the overhead lights. After sniffing the air, she nodded.

"Brandy again."

Lady Isobel was lying in the corridor in front of Sir Richard's bedroom door. She reeked of wine, and her fingers were crooked, as if she had clawed at the door as she fell.

"Good God," Thomas said devoutly.

Weldon's room was unoccupied. The lights shone softly on pure white sheets, unwrinkled, and on Weldon's navy-blue pajamas laid out on the pillow.

Frank and the rector were sprawled on their respective beds, fully clothed. The rector's crown remained defiantly in place, although his head drooped over the edge of the bed.

Philip's bed was turned down. Neither he nor his pajamas were in evidence. Thomas considered the alterna-

tives and decided that Philip probably didn't wear pajamas. Jacqueline leaped to the same conclusion.

"Where can he be?" she muttered.

"Weldon is missing too," Thomas pointed out. "And
what about O'Hagan—I mean Strangways? You haven't
looked in his—"

"Weldon," Jacqueline said in a strange voice. "He's already skipped one. Or has he?"

She trotted off down the corridor, her purse swinging.
Strangways's room was empty too.

Thomas turned to face Jacqueline.

"Now what?"

"Downstairs."

In the drawing room they found two of the missing
persons.

"Not *Hamlet,*" said Thomas. "The Sleeping Beauty. Is
everybody asleep, for God's sake?"

"Considering the hour and the activities of the evening,
that's not surprising. We're the ones who are abnormal."

Reasonable as this was, it did not dispel Thomas's super-
stitious uneasiness. The house was like the legendary castle in which all the inhabitants had been cast into a spell,
dropping where they stood. Weldon and Strangways
faced one another. Both were more or less upright in their
chairs; Weldon's crowned head had fallen against the
back of the chair. Strangways was sitting up. His eyes
were closed.

Jacqueline pressed the switch that turned on the overhead lights. Strangways flung up a hand to shield his eyes;
his reflexes were as quick as a cat's.

"Who is it?" he asked. "What . . . oh. Fell asleep. What's
the time?"

"Three A.M.," Jacqueline answered. "Have you and Sir

Richard been together all this time?"

"Together in body but not in spirit." Strangways lowered his hand.

"When did you fall asleep?"

"How should I know? He dropped off first; poor fellow has had a busy day. I was drowsy myself, so I just continued to sit." The searching dark eyes narrowed. "What's wrong?"

Jacqueline didn't answer him.

"Thomas, see if you can wake Sir Richard."

Sir Richard's slumber was sound; it took Thomas some time to rouse him, and several minutes more to explain their present errand. Strangways was on his feet by that time, and when Thomas had finished the American exploded angrily.

"Damn, I might have known. Weldon, you're a hell of a jailer. Or are you setting me up as a patsy?"

"You are jumping to conclusions," Weldon said. His voice was blurred with sleep. "We all drank too much. No doubt Philip has fallen asleep somewhere."

"Then let's find him," Jacqueline said.

In the hall they encountered an unexpected note of comedy. A procession wended its slow way across the marble floor. It was led by Mrs. Ponsonby-Jones, supported by Wilkes and one of the menservants. Her arms hung over the men's shoulders and her feet dragged. She was crooning quietly to herself, interrupting the monologue from time to time with a hoarse chuckle.

When he saw his employer, Wilkes stopped. Mrs. Ponsonby-Jones, suspended, hung like a massive red effigy. The butler's face flushed with chagrin. "Sir Richard, I am sorry to have—"

"You seem to be doing splendidly under the circumstances," Weldon said with a flash of sour amusement. "Carry on, Wilkes."

"Yes, Sir Richard."

The intertwined trio gallantly tackled the stairs. Following behind, one of the huskier servants carried Percy. The boy was upside down over the man's shoulder; the view presented to the onlookers was appalling. The servant touched his forehead to Sir Richard, who nodded formally. Bringing up the rear was Liz, stumbling and hazy-eyed. Sir Richard moved like a boy, putting his arm around her waist. She leaned against him and yawned.

"So sleepy," she murmured. "Carry me."

Sir Richard looked as if the idea appealed to him. Before he could carry out the suggestion, Jacqueline spoke.

"If she can't walk, prop her up against the wall and leave her," she said sharply. "We must find Philip."

"Phil?" The girl blinked. "What's wrong with Phil? Has something happened?"

"That's what we're trying to find out," said Jacqueline.

"I'll help her upstairs first," Weldon said.

"No." Liz was waking up. "No, I won't go up, I want to know what's happening."

"Come on, then."

From the head of the stairs the butler's voice floated down to them.

"I beg your pardon, Sir Richard, but if you are looking for Mr. Philip—"

"Have you seen him?"

"Perhaps half an hour ago I encountered the gentleman going in the direction of the library. He spoke to me; something—" The butler's voice broke in a grunt and a gasp of pain. A deep feminine chuckle reverberated;

Wilkes could be heard savagely admonishing his assistant.

"Wilkes!" shouted Weldon.

"I beg your pardon, Sir Richard. Lady Isobel is at your—"

"Never mind Lady Isobel. What did Mr. Philip say to you?"

"It was not entirely clear, Sir Richard. Something to do with the date of the death of Queen Elizabeth."

"Thank you, Wilkes. Carry on."

"Thank you, Sir Richard," said the butler faintly. The sound of elephantine progress resumed along the hall above.

"Queen Elizabeth Woodville, of course," Weldon explained, turning to the others. "It is interesting that Henry the Seventh did not put out the story of Tyrell's confession until after the boys' mother—"

"Now that's a good example of how you people try to find hidden meanings in meaningless events," Strangways interrupted.

"Are you going to stand here all night arguing?" Jacqueline demanded. "Or shall we resume the search?"

"Surely there is no need for concern," Weldon said. "We will no doubt find Philip napping over a volume of fifteenth-century history."

Jacqueline didn't wait; she had already turned and was marching down the corridor, her purse swinging in a rhythm that threatened nameless things. The others followed more leisurely, so that when Jacqueline threw open the door to the library she was the first to see what was within.

The sight struck her like a physical blow. Thomas saw her body stiffen and sway. The purse fell from her arm and hit the floor with a squashy thud.

Thomas ran. Jacqueline moved jerkily to one side so that he could see too.

The room was lit by a single lamp, on the table at the far end near the windows, and by the glow of a dying fire. Straight ahead, Sir Richard's massive desk filled one corner of the room. In front of it was a good-sized log, similar to others in a wood box next to the fireplace. Philip's body lay on the floor beside the block of wood. Trunk, arms, and legs were visible. The head stood on Sir Richard's desk, staring straight at the onlookers with wide, glassy eyes.

✤ 6 ✤

THOMAS put a supporting arm around Jacqueline. She was shaking. They crossed the room together. Jacqueline put out her hand and lifted the head by its long flaxen hair.

It was a shocking gesture, even though Thomas had realized by that time that the head was plaster. The eyes had a glassy stare because they *were* glass—or some kind of plastic. The features didn't even resemble Philip's; only the hair and the bizarre setting had lent the object enough verisimilitude to give them a brief but effective shock.

Thomas dropped to one knee beside the actor and lifted the cloth that covered his head.

It was a plain square of cotton the same color as the crimson rug. Crude as the substitute head, it had nevertheless served the same function—to lend illusion, for the necessary moment of horror. Thomas threw it to one side and passed his hands over Philip's head and body.

There was blood on his hand when he looked up. Weldon and Strangways were still in the doorway. Weldon had gone limp; only the white-knuckled clasp of his hands on the doorframe kept him erect. Strangways was kneeling beside Liz, who had collapsed into a moaning heap.

"He's alive," Thomas said.

"Thank God." Weldon's voice was barely audible.

"He's had a bad knock on the head, though, and I don't like the way he's breathing. See if you can arouse the doctor. Last time I saw him, he was passed out in the dining room."

Strangways rose and ran out. He was back in less time than Thomas would have believed possible, pushing Rawdon ahead of him. The doctor was only half awake and mumbling querulously, but the scene in the library woke him with a vengeance. Without realizing it, Thomas had taken up a position that once again concealed the fallen man's head and shoulders; and Jacqueline, leaning against the desk, was still holding the plaster head by its hair.

"Dear God," said Rawdon, coming to a stop.

He was reassured and put to work; and after examining the actor he was able to reassure the others. Between them the men got Philip upstairs to his bed. Sir Richard insisted that the servants should not be brought into it, so they used the upper stairs that led to the bedroom wing by way of Sir Richard's sitting room.

Rawdon stayed with his patient. The others returned to the library. Thomas looked at Jacqueline, who was still contemplating the plaster head. He was reminded of Margaret of Navarre admiring the macabre mementos of her dead lovers. Liz lay in a chair like a stuffed dummy; she had not spoken since she came out of her faint, nor taken her eyes from the horrible head.

"It's the sort of thing they use on department-store dummies," Jacqueline announced, looking up. "The wig was probably purchased elsewhere. It's been glued on, somewhat amateurishly."

In order to demonstrate, she suspended the head by its hair and bobbed it up and down like a yo-yo.

Liz gasped. "Please don't. . . ."

Strangeways seated himself behind the desk. "It wasn't meant to convince anyone for long," he agreed. "But it certainly did the trick for a few seconds. God! . . . He must have been sitting here when he was struck. Here's a copy of my book, open to page four hundred fifty-seven."

"But how did the assailant reach him unobserved?" Weldon was beginning to recover his control. "He was wary and nervous—"

"Not after Mr. Strangways was unmasked," Thomas said. "He felt safe then."

"Damn it," Strangways began.

"No one is accusing you," Weldon said. "Thomas is merely stating an observed fact. Philip was put off his guard, not only by the discovery of your true identity, but by the fact that Percy was attacked before he was."

"All right, all right." Strangways's eyes were as hard as those of the plaster head. It crossed Thomas's mind, not irrelevantly, that the American scholar would be a good man in a fight. "Thanks to Weldon's incompetence I can't prove my innocence in this case. If we are to believe Wilkes, this happened within the past half hour. Does anyone have an alibi?"

"I do," Thomas said. "Jacqueline was with me the whole time."

"No one has ever suspected you, Thomas," Weldon said.

"Thanks." Thomas was gratified. After thinking it over, he wasn't sure he should be gratified. After all, the joker had displayed ruthlessness, bravado, and cleverness.

"The others were all asleep when we found them," he said. "At least they appeared to be asleep. Maybe we should have looked at them more closely, although I don't know how the hell you can tell—"

"Will you stick to the point?" Strangways shouted. He exchanged a glance with Jacqueline that seemed to encourage him. "This is serious, Weldon. You've got to call the police. You should have done it last night."

"If Philip insists, I shall of course comply with his wishes," Weldon said calmly. "But I rather imagine he would prefer not to have his weakness exposed."

"Weakness!" Strangways literally threw up his hands. "Don't any of you have an ounce of common sense? Where is all this going to end? Do you think if you ignore it it will just go away?"

"Well put," Jacqueline said approvingly. She was still absently juggling the head. Thomas resented her nonchalance. She had been no more immune to the shock than the rest of them. He also resented the admiring way she was looking at Strangways.

"Look here, Strangways," he said belligerently. "Who appointed you judge and jury and public prosecutor? So far as I'm concerned, you're still chief suspect. You have the best reason of anyone for making fools of us."

"Oh, God." Strangways ran a hand through his white hair. "Let's try it another way. I've been here, on the ground floor, the whole time. Isn't it obvious that the assailant used the upper stairs here? Philip would have had his back to them if he was sitting at the desk. He was facing the door. He'd have seen anyone who came that way."

"Not necessarily," Jacqueline said. "He was drugged—probably unconscious before he was hit on the head. The blow was merely an additional precaution, to prevent him from waking and catching a glimpse of the joker while he was being arranged in that charming little tableau."

Again Strangways was quick to understand. A little too quick? Thomas wondered.

"The wine," he exclaimed. "Weldon and I had a cup before we left the Hall. I should have suspected—"

"No, why should you?" Jacqueline said. "It was late, and everyone had had a good deal to drink. Most of us would have been asleep by then anyhow. The drugged wine was meant for Philip."

"And to prevent a hardheaded drinker from poking his nose in where it wasn't supposed to be," Thomas added. "Our friend thinks of everything, doesn't he? Was there anyone who didn't drink from the punch bowl after . . . after . . ."

"After what?" Jacqueline asked. "That line of inquiry won't get you anywhere, Thomas. We don't know when the drug was added to the wine. The brandy decanter in the dining room must have been doctored too. And if I were the villain, I'd make a point of drinking the fatal brew myself—or pretending to do so."

She threw the head lightly into the air and caught it.

Liz sat up straight. "Will you please stop playing with that ghastly thing?"

Her voice was high and strained. Jacqueline looked at her thoughtfully and then put the head down on the desk. "Sorry. There is nothing to be learned from this prop."

"Except," Thomas said, "that it proves premeditation."

"I would have thought that was obvious," said Strangways drily.

"Premeditation?" Weldon repeated. "How is that possible?"

"Don't be dense, Dick," Liz said impatiently. She looked better; Jacqueline had considerately placed herself in front of the head so that it was hidden from the girl. "We must try to think. We planned this meeting in July, didn't we? After you learned of the letter. I don't remember when we assigned the various parts, or how it was determined—"

"That's important," Jacqueline interrupted. "The head was meant to represent Philip and no other. Look at the hair."

She reached for the head and Liz said quickly, "Quite right. The—the person must have known Phil would take the role of Hastings, who was decapitated. It's been settled for . . . at least two weeks, isn't that right? We needed time to prepare our costumes and so on."

"Each of you knew what part the other would be playing?" Jacqueline asked.

"Yes, of course. We had to agree so there would be no duplications."

"Then let's go back to the question of motive," Jacqueline said. "Sir Richard . . . the letter. How much is it worth?"

"Its worth is incalculable. It is proof that Richard—"

"Never mind Richard the Third," Jacqueline groaned. "Is the letter worth money? Cash? Filthy lucre?"

"Why, I've no idea. A few hundred pounds, perhaps, a few thousand . . . Not enough to justify such a complex plot, if that is what you are suggesting. Why do you believe that the letter and these tricks are connected?"

"I don't know that they are. I'm grasping at straws. But none of your friends seem to have broken out before this, and the letter is the only new addition to the proceedings. Don't you think it's time I saw it, Sir Richard?"

"No. I'm sorry."

"But that's why Jacqueline came," Thomas exclaimed. "To look at the letter."

"I know why she is here," Weldon said. He smiled at Jacqueline. It was his old smile, gentle and apologetic. "Forgive me, Jacqueline, I did not intend to sound so brusque. I'm delighted to have had the opportunity of meeting you, and we have all enjoyed your company. But you are not an expert on medieval manuscripts, any more than I am a naive fool. When Thomas mentioned you, I took the liberty of investigating your antecedents. Don't you see—I couldn't take the risk of introducing a stranger into the household unless I was sure of her. You asked about the value of the letter. When I said it was incalculable, I meant it. It is worth an infinite amount of money— to me."

"Ah," said Strangways. "I wondered when someone was going to bring that up."

Tipped back in the chair, he was totally relaxed, hands clasped on his chest and a faint mocking smile on his lips. After a moment he went on in a cool voice.

"The value of the letter on the open market is irrelevant. It is worthless to an ordinary thief because it is unique. How could he possible sell it? But he could hold it for ransom."

Liz's mouth dropped open in a look of astonishment. Jacqueline's face remained impassive.

Weldon nodded. "You are clever, Mr. Strangways." He turned to Liz. Thomas couldn't see his face, but the change in his voice, from calm appraisal to impassioned pleading, made Thomas wince. "I know most people would think me mad to care so much about a cause that has been dead for hundreds of years. But I do care. That letter must be published. You haven't seen it. You don't know. I tell you, that single document will clear Richard's name of all the charges the Tudors invented. It will restore him to his rightful place as one of England's greatest kings—a martyr, not a murderer. I would do anything—pay any amount—to make sure it is not suppressed."

He paused. For a moment the room was silent except for the hiss of the dying flames and Weldon's heavy breathing. Liz stared as if she were hypnotized. Her eyes were dilated.

"And that is why," Weldon said, "I will not take the letter from my safe until I produce it for the public announcement. I would let the house burn down before I would open that safe. It is flameproof and the letter would survive."

He turned to face the others, who were grouped around the desk. His face was transformed.

"You must be a Sherlock Holmes fan," Jacqueline said. Her matter-of-fact voice broke the spell.

Weldon smiled faintly. "Yes, Holmes pretended to set a house on fire to persuade a certain lady to open her safe. It may sound farfetched, but recent events have been even more bizarre."

"I gather the warning is meant for me," Strangways said. "Thanks, Weldon. Once again I strongly advise you to call the police."

"No."

"Then I'm going to bed." Strangways rose. His lean face was taut with anger. "I admire you in a way, Weldon, but you're the biggest fool in this pack of fanatics."

He walked toward the door, but he walked slowly; and when Liz spoke he stopped, as if he had been expecting her question.

"The letter clears Richard? How, Dick? Can't you tell us what is in it, even if you won't show us?"

"I'm sorry," Weldon said regretfully. "I've said too much already."

Strangways turned. His eyes had a wild glow that reminded Thomas of Weldon. "Can't you guess? There's only one significant charge, and only one way of clearing Richard of it. The letter is from the boys' sister. She says she has seen them or heard from them. Is that right, Weldon? The princes were still alive in the early months of 1485?"

Weldon didn't answer. He didn't have to; Strangway's deduction was the only possible answer.

"But damn it all," Strangways exclaimed. "Don't you see, Weldon? That proves the letter is a fake."

"Typical anti-Ricardian reasoning," Weldon said bitterly. "Richard killed the princes, therefore anything that proves his innocence must be false."

"But Buck saw the letter." Strangways' voice shook with suppressed fury. He was trying so hard to control himself that his face turned bright red. "He was Richard's first defender; don't you suppose he would have mentioned that in his book if it had been in the letter?"

"Ah!" Weldon whirled to face him, his slight figure braced as if for physical combat. "So you admit the letter did exist!"

Strangways was speechless. Odd strangled noises issued from his open mouth.

"That doesn't necessarily follow," Jacqueline said.

"But Sir Richard has a point. There would be no reason for Buck to invent or fake such a letter; if he wanted to invent evidence, it would have been something more conclusive—" She caught Thomas's eye and turned pink.

"My God, Jacqueline," Thomas said plaintively. *"Et tu?"*

"Well, I'll tell you one thing," said Strangways, who had recovered his powers of speech, though he was still flushed. "I'm not leaving. You'll have to carry me out of here bodily if you want to get rid of me. I wouldn't miss that meeting tomorrow for a million dollars."

"I shouldn't allow you to leave if you wanted to," Weldon said between tight lips. "You will stay and see, and admit your error before the world."

"That will be the day," said Strangways.

Liz stood up. The folds of her skirt rippled as she walked across the room and stood next to Weldon. She took his arm. "Don't waste time arguing with him."

Weldon put his hand over hers. Thomas felt a strange pang; it was as if some premonition warned him, for although he did not know it, this was the last time he would see them standing side by side in the magnificence of golden crowns and shining robes, the shadowy survival of a past that had never lived except in the legend it bred.

Arms locked, the pair moved toward the door, and Strangways stepped back to let them pass, with a deliberate inclination of his head. When they had gone, Thomas sighed. Strangways looked at him.

"Yes," he said. "I know. . . . And I'm sorry, in a way, for what is going to happen."

Thomas felt as if he had been wearing his costume for a week, but before he took it off he couldn't resist one last look in the mirror. He doubted that he would ever again appear in coronet and fur-trimmed robes.

The image that confronted him was something of a shock. The debonair duke of the preceding night was a nightmarish figure—a specter out of Clarence's premonitory dream in the Tower, dead and drowned and dragged out to dry. The wig had gone stringy, as cheap wigs are wont to do when wet; the robe was wrinkled and stained; and in the cold light of dawn the crown was obviously paste.

Thomas was about to lower himself thankfully onto his bed when there was a knock at the door.

"Come in," he said, in a resigned voice. He recognized the knock. Jacqueline's style was unmistakable, even in such normally impersonal actions.

"Are you decent?" inquired Jacqueline, through a modest crack.

"No."

The door opened. "You aren't going to bed, are you?" Jacqueline asked. She was fully dressed in battle costume—hair pinned back, glasses firmly on the bridge of her nose, purse over her arm.

"Who, me? Why would I think of doing a crazy thing like that?"

"There's no point in going to sleep now. It's morning already."

Jacqueline sat down on the bed next to Thomas. A vagrant fancy slipped through the latter's mind, but it did not find a lodging place; Helen of Troy couldn't have stimulated Thomas just then.

He yawned. "I noticed it is morning," he said. "Nothing is going to happen until three this afternoon. I have had no sleep at all, and the hours of the night have not been uneventful. I am exhausted in body, mind, and spirit."

"I figured you would be," said Jacqueline. She opened her purse.

Thomas shied back. "No," he said vigorously. "No. Not some noxious remedy from that bottomless purse. I will not sniff ammonia or drink—"

"What are you raving about?"

The only thing to emerge from the purse was a slip of paper covered with writing in Jacqueline's sprawling hand.

"Here," said Jacqueline, "is the list of Richard's supposed victims. I copied it from Markham's biography."

The list read:

1. Edward of Lancaster.
2. Henry the Sixth
3. Clarence
4. Hastings
5. Rivers, Vaughan, Grey, and Haute
6. His wife, Anne
7. The princes

"So what else is new?" Thomas asked. "They aren't in chronological order," he added.

"They are except for the princes. Markham puts that one last because it is the main charge. Now look at the list from Walpole's *Historic Doubts.*"

1st. Edward Prince of Wales, son of Henry the Sixth
2nd. Henry the Sixth
3rd. George, Duke of Clarence
4th. Rivers, Grey, and Vaughan
5th. Lord Hastings
6th. Edward the Fifth and his brother
7th. His own queen

"Yes, indeed," said Thomas. He collapsed backward onto the bed and lay staring at the ceiling with his hands clasped protectively over his stomach. "So what does it all mean?"

"Not a damned thing," said Jacqueline.

"Your tone is one of poorly repressed exasperation. I deduce that you are baffled."

"But it has to mean something," Jacqueline insisted. "I hoped you could tell me what."

"Don't give me that humble bit," said Thomas, still prone. The ceiling was singularly dull. No cracks, no stains, not even a cobweb in a corner. Not in a well-staffed house like this . . .

He came to with a start as Jacqueline's finger traced a path along the sensitive area on the bottom of his foot. He sat up.

"All right," he said resignedly. "Let me get dressed and I'll go out and detect with you. Only don't insult my intelligence by intimating that you are leaning on my superior brain. You just want somebody to listen to you and say 'yes' now and then."

"Go ahead and dress." Jacqueline turned her back. As Thomas assumed daytime attire, she continued to talk.

"He isn't following the lists, Thomas. Nobody puts the princes ahead of Hastings. Why did he break the succession there? He followed it up to that point."

"Dunno," said Thomas.

"Both lists include the queen's relatives—Rivers, Grey, and the rest. Those were executions—legal, I suppose, according to the useage of the times, but—"

"Nobody is playing those parts."

"All right, but then why not include the Duke of Buckingham? Richard had him beheaded, like Hastings. The general is playing that part."

"Buckingham rebelled against a crowned king," Thomas said. "Richard hadn't been crowned when he arrested Hastings and the Woodville crowd; and some historians doubt that they were really guilty. Buckingham was running around the countryside with an army; you can't quibble about his being a traitor. . . ."

His voice trailed off. He was standing on one foot with a sock halfway on the other.

"This character is not following the lists," he said, thinking aloud. "Poisoning Rawdon—Henry the Sixth—was out of line too. So he has some weird list of his own—obviously anti-Richard. Buckingham rebelled against a tyrant and a usurper, not an anointed monarch. You don't think . . ."

"Oh, yes, I do," Jacqueline said coyly.

Still on one foot, his shirt tail hanging out, Thomas cursed with a fluency Kent might have envied.

"Okay," he said, when he had exhausted his repertoire. "Let's go see."

It was almost an anticlimax to see the head stuck jauntily on top of one of the high carved posts of Kent's bed. The cranium was covered with a fuzzy grayish coating meant to suggest gray hair.

From where he stood in the doorway, Thomas could see Kent's entire body, or at least that part of it which was not covered by sheet and blanket. Kent had not stirred or shifted position since they had checked on him earlier, and he was still snoring.

"This isn't particularly picturesque," Thomas said critically. "Maybe I'm getting used to it. I feel cheated."

"He just tiptoed in and stuck the head on the bedpost," Jacqueline said thoughtfully. "There was a hole at the base of the other neck too."

"He might at least have covered Kent's head."

"I'm so sorry he disappointed you, Thomas darling. But I don't blame our anonymous friend for being cautious. Why should he risk waking General Kent? He got his grand effect with Philip."

"Shall we wake him up?" Thomas asked.

"Do you really want to?"

They looked at each another conspiratorially. Thomas felt a momentary pang of compunction, but it did not endure. Kent might be a bit startled to wake and see the head grinning at him, but knowing that his own skull was firmly attached to his neck bones, he would not be frightened. The man was a bore anyway.

"No," he said. "Let's just steal away."

As he closed the door softly behind them, another thought struck him. "We can wipe one suspect off the list," he said. "Philip couldn't—"

Just then, a neighboring door opened and Philip stepped out into the corridor.

He was as white as the bandage around his head, and his eyes were uncertain. After a surprised start he advanced on the staring pair with a stealthy, theatrical stalk.

"You do me wrong, being so majestical," he declaimed inaccurately, but with great feeling, "to offer up the show of force—"

"The show is not of force," Thomas said. "What are you doing out of bed? Where have you been?"

"Where do you think I've been?" Philip asked poignantly. "I'm not a ghost, actually. I've a body. 'Gin a body meet a body. . . .'"

He swayed alarmingly. Thomas stepped forward to support him.

"Good Lord," he exclaimed, as an unmistakable smell reached his nostrils. "Don't you know how dangerous it is to drink after a head injury? Rawdon shouldn't have left you alone."

"Back to bed," Jacqueline said. "Come on, Thomas, here we go. . . ."

They dragged the protesting actor to his room. When they had him safely in his bed, Jacqueline went straight to the bureau drawer and removed a bottle of whiskey. Philip was still singing "Comin' Through the Rye" as they left.

"Put him back on the list, Thomas," Jacqueline said, tightening the cap on the bottle before putting it into her purse. "He can walk."

"Not very well. Damn it, Jacqueline, I know the guy's an actor, but nobody could counterfeit injury that effectively. I felt that crack on his cranium with my own two hands. If it weren't for that . . ."

"Yes?" Jacqueline said encouragingly.

"He's malicious enough. He was spouting the most God-awful slanders about the others before we went down for the banquet."

"Such as?"

"It would take too long to repeat them. Can I go to bed now?"

"No. Can't you rise above the demands of your vile body?"

"It feels vile at the moment, I must admit. What do you want to do now?"

"I want to pay a call on Mrs. Ponsonby-Jones."

Thomas's head was fogged by fatigue, malmsey, and chronic sinus trouble. It took him several seconds to understand.

"Mrs. Ponsonby-Jones—Queen Anne. You think she—"

"Richard poisoned her, didn't he?"

"No, he did not. She died of consumption, or something equally lingering."

"Something with boiling oil in it."

"Your quotations are getting less and less appropriate. Mrs. Ponsonby-Jones is probably okay. The old witch was drunk as a skunk last night and drugged to boot. It would be gilding the lily to make her any sicker than she was."

Jacqueline didn't answer. She stopped before Mrs. Ponsonby-Jones's door and tried the knob.

The door was locked.

"I expect she locked herself in," Jacqueline said. "Thus demonstrating more intelligence than any of the others. However, we had better make sure."

She pounded on the door.

The noise sounded hellishly loud to Thomas, but at first it had no effect on the occupant of the room. He was beginning to feel apprehensive when there were sounds from within. The door was flung open.

Presumably Wilkes had summoned one of the female servants to help Mrs. Ponsonby-Jones into her nightclothes. She wore a voluminous gown of pale blue. Her face was a bilious yellow. The colors clashed hideously.

Her puffy features were set in an expression that would have made Shakespeare's villainous Richard look like a saint. With an effort that made her quiver from head to foot, Mrs. Ponsonby-Jones focused her eyes.

"How dare you?" she moaned. "How dare you, how—"

The door started to close. Jacqueline threw herself against it. "Wait a minute. Are you all right?"

"No," said Mrs. Ponsonby-Jones emphatically.

"Have you been sick?" Thomas inquired anxiously.

The question was not well phrased. Mrs. Ponsonby-Jones's eyes looked like currants sunk in a doughy slab of pudding. She slammed the door. Jacqueline removed her arm just in time.

She and Thomas stood staring at the door until it stopped vibrating. Thomas expected an irate delegation to emerge from the other rooms, but apparently the guests were still comatose.

"Was she or wasn't she?" he asked.

"Sick? Definitely. As to whether she has been visited by the comedian, I think not. He likes to have his efforts noted and appreciated. A hung-over female tossing her cookies in private wouldn't do the trick."

"How vulgar you are."

"I haven't begun to be vulgar yet. Let's get out of here."

"Can I go to—"

"No, you cannot go to bed. I need fresh air. Let's go for a walk."

"It's raining."

"So it is. How unusual."

Thomas sighed. To walk in the rain with the lady you love is romantic when you are eighteen. When you are fifty it is merely conducive to sniffles and rheumatism.

"How about the conservatory?"

The conservatory was an acceptable compromise, but it was not the happiest locale for a conversation in that house of confusion. The electric lights did not wholly dispel the gray gloom of a rainy morning, and the rain drummed on the glass panes overhead, setting up quivering echoes in the greenery. Epiphytes hung like fleshy miniature monsters. The fronds of palm trees brushed the glass roof; they had squat, spiny trunks, like deformed pineapples. Green branches reached out at them as they walked along the graveled paths. Such was Thomas's mood that he would not have been surprised if a swollen, fecund bud had opened, fringed with fangs, and snapped at his sleeve.

"What do you want to do now?" he asked.

The damp air made Jacqueline's hair curl. Little tendrils, like copper shavings, coiled distractingly over her ears and at her temples.

"What I should do is call the police," she said, in a voice that did not match the charming curls.

"And what is your complaint?"

"Half a dozen people have been physically attacked. What do you want before you call the police? A couple of murders, or . . ." Jacqueline's mouth remained open, shaping the word she had not said.

Thomas peered at her. When she did not continue, he said, "The people who have been attacked are the ones who ought to complain. If they won't, and Sir Richard won't, there is nothing much you can do. Nothing has happened to you."

"Aha," said Jacqueline, turning on him. "So that's what's bugging you. You'd like to see me upside down in a barrel, I suppose."

"No thrill in that. I've seen your legs. They are good

legs; one might even call them excellent legs; but—"
Thomas looked closely at her. "For God's sake," he said,
in a different voice, "of course I don't want you to be
attacked. You drive me crazy with your arrogance and
your sarcasm and your know-it-all airs, but I don't want
anything to happen to you. I adore you."

He kissed her. She came into his arms willingly enough,
but after a brief interval he realized that she was not
responding. If an embrace could be called preoccupied,
this one was.

He raised his head. Jacqueline's lips were parted, recep-
tive; her face had the same expression of severe cogitation
it had worn before the embrace.

Thomas sat down on the edge of one of the raised,
brick-lined flower beds. "Sorry to have interrupted your
train of thought," he said.

"You didn't interrupt it." Jacqueline sat down beside
him.

"No, you wouldn't let a little thing like that interfere
with your thinking. Who do you think is going to be murdered?"

"Why do you think I think—"

"Oh, come now. I don't mind being Watson, but I refuse
to emulate Watson's superb stupidity. Murder was the
operative word. You said it and then you went into a—if
I may say so—theatrical double-take. If this were a comic
strip, you'd have had a light bulb over your head. I think
you're bananas, but if I am to have your complete undi-
vided attention in matters of more importance, I see I
must let you exorcise this weird idea first. Who do you
think is going to be—"

"Whom," said Jacqueline. "Wouldn't it be 'whom'?"

"No. Subjective pronoun. 'Do you think *he* is going to

be murdered?' Not 'do you think *him* is . . .?' " Thomas hit himself on the forehead with the palm of his hand. "Grammar lessons," he exclaimed wildly. "No, no, no, not grammar lessons. Who, where, when, and why? Especially why?"

Jacqueline followed this incoherent statement without difficulty.

"Why depends on who," she explained. "If I knew for sure who was going to be murdered, then I would know—"

"Whether," Thomas interrupted. "Now there's a relevant adverb. What makes you suppose somebody's going to be murdered? Go ahead, I'm listening. Ratiocinate."

"What?"

"Ratiocinate. Reason. Think."

"Someone has said that only Americans could put up signs ordering the reader to think," Jacqueline said coldly. "All right, I will."

"Be the great detective," Thomas went on. His head felt better. Perhaps the damp air had cleared his sinuses. "I'm no male chauvinist; I don't mind your showing off. Throw out mysterious hints. Ask meaningless questions. I'll say I don't know the answers. I'll make admiring noises from time to time, and look as stupid as I can."

"Just be yourself," said Jacqueline, breathing through her nose.

They glared at one another. After a moment the corners of Thomas's mouth lifted, and Jacqueline's snarl relaxed. Thomas put his arm around her and she leaned comfortably against him.

"There are some advantages to being my age, even if it does make walking in the rain hazardous," Thomas said after a peaceful moment. "If we were stronger we'd have had a loud screaming fight. Then I wouldn't have learned the solution until the last chapter, after three or four murders. Why murders, for God's sake?"

"The murders of Richard the Third," said Jacqueline.

"What?"

"That's what we've seen, in the not-so-funny jokes. Richard's reputed murders."

"Well, obviously," Thomas said impatiently. "You pointed that out yourself after I. . . ." He thought for a moment. "Oh. I see what you mean."

"I don't see what I mean myself. I'm on the verge of an idea and I can't quite grasp it. But . . . murders. Why reproduce ancient deaths? Carefully, painstakingly, and harmlessly? When is a murder not a murder? *Why* is a murder not—"

"There you go again."

"I'm letting my stream of consciousness trickle on. When, why, who? Mrs. Ponsonby-Jones has to be the next victim.. . ."

"There is a more crucial who," Thomas said. "Who is the comedian? If we knew that—"

"I do know."

Thomas stood up so he could see her face more clearly. He had been getting a trifle farsighted the last few years.

"You know?"

"Oh, let's not have another one of those conversations. It's so obvious, Thomas. So obvious I can't believe it," she added in a rare burst of candor.

"So you aren't going to tell me."

Jacqueline smiled at him. Her eyes were glinting with humor; they looked like clear green water.

"Thomas, do you know why the detective doesn't tell

until the last chapter? So he won't make a fool of himself in case he's wrong. It's much easier to deduce the identity of the murderer when you catch him in the act of murdering, or when all the other suspects are dead. Ellery Queen made that mistake in one of his books, I forget which one, but it was funny; he kept presenting complicated solutions that were promptly exploded. So after a while he decided—"

"Damn Ellery Queen!" Thomas thought of something. "You can't eliminate the people who have been victims of the joker, you know. In the form of literature to which you refer the victims were dead. They couldn't commit murders after they were—"

"Darling Thomas, aren't you belaboring the obvious? As a matter of fact, that one has been done. By Agatha Christie. The murderer was one of the supposed victims. He was supposed to have been shot through the head, but he—"

"I am not going to say anything rude about Agatha Christie," Thomas told himself aloud. "I am going to continue with my ratiocinations. You can't eliminate our victims just because they were victimized. But maybe you can eliminate some of them. In my case—"

"I never suspected you, Thomas," said Jacqueline earnestly.

"I wish people would stop saying that. I couldn't have rigged myself up in that uncomfortable position."

"You could have had an accomplice. There may be two jokers."

"Maybe everybody is guilty," said Thomas wildly. "And don't tell me that's been done. I know, I read that book. Okay. For the sake of argument let's say I had an accomplice. I suppose Frank could have staged his accident and Percy could have drugged himself and the doctor could have poisoned his own mush—"

"Or just pretended to be sick. Rawdon is the only doctor in the group. No one questioned his diagnosis."

"Okay, so he could have done it himself. But Philip got a nasty knock on the head. Or are you going to tell me that his hypothetical accomplice miscalculated?"

"I don't have to say it, you did. But Philip didn't need an accomplice. Head injuries are tricky things. There are medically documented cases of people getting a blow on the head and walking around for hours, even days, before collapsing. Philip could have produced the wound by banging his head up against a firedog or something equally hard. He wouldn't realize the extent of the damage. He might have had time to arrange himself artistically on the floor before he passed out." Jacqueline paused.

"Aren't you being rather fantastical?" Thomas said.

"I'm not the one who is fantastical. Even I couldn't have thought up these tricks."

"That's been suggested," said Thomas.

"Naturally. But we know better."

"Do we? Okay, I'll eliminate you. And you will eliminate me? Thank you . . . I think. Anybody else?"

"Oh, Thomas, this is a waste of time. You're on the wrong track."

Thomas began to pace. Gravel crunched under his feet. He brushed at a trailing vine that seemed to be eyeing him hungrily.

"So what's your solution, Holmes?"

"You really can't see it? Maybe I'm wrong. . . ." Jacqueline sounded uncharacteristically meek. Thomas turned and looked at her.

"So it is going to be one of those conversations. That's one of the reasons why I hate mystery stories. The detective, or some vital witness, is always being interrupted in the middle of a clue, and the damned fool never gets around to finishing what he was about to say."

"Sometimes he gets killed," Jacqueline said cheerfully. " 'The murderer is . . .' Wham! Bang! Crash!"

"That's enough of that. Is there any reason why you can't tell me what you're thinking?"

"Several reasons. My inflated ego, for one."

"That's an accurate description, but it is not a valid reason."

"All right," Jacqueline said unexpectedly. She was sitting bolt upright, with her hands folded on her knees. Her head was cocked as if she were listening to an inner voice. "The comedian is . . ."

She stopped. Thomas stiffened. His nerves were in worse shape than he had realized; for a moment he half expected to hear a shot ring out and see Jacqueline collapse in a pool of blood. Then he heard the sound her keener ears had already picked up, over the drum of the rain. Someone was coming.

He scowled at Jacqueline, who smiled back at him. Around a palm tree came James Strangways.

"There you are," he announced triumphantly. "Wilkes said he thought he saw you heading for the conservatory. Though why the hell anyone would pick this place on a day like this . . ."

He glanced distastefully at the lush greenery. Thomas found himself warming to the man, in spite of the fact that he was looking far too bright and healthy. His sleek white head and erect body, clad in neatly pressed slacks and a blue shirt, made Thomas feel grubby.

"Jacqueline's idea," he said. "She was about to tell me—"

"Hm," said Jacqueline loudly.

Strangways looked from one of them to the other. His wide-lipped, attractive smile warmed his lean face. "The identity of the criminal? Don't let me interrupt. I've a few ideas of my own." He sat down beside Jacqueline.

"So you think of him as a criminal," Jacqueline said.

"I consider assault a criminal act," Strangways said drily. "That puts me in a minority in this madhouse, I know. I thought you two had a little more sense. That's why I wanted to talk to you."

"What about?" Thomas asked suspiciously. He sat down on Jacqueline's left. There was barely room for the three of them.

"What about? A plan of action, naturally. We three are the only ones in the crowd who have our wits about us. Or don't you agree with me that the situation is dangerous?"

"Yes," Jacqueline said slowly. "I do."

"Do you know the identity of the comedian?" Thomas asked.

Strangways looked at him without moving his head. The rolling eyes gave him a crafty expression. "It has to be one of two people," he said finally. "I'm not sure which. And even if I were sure, I couldn't prove it."

"Who?" Thomas demanded.

"Uh-uh." Strangways' smile was not so attractive. "I'm not sticking my neck out. I'm in enough trouble as it is."

"Then what do you propose we do?" Thomas asked.

"My God, I'm tired of egotists," he added.

"It's very simple," Strangways said. "The point of all these unpleasant activities is the letter. I didn't believe in the letter to begin with, and I don't now, especially after Weldon's disclosure last night."

"How biased can you get?" Thomas said angrily. "Dick is right, you are so hung up—"

Jacqueline regarded Thomas without affection over the tops of her glasses. "Who was it who was complaining about distractions and interruptions and extraneous comments?" she inquired.

"Oh, hell," said Thomas.

"Let me finish," Strangways said loudly. The last word echoed uncannily through the muggy air. "The letter is a fake. It was concocted by the character who planned the series of jokes. He is going to steal it and hold it for ransom. The jokes are merely a distraction. They focus our attention on the victims of the moment; while we stand around yelling at each other, the criminal will have his chance to steal the letter."

"From Sir Richard's safe?" Thomas demanded. "How?"

"You don't suppose the letter is in the safe, do you?"

"But Dick said . . ." Thomas stopped. "Oh."

"I can read Weldon like a book," Strangways said arrogantly. "He thinks he's Machiavellian, poor devil. He mentioned the safe to put us off the track. I'll give you ten to one that he's got his precious letter tucked away in some hiding place he innocently considers clever. I'll also bet he keeps sneaking in and gloating over it. The criminal now has everybody so frantic, they don't know what's going on. He'll play his last joke and snatch the letter. Well?" He turned to Jacqueline. "What do you think?"

"I think," said Jacqueline calmly, "that your theory has

so many holes, it leaks like a colander."

Strangways's face darkened. Thomas watched with interest. He had never seen the man so angry, even when his identity had been disclosed.

"Oh," said Strangways in a stifled voice. "So you're one of those."

"One of what?"

"Liberated women. You have to degrade men to make yourselves feel superior. I came to England to get away from them," Strangways cried. "But they're here too. What's biting you? You'd be quite a woman if you'd only accept the role you were meant for."

Thomas could have hugged himself. He watched Jacqueline's face solidify into something that could have been enlarged and carved on Mount Rushmore. Only her eyes were alive. They shot out green sparks.

"Oh, what a shame," she said in a voice of saccharine sweetness. "I've hurt your feelings. I've dared to imply you might be wrong about something. Forgive me. I will accept your admonition. I will not offend you by presenting my weak, female attempts at reason."

"Wait a minute," Thomas said, no longer amused.

Jacqueline turned on him.

"You're one too," she cried, accurately but unjustly. "You're all alike! This whole weekend, all you were after . . . You didn't think I knew that, did you? You can go to hell, Thomas, and take him with you."

She stalked off down the path, emitting sparks that were almost visible.

The two men stared at one another across the vacant space her departure had left. Strangways was still red in the face. Thomas smiled at him.

"Thanks," he said, and followed Jacqueline out.

He found her, finally, in Philip's room. The actor, fully dressed, was stretched out on the bed. He and Jacqueline were talking in low tones. They both looked up when Thomas stopped in the doorway. Jacqueline looked straight through him at the opposite wall. Thomas went away.

Bed was out of the question now. He was too keyed up to sleep. He wandered downstairs in search of coffee and found Wilkes replenishing the serving dishes. The butler greeted Thomas with his usual smooth imperturbability, but his shadowed eyes held a horrible memory.

Thomas accepted coffee and refused food. He had just seated himself when Frank came in. He greeted Thomas curtly, poured himself a cup of tea, and sat down at the far end of the table.

"No breakfast?" Thomas inquired.

"Gawd, no," Frank said feelingly. "What was in that last posset of punch?"

"More than you know." Thomas realized the other man didn't know what had happened. He rather fancied himself as a raconteur, and the tale lost nothing in his telling of it. By the time he finished, Frank was wide awake and staring.

"I can't believe it. This fellow must be insane. You mean we were all drugged?"

"Most of us, anyhow."

"Jacqueline wasn't drinking," Frank muttered. He looked up, caught Thomas's eye, and said quickly, "No, old chap, I'm not accusing her, I simply meant . . . You say Sir Richard still refuses to call in the authorities?"

"That's right. I disagree, but I understand his feelings. Ridicule would mar the grand effect he hopes to make today."

"That isn't the only reason." Frank hesitated. "I may be betraying a confidence, but in my opinion matters have gone too far for normal reticence. Sir Richard has family reasons for wanting to keep this affair quiet."

"Percy?"

"The Ponsonby-Joneses are Sir Richard's only relatives," Frank said. "If the boy did plan these tricks, he should be in an institution. He's not legally responsible for his actions."

"Then you're against calling the police too?"

"I'm about to marry the boy's sister, after all. And there are humanitarian considerations. He will end up in a nursing home in any case. Why not do it quietly, without scandal?"

"But in the meantime he's potentially dangerous."

"I'll see to it that he's not dangerous," Frank said grimly. "I plan to watch him from now on."

"It might be more useful to watch his mother. She's next on the list—"

He broke off with a start. Mrs. Ponsonby-Jones had entered the breakfast room.

Her night of dissipation had left her looking as haggard as a person one of her fleshy girth could look, but it was not her ghastly face that made Thomas's eyes bulge. Arm in arm with Mrs. Ponsonby-Jones was Jacqueline. She guided the older woman to a chair at the table—a tug boat steering a liner—and helped her into it.

Mrs. Ponsonby-Jones obviously knew of her new status as the next victim. The woman was not only queasy and ill; she was terrified. Only the stiff upper lip required of her class kept her from howling, but she clung to Jacqueline with pathetic desperation.

In what could only be called a misguided attempt at distraction, Frank greeted his future mother-in-law.

"Good morrow, madam. How does your Grace?"

"Aoow!" The sound might have come from Shaw's Eliza Doolittle. Thomas contemplated Mrs. Ponsonby-Jones with new interest. Had Sir Richard's cousin married beneath him? If so, the guttersnipe had learned her lesson well. Mrs. Ponsonby-Jones recovered herself; with one hand on her palpitating bosom, she glowered at Frank. "How can you continue this jest?" she boomed. "Must you remind me—"

"I'm frightfully sorry. But there's nothing to worry about, honestly. Forewarned is forearmed. We'll not let anything happen to you."

Thomas noticed that Frank did not address Mrs. Ponsonby-Jones directly, avoiding the use of any terms of affection or even familiarity.

"Frank is right," he said. "We'll all look after you."

The offer did not soften Jacqueline, who was still looking at him as she might have looked at a squashy beetle.

"Where is Sir Richard?" she asked coolly.

"He'll be down before long," Frank said. "I passed him in the hall."

However, the next to come was not Sir Richard, but Kent. Alcohol couldn't hurt him much, Thomas thought; he was probably pickled in the stuff. Bright-eyed and beaming, he headed for the sideboard and loaded his plate with a heap of food that induced a unanimous shudder among the others.

"How are you all this morning?" he asked genially.

"Apparently you don't know," Thomas began, hoping to tell the tale again.

"Apparently *you* don't know," Kent said coolly, "that when I awoke a short time ago, the first thing I saw was a severed head."

He took a huge bite of coddled egg and was silenced, briefly. Then he went on, "Rather inadequate job, that one. More annoying than frightening. I understand the other joke of the evening was more effective. Met Weldon upstairs and he told me about it. Sorry I missed the excitement."

Mrs. Ponsonby-Jones muttered something in which only the words "cold-blooded monster" could be distinguished. Kent raised his head.

"Yes, I am cold-blooded," he said, sounding pleased. "Rather that than soggy emotionalism. None of this would have happened if you hadn't been such bloody sentimentalists."

"What do you mean by that?" Frank demanded.

"Good morning, good morning." The appearance of the rector saved Kent from answering, if he had intended to; he smiled enigmatically and returned to his breakfast.

Rawdon and the rector had come down together. They had met Sir Richard and heard the latest news. Beneath their formal expressions of shock and regret, Thomas observed a certain morbid enjoyment of the new sensation. He had to remind himself that neither of them—nor Kent, for that matter—had actually seen the appalling tableau in the library. Second-hand sensations were hard to take seriously.

The newcomers were immensely interested, however, and Rawdon was about to plunge into an animated discussion of the latest atrocities when Ellis, glancing at the quivering bulk of Mrs. Ponsonby-Jones, tactfully intervened. Conversation became casual. Jacqueline succeeded in distracting Mrs. Ponsonby-Jones by discussing dressmaking. It was the last subject Thomas would have supposed either lady to be interested in; if he had thought about the subject at all, he would have expected that Mrs. Ponsonby-Jones patronized professional dressmakers. But she discussed patterns and pinking shears and other technical matters with growing enthusiasm, as Jacqueline's skillful questions drew her out.

"Do you mean," Jacqueline asked respectfully, "that you made those lovely costumes Liz has been wearing?"

"Yes, indeed. After all, dressmaking was once my—" Mrs. Ponsonby-Jones stopped in the nick of time. "My hobby," she went on, with an artificial cough. "As a young girl. Costume design, I mean to say."

"Where is Liz?" Thomas asked.

"Still asleep." It was Frank who answered. Mrs. Ponsonby-Jones glared at him.

"And how do you happen to know that?"

"I looked in on her before I came down." The young lawyer looked her squarely in the eye. "And on Percy. I intend to continue looking in on them, all day."

"An excellent idea," said a voice from the doorway. "But it won't be necessary, Frank."

Weldon was wearing the standard uniform of the week-ending old-fashioned Englishman—shabby, well-cut tweeds. Only his shoulder-length hair reminded them of the Plantagenet monarch—the hair and the grim expression. Weldon had changed. He was no longer the light-hearted host, but a man deeply involved in a cause.

He had collected his two young relatives and stood between them. Percy looked sulky and reluctant, but his face brightened at the sight of food. Pulling himself free of Weldon's grasp, he shambled toward the chafing dishes and began heaping his plate.

Liz wore a pants suit of a shade of ash rose that set off her exquisite complexion. The knit fabric fit like a glove from shoulder to hips. Thomas noted that although Sir Richard had had an arm around Percy's shoulders, he did not touch Liz.

Liz drifted toward the table. Her eyes had a blank, unfocused look, as if she were still feeling the effects of the drug. Frank got quickly to his feet and guided her to a chair.

Sir Richard remained standing. Even without the help of crown and royal robes, he was an imposing figure. "I hope you all enjoyed the banquet," he asked genially.

There was an unconvincing murmur of agreement.

"Splendid. We'll have an even better meeting this afternoon."

Thomas happened to be looking at the rector. He saw that ingenuous gentleman's face fall. Had Ellis hoped Weldon would cancel the meeting? If so, he didn't know his host. Thomas did. He had little hope of success, but felt he had to make the attempt.

"Dick," he said, "I really think you ought to call off the meeting today. Or if you insist on going ahead with it— do the whole thing yourself. Get everyone out of here— the lot of us."

"An excellent suggestion." Lady Ponsonby-Jones nodded her head. "Of course your family will not desert you at such a time, Richard, never fear. But the others—"

"I resent the implication," said the doctor angrily. "Good Lord, you can't suspect me, Dick? We've known one another for—"

His was not the only dissenting voice. Thomas caught Jacqueline's eye and was encouraged by its expression. She had decided to forgive him for the dastardly sin of being male.

"Just a moment," she said, her voice cutting through the rising chorus of complaints. "Thomas is right, and you are acting like a group of spoiled children. Do you enjoy being knocked around, humiliated, frightened? If Sir Richard has any sense, he'll throw us all out."

Weldon's smile only touched one side of his mouth.

He's getting to look more and more like that damned portrait, Thomas thought in alarm. It's not a hobby any longer, it's an obsession. Was it possible that Sir Richard had come to believe . . .

The sudden suspicion was obscene; yet Thomas couldn't get it out of his mind, even when Weldon spoke in the familiar, gentle voice. The timbre of the voice had not changed, but its tone had. Where had he acquired that unmistakable voice of command?

"My dear Jacqueline, I appreciate your concern, but I cannot accept your suggestion. In any case, it is too late for the course of action you suggest. The television people have arrived."

In the silence Thomas heard vague sounds outside. Loud voices muffled by distance, the rumble of vehicles . . .

"They are now beginning to set up their equipment," Weldon said. He was still smiling that disturbing, distorted half-smile. "But believe me, all reasonable precautions have been taken. Two of my stoutest young servants are guarding the doors of the Hall; no outsider can penetrate into the rest of the house." His steady eyes swept the assembled group. "I have taken another precaution. Mr.

Strangways is locked in his room. No "—he was addressing Kent, who had started to rise, his ugly little face set—"no, General, you are not to go near Mr. Strangways. I am not sure he is guilty; I am merely eliminating a possible source of danger. I intend to take the same precaution with Percy, as soon as he finishes feeding himself."

Percy dropped his fork. Bits of scrambled egg flew like snowflakes.

"What did you say?" he demanded shrilly.

"I am about to lock you in your room," said Weldon. "Have you finished? Take along some toast, if you like; you will be incarcerated for some time, and I know you are not accustomed to going without food for more than a quarter of an hour."

"But Richard . . ." said Mrs. Ponsonby-Jones.

"No, my dear, my mind is made up. It is for Percy's own good," he added gently.

Mrs. Ponsonby-Jones subsided, with an agonized glance at Percy. Her meekness maddened her son. He burst into a furious speech whose epithets were more or less equally divided between his mother and his couin. He backed slowly away from the table as he shouted. Thomas had never doubted Percy's emotional instability; now he was ready to believe it might be more than a mild neurosis.

"Percy," said Weldon quietly.

Percy stopped shouting. He was drooling with rage and excitement. "You can lock me up," he said, licking his lips. "But you can't keep me there."

"I can but try," said Weldon equably. He gestured. One of the footmen stepped into the room. He was the same husky young man who had carried Percy the night before. Apparently Percy recognized him; his damp chins quivered.

"Go along with Charles," said Weldon.

"Oh, very well." Percy made a lunge at the table. Lady Isobel, who was closest to him, shrieked and shied away, but Percy's designs were on the food. Snatching a handful of bread, he sauntered toward the door. Thomas did not find his change of mood reassuring. The boy's furious frown did not wholly conceal the glint in his eyes. Percy enjoyed being the center of attention—the suspect—and he was already planning his next move.

He swaggered out, with the embarrassed footmen in close attendance. There was a long, universal sigh. Mrs. Ponsonby-Jones, huddled in her chair, did not speak.

"And those are the precautions you mean to take?" Jacqueline inquired.

"You think them inadequate?"

"I do."

"What do you suggest?"

"Disperse the house party."

"I can't do that," said Weldon good-humoredly. "This is a supreme moment for all of us. Nor will I insult old friends by seeming to suspect them."

Jacqueline's glasses were slipping. She stared over them at Sir Richard, who smiled affably at her.

"You wouldn't believe me if I told you—"

Weldon laughed. It was a pleasant, low-pitched laugh, but Thomas didn't like the sound of it.

"My dear—no, I wouldn't. I know some of the surmises that have been flying about. Fantastic theories! They do more credit to the imaginations of my friends than to their intelligence. I feel quite sure of the identity of the person who has been playing these nasty little tricks on us. That is all they are; nothing harmful was ever intended. If any of you wish to leave, of course I shan't stop you. But

I do most sincerely hope you will all stay and share this day of triumph."

Thomas was hypnotized by Jacqueline's glasses, which continued to slide slowly down her nose. At the last possible moment she put her finger on them and pushed them back into place.

"Oh, I'll stay," she said. "Either everyone goes, or we all remain. But may I suggest that we gather in groups from now on? That particularly applies to you, Sir Richard."

Weldon continued to smile. Thomas thought he heard Jacqueline's teeth grind together before she spoke again.

"I presume the famous letter is safe?"

"Oh, yes. I have just looked to be sure."

"Damn it," Thomas burst out. "You said you wouldn't go near it until—"

"So I did." The smile seemed to be stamped on Weldon's face. "You must allow me my little subterfuges, Thomas. And now, shall we all retire to the drawing room to await the great moment?"

He walked out, moving as if in time to the strains of a slow, majestic march. Jacqueline jumped to her feet and followed. The others moved like a herd of animals after a leader.

Thomas remained in his chair. The more he thought about his new theory, the more disturbed he became.

All of them had been affected by the bizarre atmosphere of the past few days. Thomas had felt his own grip on reality slip once or twice. Could an innocent avocation such as historical research fan the spark of incipient schizophrenia? That story of Jacqueline's about the scholar who worshiped at the shrine of Mary, Queen of Scots . . . That was not an extreme case, but the asylums, he had heard, were full of people who thought they were Julius Caesar or Napoleon. Abnormality sends out invisible waves that touch the people within its range. One seriously disturbed personality could sensitize others and make them behave abnormally too.

Weldon was an authority on medievel manuscripts. He had called the meeting; naturally he knew the roles the others had assumed. He himself was King Richard, and the victims of the jokes were Richard's victims. Had Weldon's sense of identification with his Plantagenet prototype passed the bounds of sanity? Was some sly, submerged segment of Weldon's personality, beset by doubts as to Richard's innocence, denied by Weldon's conscious mind, seeking an outlet? An outwardly dutiful son, subconsciously rejecting and resenting his father's belief . . .

Thomas knew he was weltering in a morass of absurd Freudian contradictions, but he couldn't get the idea out of his head. He felt an urgent need to talk with Jacqueline.

A windblown spatter of rain against the windows made him start. The room was horribly quiet. All at once he was afraid to be alone.

✻ 7 ✻

WHEN Thomas reached the drawing room he was out of breath, in part from distress of mind, in part from the speed with which he had traversed the long, empty corridor. He tried to catch Jacqueline's eye, but did not succeed; she was chatting with Mrs. Ponsonby-Jones and Lady Isobel. From the shape of the latter's smirk, Thomas deduced that Lady Isobel had taken a nip or two to brace herself for the day's activities.

All the guests were present except the two who were incarcerated upstairs. Even Philip had come down. His eyes closed and his bandaged head resting against the back of the chair, he was expressing courageous suffering. Liz and Frank were seated side by side on a sofa. The rector and Rawdon were discussing music. Kent stood by the window, his back to the room, looking out at the rain; the set of his shoulders expressed anger and frustration. He probably wants to drag Strangways down and torture him into a confession, Thomas thought.

Weldon wandered around the room, rearranging a pillow here and an ornament there. No one seemed anxious to engage him in conversation; Thomas wondered how many of the others had had the same idea he had. As Weldon passed the sofa on which Liz and Frank were sitting, Thomas thought he saw the girl shrink back. Weldon saw it too. A touch of color came into his face and he walked away.

Finding that his performance was not getting the proper attention, Philip got up and joined Liz and Frank. He said something to Liz. She looked at him with an expression of such fury that Thomas hastened toward them. Her comment reassured him as to the nature of the offense; it was Richard the Third again.

"But that is the crux of the matter," she exclaimed. "Don't you see—all the other accusations fall to the ground! No one believes in them today. Nothing tarnishes his reputation except the disappearance of the boys. Everything else hangs on that, even the so-called usurpation. Historians admit that the story of the precontract is probably true, and yet they continue to refer to usurpation. Why? Because afterward the princes disappeared. Yet Richard's seizure of the throne was not only justified legally, it was a moral imperative, given the attitude of the period. The kingship was a divinely sanctioned gift of God. For Richard to stand aside and see the throne go to a bastard would have been to commit an act of impiety, blasphemy! It is true that bastards could be legitimized by royal decree, but a person so legitimized could hardly hope to inherit the throne. And ironically, the only person who could legitimize the children of Edward the Fourth was Richard himself, as king. He may have planned to do just that, if he had lived longer. Everything indicates that he was a man of integrity, courage, and kindness; and yet he has been accused of one of the most dastardly murders of history, on grounds that wouldn't convict a dog. No wonder we harp on it! And we'll clear him of it, too!"

In spite of the fact that he recognized the speech as a quotation from one of Weldon's more pompous articles, Thomas couldn't help cheering.

"Hurray!" he shouted, and began to clap.

The applause was echoed from behind him. Weldon brushed past, his shining eyes intent on the girl. Kent also joined the group. Thomas heard him urging the claims of the Duke of Buckingham as murderer. He went to Jacqueline, who had left the other women and was standing by the window.

"Why don't you put Weldon up as Pretender to the throne?" she suggested, before Thomas could speak. "After all, if Henry the Seventh succeeded, as the descendant of an illegitimate son, then Sir Richard—"

Thomas was not amused. "I've just had a horrible thought," he said. He went on to explain his suspicions of Weldon. Jacqueline listened without a visible change of expression.

"Hmmm," she said, when he had finished.

"What do you think?"

"I think you're very ingenious."

"What the hell does that mean?"

Jacqueline sat down on a hassock and reached into her purse.

"Not the tatting," Thomas begged. "My dear old grandmother used to do it. She did it beautifully. I can't stand watching your fingers turn blue. Why don't you take up whittling?"

Jacqueline produced her cigarettes.

"I hate myself," she said sadly. "If people would just leave me alone and not strain my nerves, maybe I could—"

"What about Weldon?" Thomas insisted.

"Watch him. Like a hawk."

"Then you agree—"

"I will say no more, *mon ami*," said Jacqueline. Her French accent was execrable. "The walls have ears."

Her eyes rolled meaningfully, and Thomas saw Kent bearing down on them. He held a half-filled glass; the amber liquid sloshed with every step.

"Where are you going?" Jacqueline asked.

"Out," Kent said.

"You mustn't go alone. I'll go with you, to protect you." Jacqueline batted her lashes and pouted. Thomas thought it a disgusting display, but Kent was not so fastidious.

"I can hardly reject an offer like that," he said, leering.

Jacqueline took the arm he extended and they went toward the door. Over her shoulder Jacqueline looked at Thomas and winked strenuously.

Thomas wondered what the hell she was trying to tell him. To watch Weldon? That was the only positive suggestion she had made, but it was not as easy as it sounded. The room was large, and the Ricardians paced like restless lions. Sir Richard was the worst of the lot. Thomas kept losing sight of him—first behind the draperies, where he stood for a while peering out into the rain-drenched garden; then momentarily hidden behind Mrs. Ponsonby-Jones considerable form. Then he darted for the door, ostensibly to check on the preparations going on in the Great Hall, which were reaching a peak of activity audible even in the drawing room. Thomas headed him off and guided him toward the table where sandwiches and coffee had been laid out.

He was sweating with nervousness by the time Jacqueline and Kent returned; the smug look on the general's face did not quiet his irritation.

"Have a sandwich," he snarled, shoving a ham-and-cheese concoction into Kent's hand.

The general looked startled. "I don't want a sandwich."

"Have one anyway. You too, Dick."

"I don't want—"

"Have a sandwich!" Thomas shouted.

"Now don't get excited, Thomas," Jacqueline said soothingly. "We'll all have a sandwich. We'll eat sandwiches all day if that will make you happy. And Sir Richard will tell me about the entries in the royal household account books that indicate the princes were still alive in 1485."

Weldon's puzzled frown smoothed out.

"The payment to the footman of the Lord Bastard—is that the one? Yes, I'm certain it must refer to young Edward. In an earlier entry he is called Lord Edward, and on another occasion, Edward bastard. The 1485 entry—"

"Balderdash," Kent interrupted. "The boys were dead by then. Buckingham killed 'em. The Lord Bastard must be Richard's illegitimate son John."

"Who was not a lord," Weldon snapped.

"As a king's son he may have been given a courtesy title—"

Thomas took Jacqueline's arm and removed her. "What were you doing out there with the general?" he asked. It was not what he had meant to say.

"Distracting him," Jacqueline said coolly. "He was heading for Mr. Strangway's room. He's quite drunk, and spoiling for a fight."

"But Strangways is locked in, isn't he?"

"So far." Jacqueline was clearly worried. "Thomas, Sir Richard doesn't have anyone guarding his prisoners. The locks are clumsy old things; I'm sure they could be picked."

"My dear, don't you think you had better tell me what is worrying you?"

"I may be wrong," Jacqueline said rapidly. "But I don't think so. Thomas, surely you must see it too; it's so obvious! I'd be much more confident if you arrived at the same conclusion."

Thomas shook his head. "I told you my idea. You haven't told me a damned thing that makes any sense."

"Oh, dear. Well, then, there are three people whose movements during the next couple of hours are of crucial importance. If we can keep them under observation, we should be all right."

"Who?"

"Percy, Sir Richard, and Frank."

"Frank?" Thomas repeated, in surprise. He turned.

The others had gathered in a group around the refreshment table. Richardian debate raged, scarcely interrupted by sandwiches and coffee. Weldon stood a little apart, watching. . . . It was Frank he was watching.

Thomas had suspected that Weldon was in love with his young cousin, but the corollary had not struck his essentially law-abiding mind until that moment. The look on Weldon's face . . . Thomas saw a possible motive for murder, as well as explanations for the other mystifying events of the past few days.

"I can't believe it," he whispered. But unwilling conviction showed in his eyes, and Jacqueline let out a little breath of satisfaction.

"At least you see the possibility. That's a relief."

"But it doesn't make sense. Frank was the first victim—"

"Forget the Ricardian lists. Forget the whole Ricardian mess, it doesn't have anything to do with the problem. Or rather," Jacqueline amended, "it does in a way, but not in the way you mean."

"Wait a minute," Thomas said, his head spinning. "I'm not sure I do see what you're aiming at. Where does Percy come into it?"

"Oh, for goodness' sakes," said Jacqueline in ladylike exasperation. "I'll have to spell it out. As soon as Percy gets out of that room—which he will do, you can count on that—then—"

"Here comes the rector," said Thomas huskily. "Let's—"

It was too late. Mr. Ellis, smiling and refreshed, was upon them.

"The moment approaches," he said cheerfully. "I confess my agitation is mounting."

"If my agitation mounts any higher I'll have a stroke," Thomas muttered. "Oh, my God—there goes Frank. Jacqueline . . ."

"Go with him." Jacqueline was just as disturbed. "Don't let him go alone, Thomas."

Thomas darted off, leaving Jacqueline to make excuses to Mr. Ellis, who was starting at them in understandable confusion. He collided with Frank in the doorway and caught his arm in a steely grip.

"Ouch," Frank said. "Thomas, what are you—"

Thomas could think of nothing to say except the simple truth.

"Jacqueline thinks we shouldn't wander around alone."

"Oh? Perhaps she's right."

Thomas sagged with relief. It was a pleasure to deal

with someone reasonable. "I was going upstairs to have a look at the prisoners," Frank said. "Come along if you like."

They went to Strangways's room first, since it was nearest. The upper halls were strangely deserted. Thomas glanced uneasily over his shoulder.

"Where are the servants?"

"Gawking at the telly," Frank said briefly. "The place is in an uproar."

Thomas knocked on the door. After a moment Strangways answered.

"Who is it?"

"Thomas. Are you all right?"

There was a rich chuckle from within.

"I'm fine and I intend to stay that way. You haven't come to let me out, have you?"

"No."

"Good. Because I wouldn't come. Anyone who enters this room for any reason whatsoever is going to get crowned with a poker."

"Are you planning to remain there indefinitely?" Thomas inquired.

"Only until time for the meeting. All hell will have broken loose by then, but I'll have my alibi. How is Jacqueline?"

"Fine," said Thomas stupidly.

Another chuckle. "She'll be feeling humble and depressed when my predictions are confirmed. But I'll console the little darling."

Thomas's eyes opened wide. It seemed incredible to him that anyone could think of Jacqueline in those terms.

"Oh, come along," Frank said impatiently. "We haven't time for games. Percy is the lad I'm concerned about."

Percy's incarceration was audible some distance away. Apparently he was kicking the door. The rhythmic thuds reverberated along the hall, and for some reason the noise maddened Thomas. He pounded on the door with his fist.

The thuds stopped. Percy's voice inquired ominously, "Are you going to let me out?"

"No."

The kicking began again.

"Listen to him," Frank said angrily. "The way things are going he could ram the door down with a battering ram and noone would notice. There are a dozen ways of getting out of that room. The windows lock only from the inside. . . ."

He had to raise his voice to be heard over the kicking. Thomas shouted back, "Luckily he's too angry to be rational. Let him wear himself out kicking."

They went back down the hall with the thuds following like drumbeats. Thomas resisted the temptation to comment on restless natives.

The restlessness extended into the drawing room. Only Weldon and Kent, the two diehards, were still arguing. The others prowled around the room. Jacqueline was pacing up and down. The rector chugged along beside her; he had to take two steps to each of Jacqueline's strides. The purse, a shoulder bag with a long strap, swung back and forth in rhythm.

Thomas caught her eye and nodded, but her face did not lose its worried frown. She slowed her step as Thomas joined them.

"Splendid exercise," said Ellis guilelessly. "Since we cannot be out of doors."

Jacqueline continued to walk. She was humming

drearily to herself; again, Thomas wondered why her sub-vocal performances sounded so lugubrious. It took him some time to identify the music as Gilbert and Sullivan.

". . . I'd an appetite fresh and hearty," crooned Jacqueline.

She caught the rector's astonished eye and lowered her voice, but the look she gave Thomas was not at all abashed.

"Very appropriate," Thomas said approvingly.

"How nice to find that others appreciate Gilbert and Sullivan," said the rector."They are rather underrated these days, I believe. Personally I find Mr. Gilbert's lyrics extremely witty. Do you know that charming song," and at the top of his voice he caroled,

> *"Spurn not the nobly born*
> *With love affected,*
> *Nor treat with virtuous scorn*
> *The well connected. . . ."*

Thomas choked. Jacqueline had met her match. Characteristically, she was delighted to find a kindred spirit. She joined in.

> *"High rank involves no shame,*
> *We boast an equal claim*
> *With him of humble name*
> *To be respected."*

The rector was equally delighted. The singing turned into a contest, with each of them dragging out the most obscure songs they could think of in order to stump the other. Jacqueline caught the rector on the second verse of the sentry's song from *Iolanthe;* Thomas, who was accustomed to the trivia with which her brain was clogged, was not surprised that she should know all the words to a bass solo. Then it was the rector's point, with an obscure ditty from *The Sorcerer,* which Jacqueline did not recognize.

As a divertissement the exercise was highly successful. Even Weldon stopped arguing about Richard, and listened with a smile. Thomas was torn between amusement and embarrassment; W. S. Gilbert had a shaft for everyone. He had carefully avoided looking at Weldon when the rector chirped out his plea for the romantic rights of the rich, but that wasn't the only appropriate verse; Gilbert had much to say about overweight elderly ladies, cowardly generals, and inept practitioners of various professions. He even satirized the Women's Lib of his day, and when the rector quoted from *Princess Ida,* Jacqueline stopped singing.

As the time for the broadcast approached, a rising hubbub proclaimed the arrival and raucous discontent of members of the press. According to Weldon, they were to be shepherded straight into the Hall, but on at least two occasions Thomas thought he saw a vague form pass swiftly through the mist and drizzle without.

The nursery-school image occurred to him again; he felt like a helpless teacher taking a group on an outing. As he rushed to head one stray back into the flock, another slipped away. He thought he had kept track of them fairly well. Weldon and Frank, at least, were present and hearty when the fun began.

Although Thomas had been watching the windows off and on, he was not looking in that direction at the crucial moment. It was Frank who saw the face. His shout alerted the others. Lady Isobel screamed. The countenance pressed against the streaming glass was dreadful enough to justify her cry. Wet, dank hair was plastered against the rounded skull, nose and lips were flattened and whitened. The eyes shone with a steady glare.

"Damn that wretched brat! I knew he'd get out!"

Frank ran toward the window. He was thrust aside by Kent, who wrestled with the fastenings. Pandemonium ensued. Lady Isobel hid under the table. After a moment of indecision Mrs. Ponsonby-Jones decided to faint. She did so, falling heavily against Philip as she collapsed. They fell to the floor, Philip swearing in a loud voice as he tried to untangle himself. Kent finally got the window up and vaulted over the low sill. He was followed, more slowly, by the doctor. The rector vibrated uncertainly on the hearthrug, like a modern dancer expressing Doubt and Insecurity; then he bolted for the door, possibly with the idea of heading the fugitive off from the front of the house. The lights went out.

Thomas knew that the moment was upon them. Something was about to happen. He had no intention of pursuing Percy; there were enough people engaged in that futile exercise already. But he didn't know what to do. The room was a gloomy cavern through which shadowy forms moved and shouted. He could not identify any of them.

Someone grabbed his arm. Thomas recognized the perfume, the grip, and the faint gleam of coppery hair.

"Quick," said Jacqueline. "Quick, for God's sake."

She crossed the room like a cannonball, towing him with her and ruthlessly brushing aside interference. Someone reeled back from her outthrust arm. A voice rose in a banshee wail as they ran past the long table. Thomas deduced that Jacqueline had trodden on Lady Isobel's hand.

There were lights in the hall. Jacqueline began to run faster, the purse swinging wildly. Thomas ran after her. She passed the doors to dining room and breakfast room and flung herself at the oak panels of the library door. It was locked.

Thomas didn't offer to break it down. "Upstairs," he said. "Through Weldon's sitting room and down the library stairs."

Jacqueline shot him a glance of approval and took off. As they reached the central vestibule and the stairs, they saw Wilkes struggling with a determined mob. Actually, there were only a dozen people present, but they conveyed the impression of a mob. The press had broken in.

Jacqueline put her head down and went through like a fullback. Thomas was on her heels. Several of the more alert reporters followed them, but Jacqueline lost them in the maze of corridors above. Thomas could hear them bellowing for a guide as he and Jacqueline entered Sir Richard's room. He was puffing like a grampus. Speed and apprehension had winded him. Jacqueline beat him to the library stairs. He had to follow her down; the stairs were too narrow for more than one person.

He had had no time to think ahead, to imagine what he might see; but his wildest imaginings could not have prepared him for the scene that met his eyes.

The heavy draperies were drawn, but the room was well lit by the chandelier overhead and by the lamp on Weldon's desk. Flames flickered on the hearth—not the blaze of a well-laid fire, but the isolated, smaller flame of something burning—something like a piece of paper. In the center of the room Sir Richard lay on his back, his arms outstretched. His shirt had been ripped open; his chest streamed with blood from at least two wounds.

Standing over him, a naked blade in his hands, was Frank.

Thomas closed his eyes. When he opened them again, the tableau had not changed. He had hoped he was having a hallucination.

Jacqueline ran forward, emitting cries of distress. Thomas thought she was wringing her hands, although he didn't see how she could, with her purse in the way; she was certainly doing everything else a frightened woman is supposed to do. She flung herself down beside Weldon's bleeding body, under the lifted blade.

Frank fell back a step before her impetuous rush. The weapon wavered. It was the huge two-handed sword that had hung on the wall, and he needed both hands to hold it. The blade was no longer clean and shining. As Thomas watched, petrified, a drop fell from its tip and made a small red stain on the back of Jacqueline's white blouse.

"Thank God you got here in time," she exclaimed, glancing up at Frank. "Did you see him?"

"Who?" Frank looked as if he were in a state of shock —which, Thomas thought, was not surprising.

"Percy," Jacqueline answered. She was still on her knees; her hands, horribly stained, were moving over the unconscious man's breast. "It was Percy, wasn't it?"

"I don't know," Frank said slowly. "I didn't see anyone. The—the damned sword was lying on the floor. I picked it up. I never really believed people did idiotic things like that."

"Shock," Thomas said. "Put it down, Frank."

He spoke gently; he didn't like the young man's looks. Frank was abnormally flushed; his body shook with his quick breathing. Instead of lowering the blade, he turned it, studying it with bemused interest. Another drop fell. Jacqueline had straightened; the crimson drop struck her forearm and trickled slowly down toward her wrist.

"He burned the letter," Frank said, indicating the fire-place.

"That doesn't matter now," Thomas said. "Sir Richard —is he still alive?"

Jacqueline didn't answer. She didn't look at him; her eyes were glued to Frank's face. Thomas realized that the young man was perfectly dry. He had not been out in the rain. He had come directly to the library. . . . And the library door had been locked when Jacqueline tried it.

Thomas knew then. In spite of his habit of self-control, a gasp escaped him. It was as if an invisible tendril of thought crossed the room, from his mind to Frank's. The younger man turned his head and looked directly at Thomas. Sir Richard stirred, moaning.

"Yes," Frank said gently. "He's still alive. You had better fetch Rawdon, Thomas."

Thomas didn't know what to do. It was too late for pretense; Frank had read his cursed open face. He couldn't leave anyway, not with Jacqueline and the helpless man under the sword. He couldn't jump Frank; he was too far away, and the dripping blade hovered over Weldon's lifted face. The huge sword was as heavy as a sledgehammer; Frank didn't have to thrust, all he had to do was let go. Shock and nervous strain might excuse the failure of his grip. A sudden move from Thomas certainly would.

As his overtaxed brain struggled with split-second alternatives—all of them impractical—Jacqueline broke out again, wringing her hands and keening like an old lady at a wake. Trivialities assault the mind at such moments; Thomas was disproportionately vexed by the purse, whose strap kept slipping and getting entwined with Jacqueline's hands.

Then he caught a gleam of emerald as Jacqueline turned her head slightly; and he found that the expression "his heart sank" was not a poetic flight of fancy. Something inside him seemed to drop with a thud and press agonizingly into the pit of his stomach. She was going to move. A bare-handed, middle-aged woman against a husky young man armed with a six-foot sword . . .

"No," he shouted. "No, don't—"

The cry helped, distracting Frank's attention for an instant. Jacqueline was already in action. Only her arm moved. Her arm—and her purse, whose strap was now wound around her fist like the cords of a sling. The massive, weighted object sailed in an accurately calculated arc, striking Frank's hands and the hilt they clasped. The impetus carried arms and sword up and back, away from Weldon's face. In a single smooth movement Jacqueline rose and took a long stride. She lifted her knee.

Thomas stood frozen, not with fear but with consternation. The brutal, effective blow and Jacqueline's white-clad elegance made a rather horrid combination.

Jacqueline herself seemed surprised. Looking down at the moaning form at her feet she remarked, in a wondering voice,

"Amazing. It really works!"

✤ 8 ✤

"YOU never studied karate," said Thomas. It was not a question.

"I read a book."

"You cannot learn karate from a book," said Thomas. His voice vibrated with passion. "It is impossible to learn karate from a book. No one has ever learned—"

"Well, I saw it on television, too," Jacqueline said calmly. "I'm not even sure that particular move is karate. Judo, perhaps? Or that other thing, the Chinese—"

"Where I come from, it's plain dirty fighting," said Strangways, grinning. "I wish I'd seen you in action, Jacqueline. Not that Thomas's description lacked verve . . ."

They were barricaded in the drawing room while Wilkes and the other servants searched out and expelled lurking reporters. The meeting had been canceled; the roars of trucks and the expletives of frustrated media men reached them faintly, even through the closed and bolted windows. It had stopped raining.

"Someone will have to give them a statement," Kent

said, as a particularly outraged expletive echoed along the hall.

"Inspector Whatever-his-name will handle that," Jacqueline said. She looked apologetically at the new member of the group who stood, in formal rigidity, by the door. "I'm afraid I don't know your name either, Sergeant . . . Lieutenant . . ."

"Constable Stewart, miss," said the young man, moving only his mouth. A wave of color ran up his thin face, from his tight collar to the roots of his sandy hair. Thomas had noticed that he blushed every time someone spoke to him. He wondered if the young fellow was really cut out for his profession.

"Thank you." Jacqueline smiled. "You don't mind if we talk, do you?"

"I have had no instructions as to that, miss."

"I'm going to talk whether it's allowed or not," said Philip decidedly. "I'm confused. What the hell has been going on?"

"Weldon will live," Thomas said. "He was stabbed three times and lost a lot of blood, but none of the wounds were fatal. The fourth—or fifth, or sixth—would have been."

"But why not dispatch him at once?" Mr. Ellis looked lost without his usual companion. Rawdon was still upstairs with the wounded man. "The unnecessary brutality . . . the cruelty . . ."

"Richard was killed by a dozen blows," said another voice. "They hacked at his body after he had fallen."

They had forgotten about Liz, who sat quietly in a corner of the sofa. Thomas stirred uncomfortably as she turned her pale face toward them. She was pale, but composed. Weldon's survival was the only thing that really mattered to her; the mad events of the day had clarified her feelings.

His candid, sympathetic face gave his thoughts away. Liz smiled at him.

"I'm quite all right, Thomas, Mother is still having hysterics upstairs, but that's simply habit. She never liked Frank." A touch of bitterness cooled the girl's voice, but it disappeared as she went on. "Isn't it strange, how the most frightful things can have positive results? Percy has been absolutely marvelous. He's with Mother now. Perhaps all he needs is responsibility. She's coddled him too long."

"There's nothing seriously wrong with Percy," Jacqueline said. "He's pampered, frustrated, and overweight. He needs a few good hard kicks in the rear, and the chance to do his own thing."

She looked as smug as a copper-furred cat, curled up in a leather armchair and smoking like a chimney. For once Thomas didn't resent her arrogance. It occurred to him that perhaps Jacqueline sometimes sounded overconfident and autocratic because that was what people wanted from her. Certainty can be reassuring.

Liz's face relaxed visibly; and Thomas, unable to resist a small dig, remarked, "Is that how you raise your children, Jacqueline? By God! That's how you learned karate! From David."

"He lets me practice on him," admitted Jacqueline.

Thomas hadn't seen Jacqueline's son for five years. He had been a dirty, freckled urchin then; he was about eighteen now, and if he was Jacqueline's son he would be a match for her in everything but experience—neatly built and mentally agile. He had a vision of Jacqueline heaving her tall son over her shoulder in her cool pastel living room. It was a delightful thought.

The rector was still struggling with the incredible truth.

"Then it was King Richard's death the—the criminal was attempting to reproduce—as he had reproduced the deaths of the others?"

"Only this was to be a fatal accident," Jacqueline said. "Sir Richard's death was the point of the whole bag of worms. The list of the people who died violent deaths during the reign of Richard the Third is incomplete unless you add Richard himself. If you follow the pro-Richard line, Richard was not a murderer; rather, he was a victim of the treachery and self-interest that doomed the other victims. The real villains were kings like Edward the Fourth and Henry the Seventh—your favorite candidate for the murderer of the princes.Henry was also responsible for Richard's death, although he didn't strike a blow himself. 'He led his regiment from behind. . . .' "

Thomas looked sharply at her. After a moment of silence Strangways spoke.

"And that is how you deduced what was going to happen?" he inquired skeptically. "Because the logical victim of the series was Richard himself?"

Jacqueline raised cool green eyes to his face and he threw his arm up in a mock gesture of defense.

"I'm not arguing. You lucked out—I mean, you were right and apparently I was wrong. I'm just asking."

"Ah," said Jacqueline, with satisfaction. "In that case, I will explain.

"The idea that the comedian's ultimate victim might be Sir Richard wasn't deduction; it was a crazy hunch. Thomas, do you remember our discussion in the conservatory? We were both groggy with wine and lack of sleep and we talked a lot of nonsense; and yet everything we discussed, from grammar to detective fiction, had bearing on the problem of the final victim. We debated about pronouns and adverbs; but when I spoke of 'the murders of Richard the Third' I realized that two other grammatical points were pertinent—the plural and the possessive preposition. If I say 'the murder of Henry the Sixth' you understand that I am describing Henry the Sixth's violent death. But if I say 'the murders—plural—of Richard' you assume I am accusing Richard of committing the murders, not of being killed more than once. 'Of' has two different meanings. In the first case, the possessor has suffered violence; in the second, he has committed it. There is a classic detective story called *The Murder of My Aunt.* . . . Think about it.

"Of course in ordinary speech the plural word 'murders' restricts the meaning of the possessive to the active form. Ordinarily people aren't murdered several times. But here in this house, Clarence, Henry the Sixth, and the others *were* 'murdered' a second time. So, I thought to myself, what about King Richard the Third? According to the York records, he was "piteously slain and *murdered*, to the great heaviness of this city. . . .' An unusual epitaph for a tyrant, and a better one than Henry Tudor ever got. . . .

"In the view of the pro-Richard school, Richard was a victim, not a villain; a murderee, not a murderer. What if he, like the others, was due to be 'murdered' again? Sir Richard Weldon was King Richard. I had already figured out that the comedian was Frank—"

"Wait a minute here. You're skipping. How did you know that?" Strangways demanded.

"The heads," Jacqueline said. "Frank was the only one who had a car."

There was a damp silence. Strangways was the first to catch on. He swore. "Ditto," said Thomas. Jacqueline looked from one disappointed face to the next, and lifted the corner of her lip in a silent snarl.

"I know how Holmes felt after he explained his deductions and Watson told him how obvious they were," she said.

"But it is obvious," Thomas said. "I expected—"

"A pseudopsychological mishmash of Ricardian data? Oh, I suspected Frank before that; but I could have made out a plausible case against most of the people here. When will you get it through your academic head that possibilities are not proof?

"The plaster heads were the clincher. You yourself complained about the lack of privacy in well-staffed houses—the servants always unpacking for guests. The criminal knew this; he would have taken an awful risk trying to smuggle the heads into the house without their being seen. It might not have attracted comment or attention initially, but after the heads made their public appearance, a servant might have remembered them. Even if the criminal could count on sneaking his luggage in and unpacking it himself, where would he hide the things? A bureau drawer? A closet shelf? Under the bed?"

"What about secreting the heads somewhere in the grounds?" Thomas asked.

"Possible, but equally risky. Also inconvenient. If the heads were found, by one of the outside staff, they might not be traced to the person who brought them, but they would be unavailable thereafter, and he needed them. He had to be able to get at them in a hurry when the opportunity arose. If it would rain, he would get wet and muddy, which might arouse suspicion. . . . But there was one hiding place that was practically foolproof. The locked trunk of a car. You call it the boot, I believe," Jacqueline explained to Mr. Ellis, who nodded dumbly.

"When did you first suspect Frank?" Thomas asked.

"Let's begin at the beginning," Jacqueline said, with infuriating patience. "At first we didn't have a criminal; we had a comedian with a strange sense of humor. As soon as the pattern of the tricks became clear, I asked myself the obvious question: Were the incidents simply sick jokes, or were they camouflage, to mask a serious purpose? I really couldn't believe the first interpretation. Only a madman would perpetrate such tricks. I hope you don't mind my using that word. It isn't approved these days, but it takes too long to say 'mentally disturbed individual.' "

"Call him a Bedlamite if you like," Thomas said impatiently. "Only get on with it."

"Now madness, though its acts may seem irrational to normal people, has its own rationale. The acts become explicable when one comprehends the underlying obsession. A paranoidal schizophrenic attacks strangers because he believes they are members of a conspiracy aimed at his life. A religious fanatic may murder prostitutes. If we were dealing with a man of this type, the rationale could only be hatred of the society, or of Richard the Third—as you know, he still inspires strong emotions. Your members are all dedicated Ricardians. If any of you developed a monomania—which I could well believe—it would hardly take the form of a plot based on vicious slanders of your hero, or one that mocked the organization formed to defend him."

"Do forgive me," the rector said in his gentle voice, "but I believe there is a contradiction. You said, a few moments ago, that Sir Richard was the ultimate victim of this dreadful plot. By killing King Richard's alter ego, the criminal made him a martyr, not a murderer. Of course I cannot agree that any of us would be capable of such atrocities, under any circumstances, but in a perverse sense Sir Richard's death might suggest a pro-Ricardian bias, rather than the reverse."

"I see what you mean," Jacqueline said, smiling at him. "But I think you are being a little too subtle, Mr. Ellis. However, I had other reasons for believing that the tricks were not the work of a monomaniac. Although they imitated the deaths of Richard's purported victims, they deviated from the known facts in several ways. The accepted Tudor legend accuses Richard of stabbing Henry the Sixth with a sword or dagger. Yet the trick played on the doctor was meant to imply poison.

"Even more significant was the change in the chronological sequence. It is impossible that the young princes should have been murdered before Lord Hastings was beheaded; the younger boy did not leave sanctuary until after Hastings was dead. Now a monomaniac is usually consistent in his aberration. He will take the most appalling risks in order to stick to his self-determined rules. But our joker attacked Percy before he struck at Philip, who ought to have been the next victim. To me, these deviations suggested expediency rather than madness. It was much easier to slip some substance into the doctor's special food than to lure him away to a spot where he could be safely 'stabbed.' Philip is young and strong—a dangerous man to attack. By appearing to skip him, the comedian put him off guard.

"It was clear that the comedian was a member of the house party. The mysterious figure who lured Frank into the cellar—"

"That's when you began to suspect Frank," Thomas interrupted.

"I didn't suspect him then; I didn't suspect anyone until the pattern of the tricks made it evident that there was need for suspicion. But when I looked back on Frank's 'accident,' I found some grounds for doubt. Anyone in the house could have put on a raincoat and hat. And blows on the head often do induce mild amnesia. But it was singularly convenient for the attacker that Frank should suffer such amnesia. Remember, there were marks on his *face*. At some point he must have confronted his attacker. His injuries could have been self-inflicted; as he himself insisted, they were superficial. Any schoolboy who is lucky enough to suffer from a propensity to nosebleed soon learns how to induce that phenomenon at will. It's useful for getting out of exams and other embarrassing situations.

"The attack on Philip and the appearance of the plaster heads confirmed my suspicions of Frank, but I still didn't know what the point of the whole business could be. It was the reverse of the normal detective-novel situation, where the sleuth must deduce the identity of the criminal after he has committed a crime. I knew the criminal; but I didn't know what crime he planned to commit, or the identity of the victim, if any. So I went at the problem from another angle.

"The jokes were not the only unusual factors in this meeting of the society. There was also the famous letter. It was possible that the letter and the jokes were not connected; but I felt justified in assuming, as a working hypothesis, that one had led to the other.

"Whether the letter was false or genuine, it was valuable. We discussed that angle before." She looked at Strangways, who nodded. "The motive of the criminal joker, in that case, was profit. He meant to steal the letter and hold it for ransom.

"But surely, if that was the case, the jokes defeated the thief's aim. It would have been comparatively simple to sneak up on an unsuspecting Sir Richard while he was gloating over the letter, bang him on the head, and take the prize. The preliminary jokes made all of us, especially Sir Richard, wary and suspicious.

"The letter might have instigated the jokes in another way. If the criminal was a fanatical anti-Ricardian, he might wish to destroy evidence favorable to Richard. I know it seems incredible that anyone would go to such lengths for such a trivial purpose, but believe me, scholars are capable of insanities much more peculiar than that one. However, it was virtually certain that the joker was a member of the house party, and the only guest who opposed Richard was Mr. Strangways."

"Well?" Thomas said belligerently. "Why not Strangways?"

The maligned American grinned broadly. Jacqueline shook her head.

"Mr. Strangways is perfectly capable of playing nasty tricks," she said sweetly. "But he is not stupid. If he had wanted to steal the letter, he would not have played the tricks, for he would have seen the objection I raised in the first case. He certainly is too intelligent to continue a career of crime after being unmasked. If the letter disappeared, he would be the prime suspect.

"No; I could not believe that the tricks were perpetrated by a criminal who wanted to steal the letter, for whatever reason. They were senseless. A thief would have a better chance of success without them.

"I felt from the first that the appearance of the letter was suspiciously fortuitous. Suppose the letter was a forgery. What did it accomplish? First, it brought the members of the committee here, into a setting appropriate for the staging of the jokes. Then letter and jokes might both be elements in a complex plot.

"What plot? What was its aim, and what was its planned culmination? One answer—to discredit Richard and Ricardians. A fake letter and a series of embarrassing incidents would certainly do that. But again we return to the fact that only a confirmed anti-Ricardian would plan such strategy, and that the joker had to be a member of the house party."

Thomas cleared his throat. Jacqueline followed his glance. This time she gave the grinning Strangways a faint smile.

"You forget, Thomas, that by this time I was reasonably certain of the criminal's identity. Moreover, Mr. Strangways is the only guest who had no control over the arrangements for the meeting. The complexity of the jokes meant that they had to be planned well in advance. It wouldn't be hard for a member of the committee to unobtrusively manipulate his fellow members into accepting the idea of costumes and role playing; other amateur historical societies do it all the time. The comedian had to know, not only what roles you were playing, but your personal idiosyncracies. I couldn't imagine an outsider managing the business.

"So," Jacqueline continued, "I was left, finally, with a possibility that had haunted my low cynical mind from the first—that the jokes were misdirection, planned to distract witnesses from an act of violence against one of the persons here.

"I loved the idea," Jacqueline said dreamily. "It was beautiful. You are all familiar with the classic mystery-novel ploy of a series of murders designed to conceal the motive for one particular killing. But really, it is not a very practical method of committing a crime. As soon as the first murder occurs . . ."

She indicated the constable at the door, who promptly blushed—and with reason, for he had forgotten official dignity as he got interested in her lecture, and was leaning over the back of the nearest chair.

"As soon as a murder is committed, the police are called in," Jacqueline said. "The whole sophisticated apparatus of crime detection comes into play. Not even a madman would keep on committing murders when the house is swarming with police. If our criminal planned to kill, he couldn't hope to conceal his crime among a series of killings; the first murder would be the last. But he could carry out a series of nonfatal jokes and be sure, knowing his fellow Ricardians as he did, that official interference would not be tolerated so long as no one was seriously hurt. When someone was hurt or killed, the police would be summoned and the jokes would end; but the fatality would seem to be only a joke gone wrong, one of a series of baffling incidents rather than a cold-blooded murder. I knew then that the crime would be the last of the jokes—"

"Wait a minute," Strangways said. "Your theory, if I may say so, has so many holes, it leaks like a colander. To begin with, Philip was seriously hurt. If he had insisted on calling the police . . ."

Jacqueline inspected him coldly over the rims of her glasses. "But he wouldn't do that," she said. "Would you, Philip?"

"No," the actor said wryly. "Apparently my little foibles are no secret."

"Frank didn't mean to hit you so hard," Jacqueline said consolingly. "He got carried away. You must admit you had been irritating."

"So you decided that the murder—if there was to be a murder—would be the last of the jokes," Strangways said. "So what? You couldn't know ahead of time where the comedian meant to stop."

"It is true that that particular deduction told me very little," Jacqueline said with freezing dignity. "But I had already decided that Sir Richard might be the intended victim. For in a sense, Richard the Third was the last of this cast of characters to die a violent death. The others all survived into the next act. Shakespeare never wrote that play."

Strangways muttered something that sounded like "fanciful." But he didn't say it aloud, and Jacqueline did not take up the gauntlet.

"Now I'm going to anticipate Thomas's objection," she said briskly. "I can see it smoldering in his eagle eye. 'The best-laid plans of murderers go oft a-gley'—whatever that means. Perhaps one of the jokes was meant to be a fatal one, but it misfired. Is that what you were thinking, Thomas?"

"Forget it. I can see the counterarguments. The comedian had plenty of time to correct a mistake. He must have known I was still breathing when he put me in the barrel. Percy had a mild dose of the drug, and Rawdon's emetic couldn't possibly kill him. Furthermore, the plaster heads show that the joker had planned to continue through the 'deaths' of Hastings and Buckingham. He wouldn't have bothered with the heads if he planned to commit a murder before that. Murder would mean the police, and a thorough search of the house and grounds."

"It seems to me you are still on shaky ground," Strangways said. "You have postulated a murder—on somewhat vague evidence—and decided that none of the victims of the jokes was the potential murderee. That still leaves a number of possibilities—all the women, Mr. Ellis—and me."

"Oh, I considered you," Jacqueline murmured. "You'd be a splendid murderee."

"Hmmm. Then—"

"No one knew your identity until Saturday night," Jacqueline pointed out, in the mildest of voices. "How could anyone plan to kill you when they didn't know you would be here?"

Strangways did not reply.

"Of course the others were potential victims. But— Frank as the villain and Sir Richard as the victim—why, the motive practically hit me in the face. Not paranoia or historical mania, but two of the most comprehensible, commonplace motives for murder. Lust," said Jacqueline with relish. "Lust and greed.

"As Thomas has reiterated, Sir Richard is an extremely rich man. The Ponsonby-Joneses are his only relatives. Who else would inherit his fortune? And who would know the contents of his will better than a member of the firm of solicitors Sir Richard employs?

"True, for all I knew, Sir Richard might have left his millions to animal shelters, or to a foundation perpetuating the memory of King Richard the Third. He doesn't think much of young Percy. But his kindness and patience toward Percy's mother are manifest. He wouldn't leave her in need after his death. His feelings for Liz—"

Jacqueline paused, glancing at the girl. Liz rose.

"You'll be able to discuss it more comfortably if I'm not here," she said. "No, it's quite all right; I was about to go in any case. I'm going to Richard."

She walked slowly to the door and went out.

Thomas was struck rather painfully by the change in the girl. Even in old-fashioned robes she had been alert and alive, vibrant with health. The events of the past days might explain some of her pallor and her new air of fragility; but Thomas felt as if a ghost had passed. When the door closed, he turned to Jacqueline.

"Is she in love with Weldon, or with the reincarnation of Richard the Third? I'm not sure I like this."

"I'm sure I don't like it," Philip murmured. "But there's nothing I can do about it. Never mind, Thomas; they will always be united by their mutual passion for a dead man."

The rector made a little sound of distress.

"They'll do as well as most couples," Kent said callously. "Ridiculous business, marriage . . . At least young Frank had wits enough to fall in love with a girl who had expectations."

"Oh, he's a practical fellow," Jacqueline agreed. "He loves her—if you can call it love—but I'm sure her attractions were not lessened by Frank's discovery that Liz would inherit a sizable fortune. I don't suppose he thought of murder immediately. As Liz's husband he could expect to profit, financially and professionally, from Sir Richard's fondness for the girl.

"Then, at your last meeting, he realized that fondness was not the right word. The villagers are gossiping now about Sir Richard and Liz. Frank could hardly have missed seeing how Sir Richard felt, or the fact that Liz was beginning to reciprocate. He realized that he stood to lose, not only the girl he wanted, but the money he hoped to get with her.

"Liz and Sir Richard would have come to an understanding much earlier if it had not been for Sir Richard's modesty and the determined pushing of Liz's mother. Liz would violently resent her mother's attempts to promote a 'good' marriage. Oh, yes," she added, smiling at Thomas. "You thought Mrs. P.-J. was after Sir Richard for herself, didn't you? She's stupid, but she's not that stupid. Her hostility toward Lady Isobel—who was unfortunately naive enough to think she had a chance with Sir Richard —was on Liz's behalf. My dear man, the signs were plain to see! Do you remember our discussion about the dress Elizabeth of York wore to the Christmas party? Women know the importance of clothes. Mrs. Ponsonby-Jones supplies her daughter's wardrobe. And the costumes Liz wore were lovely, not cheap, ill-fitting things from a costumer's stock, but made for her out of expensive fabric, by her mother.

"Liz is Sir Richard's second cousin once removed, or something of the sort; the relationship is not close enough to matter. Mrs. P.-J. must have been ecstatic when she realized Sir Richard loved her daughter. Even if she had approved of Frank, she would have dumped him ruthlessly in favor of a match with a titled millionaire. What mum wouldn't? And maybe there is something to the baloney about maternal instinct. There are a few unsavory stories about young Frank's habits with money. . . ."

Thomas glanced at Philip. The actor didn't look at him;

he continued to watch Jacqueline, with an amused smile on his long mobile lips.

"When Frank realized the position, he must have considered alternatives," Jacqueline continued. "He might have talked Liz into a hasty marriage. But that wouldn't solve his problem. Marriages are easily dissolved these days. Sir Richard might marry and produce children. . . . Frank saw there was only one sure way of getting the two things he wanted—Liz and a fortune. The death of Sir Richard seemed a ludicrously easy solution.

"As a lawyer, Frank knew quite well that if Sir Richard died by violence, the first people the police would investigate were Sir Richard's heirs. The murder had to be very carefully planned. As the enthusiastic Ricardian debate raged around him, Frank began to see the outlines of his plot.

"He forged the famous letter. It is not as difficult as you might suppose to produce a convincing fake. Genuine parchment can be obtained, from specialty shops, and the method of aging it is described in several books. I can give you the references if you—"

"Never mind," Thomas said resignedly. "I believe you."

"As for the content of the letter, that was equally simple. Buck gives a summary of it in his book, and we have genuine letters of the period, including letters written by Richard himself. These provided Frank with models for the correct phrasing, spelling, and so on. He found everything he needed right here, in Sir Richard's library, including technical volumes of manuscript authentication, and a copy of the rare Kennett *History of England*, which includes Buck's work. As Liz's fiancé and a loyal Ricardian, Frank could work in the library whenever he liked.

"Remember that the letter was never intended to pass

expert scrutiny. In this case Sir Richard was not an expert; his critical sense was dulled by his desire to believe in the letter, and the sentences Frank added exculpating Richard—probably on a second sheet of parchment, so that Weldon would believe it had been overlooked by Buck—made Weldon's acceptance virtually certain. Frank never meant an outsider to see the letter. It would be destroyed at the time of the murder, not only to eliminate any possibility of its being traced back to him, but also to confuse the motive."

"Good Lord," Thomas said, starting up. "It's a wonder Frank didn't attack you, Jacqueline. If I had realized—"

"I was never in any danger." Jacqueline sounded a little regretful. "Frank couldn't spoil the 'murders of Richard the Third' by attacking someone who wasn't on the list. Besides, Sir Richard knew from the start that I was no expert, and Lady Isobel made sure everyone else knew it. Where is she, by the way?"

"Resting," said the rector. "She was totally prostrated, poor lady, by the excitement."

"Prostrated with frustration," Kent corrected, with an unpleasant laugh. "She's lost her quarry. By this time she is probably drunk."

"Never mind her," Thomas said. "Go on, Jacqueline."

"Frank dispatched the letter," Jacqueline said. "Not to Sir Richard—that would have been too obvious—but to Mr. Ellis. I suppose he invented some tale of noble families brought down in the world, of theft and mild skulduggery, in order to explain his desire for anonymity. . . ."

Mr. Ellis looked down at his folded hands. "I was culpable. And gullible. I cannot excuse myself; I have allowed a worldly interest to assume monstrous proportions. I wanted so much to believe . . ."

"You mustn't blame yourself," Jacqueline said, with the gentleness she always showed to the little man. "Whatever your reservations, you had to show the letter to Sir Richard; you had no choice. You tried to stop the show when it started to turn into a circus. . . .

"Of course Frank sent the letter in order to bring about an early meeting of the executive board. He didn't dare wait until October; Liz was showing signs of restlessness. He planned to commit the crime during a weekend house party, when the place was teeming with eccentric Ricardians. He did not expect that Sir Richard would fall completely for the forged letter and invite the press to the meeting, but he saw that this development could be useful. More confusion, more people wandering around, more suspects.

"The jokes were designed for the same purpose—confusion. But they served several other purposes. The whole setup suggested a joker with a mania about Richard the Third. Sir Richard's death, which horribly simulated the bloody end of his prototype, was supposed to be only a joke gone wrong. Thus it would appear to be one of a series, and the police would look for a monomaniac, not a killer who profited by Sir Richard's death. And if the worst happened and Frank was caught, the jokes gave him several choices of defense. It would be hard to prove premeditated murder. Insanity, accident—this poor young chap, troubled by his fiancé's sick passion for a dead man . . .

"I'm sure all this was in Frank's mind, but of course he didn't mean to be caught. The bizarre nature of the jokes suggested Percy as the joker. Adolescence is an unstable period, and adolescent killers commit crimes for the most trivial reasons. That was why I was sure no attempt would be made on Sir Richard today until Percy was free. It took him longer than Frank had anticipated. He got so impatient he went upstairs and shouted directions at the boy."

"Right under my nose," Thomas said disgustedly.

"If you hadn't been with him, he might have unlocked the door," Jacqueline consoled him. "Percy would have gotten out eventually, and Frank took advantage of his appearance at the window. He knew Sir Richard would immediately rush to check on the safety of his precious letter."

"What if Percy hadn't shown himself?"

"Frank would have thought of some other method of distraction. All he had to do was point and shout, "My God, there's Percy,' or 'I see Strangways in the garden.' The important thing was that Percy should be out, on the loose, and unable to prove an alibi. I kept Mrs. P.-J. under surveillance, just in case, but I didn't think Frank would bother with her. He had altered the correct sequence before, with Percy and Philip."

"You had it all figured out," Thomas said. "My God, yes —that Gilbert and Sullivan thing you were humming."

Jacqueline raised her voice in song.

> " 'When I, young friends, was called to the bar,
> I'd an appetite fresh and hearty,
> I was, as all young barristers are,
> An impecunious party.'

"I was trying to give you a hint, and you made a nasty remark about my perfectly normal appetite," she added severely. "You were very dim, Thomas."

"I was obsessed by my own theory," Thomas groaned. "I was sure Sir Richard had slipped a cog, and that he meant to kill Frank. I don't know about you, Jacqueline, but when we first saw Frank flat on his face in the wine cellar, I was sure he was dead. That was the one 'joke' that could have gone wrong. And Frank was Edward of Lancaster, the first husband of the girl King Richard loved, as well as the fiancé of the girl Sir Richard loved . . ."

"That's a good example of pseudopsychological Ricardian mishmash," Jacqueline said critically. "Really, Thomas, you ought to know better. The brilliant, insane murderers are in books. In real life people kill for practical reasons."

"Why didn't you tell me?" Thomas shouted. "Just tell me! You let the thing go on—you knew Weldon was in danger—"

"I'll never criticize detective stories again," Jacqueline said. "It was impossible to tell you, Thomas, with everyone wandering around the room. I couldn't hiss, 'Frank is the comedian and he's planning to murder Sir Richard,' now could I? You would have thought I was crazy. You wanted to think I was crazy. You wouldn't have believed me without a long, detailed buildup such as the one I've just given you. And . . ."

Her voice changed, and so did her expression. Watching the still, austere face, Thomas felt a chill. He had never seen this facet of Jacqueline's personality before.

"I had decided, by then, that it was necessary to let him proceed," she said quietly. "I chickened out, at first, and tried to talk Sir Richard into breaking up the house party. That would have eliminated the immediate danger; but if Frank meant to kill, he would have tried again. There was no proof. The only way to ensure Sir Richard's safety was to let Frank go ahead and catch him in the act."

"So you risked Weldon's life."

"I had to. The man who will kill for money may kill again. If I let Frank get away this time, I was risking not only Sir Richard's life, but Liz's as well—and God knows how many other lives that might one day stand between Frank and what he wanted. I hoped to stop Frank before he killed; but I was sure of convicting him whether he succeeded or failed. It was, if you like, a ruthless act. But the alternative was worse."

The rector was the first to speak.

"It was not ruthless," he said. "But it was—if you will forgive me—arrogant. 'Vengeance is mine. . . .' "

"I'm not justifying my decision," Jacqueline said. "I'm not such a hypocrite as that. I act as I must—and I pay for my mistakes, Mr. Ellis."

"We all pay," Strangways said. "But few of us have the guts, or the naked honesty, to eschew pious rationalizations."

Jacqueline looked at him. Thomas didn't like the look; it was almost kindly. He coughed. Jacqueline glanced at him, and then reached down into her purse. Thomas watched, fascinated. What would emerge from the unknown depths now?

A paperweight emerged. Shaped like a replica of Barnard Castle, it was made of bronze and measured approximately eight inches square.

"Goodness, that's heavy," Jacqueline said, putting the object back on the table where it normally stood.

"I wouldn't have thought you'd need that," said Thomas. "Your purse must weigh twenty pounds in its normal state."

"It's a very effective weapon," Jacqueline said calmly. "I prowl the campus by night, hoping to be attacked by muggers."

Monday morning is supposed to be a dismal time, but on this particular Monday, Thomas's mood was almost cloudless. The sun was shining, which in England is enough to make anyone euphoric. Sir Richard was coming along well, and his nearbrush with death had won him the girl he loved. Very romantic.

As for Thomas's own romantic situation . . .

He hummed tunelessly to himself as he went buoyantly down the stairs. The house party was breaking up that morning; they had stayed the night, having their statements taken and resting up after the excitement of the day. He and Jacqueline hadn't discussed their plans, but he assumed they would travel back to London together.

She was not in the breakfast room, but Wilkes was able to inform Thomas that she had been and gone.

"She and Mr. Strangways went off together," the butler said. "I believe they said something about the library."

Wondering, Thomas went in search.

He could hear the voices through the closed door of the library, which, in view of the solidity of that structure, suggested tones of considerable passion. Opening the door a crack, he listened. He recognized the voice and he knew the subject as well as he knew his own name. It was the two in combination that stupefied him.

"Richard has been cleared of all the other charges. No one seriously believes them. As for the murder of the boys, the weight of the evidence, such as it is, is strongly in his favor. If you could consider it dispassionately . . ."

"Now wait a minute." Strangways sounded a little desperate. "Whether Richard murdered the boys or not, he was morally guilty. By deposing young Edward the Fifth, he essentially signed the kid's death warrant. He—"

"Are you a historian or an early Church father?" Jacqueline inquired disagreeably. "You are not concerned with ethical questions, but with evidence. Maybe the word isn't familiar to you—"

"You have a tongue like an adder," Strangways shouted.

The sentiment seemed well expressed. Thomas opened the door.

Jacqueline and Strangways were standing at opposite ends of the room, Jacqueline behind Weldon's desk and Strangways near the long library table. Desk and table were covered with books, most of them open. Jacqueline's hair had been twisted back in a bun, but it was starting to disintegrate; agitated tendrils curled over her ears. Her glasses hung from the tip of her nose. Strangways, attired for travel in the proper English costume of suit, tie, and vest, had wrenched open the collar of his shirt. His navy-blue tie was under one ear.

Neither of them paid the slightest attention to Thomas.

"The hypothesis of Richard's innocence explains every anomaly in the case," Jacqueline said. "It is the only hypothesis that does so."

"The fact that the boys weren't seen again . . ."

"They were seen, or at least heard from. But you ignore that evidence, because it doesn't fit in with your fat theories. Oh, I understand," Jacqueline said. Her voice was as smooth as cream and as deadly as acid. "You started out being a logical observer. You believed the facts. Then the historical establishment got hold of you. It's hard to fight men like Kendall and Myers and—"

"It is not," Strangways bellowed.

"What evidence?" Thomas asked, advancing into the room.

Jacqueline didn't look at him, but she answered his question because it happened to suit her purpose.

"The household accounts. The reference to the Lord Bastard, in 1485, must refer to young Edward. That's what I mean about cheating; you say the entry refers to Richard's bastard son, who was never in any other place referred to as a lord, because you can't admit that Edward the Fifth was still alive. If you had not begun with the assumption that he was dead, you would never question the meaning of that entry. You are tailoring facts to fit a theory, not basing a theory on known facts."

Strangways' mouth opened and closed like that of a fish gasping for water. He was too furious to talk. Jacqueline proceeded.

"Another entry whose significance no one seems to have seen is the list of fancy clothes ordered by Richard for 'Lord Edward.' Edward was alive then, and getting expensive gifts from his uncle—and those gifts included equipment for horses.

"Was the boy going to practice equestrian exercises in the Tower of London? The inference is plain. Richard was planning to move the boys out of London, no doubt to one of his castles in the north, where the population was loyal to him. We know that certain children of the royal household were at Sheriff Hutton in 1485—but all you historians"—the words was an epithet—"insist that the princes were not among them because Sir Thomas More says the princes were dead by then! If that is scholarship, then give me ESP!"

Her glasses fell off the end of her nose.

"Jacqueline!" Thomas exclaimed. "Darling!"

He rushed across the room and flung his arms around her.

"Hello, Thomas," Jacqueline said. "Now, then, James, there is another point you—"

"You're converted," Thomas said. He held her at arms' length, his hands on her shoulders, and beamed at her. "You're one of us. By God, if nothing else had happened this weekend . . ."

Jacqueline squinted at him. The effect was rather charming.

"My glasses," she said. "I don't have my glasses on."

"Here they are." Thomas bent and picked them up. "Let's go, love. There's a train at eleven. Get packed. I'll ask Wilkes to send the car around—"

"Oh," Jacqueline said. "I am packed, Thomas. But I'm afraid I can't go to London with you. James and I are going to York for a few days."

"James—and—you—"

"Purely Ricardian, old boy," said Strangways. Thomas turned to stare at him in outraged disbelief. Strangways winked.

"There's the car, Jacqueline," he said, straightening his tie. "Let's be off."

Thomas stood in silence. Strangways strolled across the room, exuding self-satisfaction. He took Jacqueline's arm and led her to the door.

Jacqueline glanced back. "I'll see you in London on Thursday, Thomas," she said, and was gone.

Thomas stood unmoving. Car doors slammed and the faint sound of voices came to him through the open windows. The soft, expensive purr of the Rolls engine moved away into the distance.

The voices had not been mellifluous.

Gradually, unpredictably, a malicious smile transformed Thomas's face.

Purely Ricardian. Strangways had spoken in jest, but Thomas had a feeling the joke was on Strangways. Never before had he seen Jacqueline's glasses actually fall from her nose. He knew her well; she had a memory like an elephant and a passion for contrived revenge that would have suited a Borgia. He could see Strangways being whipped around York from Micklegate to the Minster, viewing the remaining memories of Richard the Third and reeling under the remorseless lash of Jacqueline's voice.

A sigh of virtuous satisfaction escaped Thomas's lips, and he went upstairs to pack.

Thursday in London, Jacqueline had said. Thomas had high hopes for Thursday.